TALES FROM THE WORLD'S END

Liam A. Spinage

TALES FROM THE WORLD'S END

FICTION4ALL

Red Scare

Turning and turning in the widening gyre

"Being at one with nature."

He answers the question simply, quickly, with the confidence that comes naturally to someone of his youth and his tanned, lean physique. He leans slightly on the edge of his surfboard with his left hand whilst, with his right, he runs his fingers through his bleached, damp hair, a move no doubt practised in the mirror and honed before every camera that he ever stood in front of. Roughly what you'd expect from a local-boy-made-good surf champ. He's easy-going and easy on the eye. His faded yellow tee reads "Party Wave", with a picture of a stylised wave, a palm tree and a generic cocktail icon. He smiles at me again, pearly white teeth standing out against a deep brown tan; beyond that, white sand and endless blue skies.

"It's the calmness of the ocean. Nothing like it. Nothing can prepare you for that." A second, taller, figure walks up to us on the beach, stepping effortlessly from the sea foam as if she were Venus herself. Her sleeveless vest reads "Gnarly Break" in black, outlined in a deep aquamarine on a sky-blue base. Another sponsor, presumably. I look over to her, wondering whether to say anything: I'm wondering how a sport that thrives on the lack of calm brought by big breaker waves can reconcile that with a zen-like worship of calm.

I'm interrupted, though, by a third figure pacing up the shore behind Venus, this time in a wetsuit emblazoned with the logo 'J'adore le surf'. Younger than the others, only by a couple of years I think, but if I've learned anything from the last couple of days, he'll be giving them a run for their money pretty soon. Youth has a distinctive advantage which can often trump experience. It's a young peoples' sport and there has recently been some harsh name-calling toward some of the older participants, where 'older' means 'late twenties'.

"Yeah, it's like no other feeling in the world. You gotta step into that sea and own it. Own your power. Fearless." He nods an acquaintance to the other two surfers, and they nod back.

"That's it. He gets it." Venus lays a hand on her colleague's shoulder. "But it's more than that. Surfing is a community. Even when we're competing against each other for a trophy, we know what we're really competing against, and it isn't each other, it's not even against the ocean. It's triumphing over your own will." She casts her eyes back to the curve of the bay. "It's about an intimate connection with each other and with the sea." She smiles for the camera.

"That's a wrap." I lower the mike and thank them all profusely. There's one more interview I need to do before I'm done, then I can relax for a while and dear lord this is a great place to relax. It may well be the most picture-postcard beach in the world, sun and sea and sand and surf in perfect paradise.

6

"Is that old guy out there on the point who I think it is?" It can't hurt to ask, even if I know the answer. Only our third surfer needs to turn round, hand over his eyes to shield himself from the glaring midday sun. The others already know.

"Yeah, that's Guy." Venus is the first to reply. She looks over at surfer one, nudging him in the ribs. "No need to be shy, Bradley. Let Madeline know."

"He's my dad." If possible, his smile is now wider, whiter, the pride evident in that winning grin, the tone of his voice. "But I think you already knew that!" He's teasing me, but I let him. An interview with 'the godfather of surf' will boost my article's reach a hundredfold. "You wanna talk to him?"

He already knows my answer, but I nod anyway. I'm trying to keep my cool.

"I'll walk you over. I'm done for the day anyway." Turning to the other two, he offers a boyish smirk. "I'll leave you two to tango with the afternoon tides." The others grin and wave us off. He offers an arm, and I take it, walking with him hand-in-hand. Now the beach really is picture perfect. It takes us five minutes to walk along that beach, a slow and amicable amble, and we make that journey in silence, just the gentle splash of waves along the shoreline. I'm pretty sure everyone left on the beach after the morning's competition - everyone that hasn't retired to the hotel in the noon heat - is watching us at that moment. It's not just the sun that's giving a warm red glow to my cheeks.

"Dad, this is, er, Madeline. She's been quizzing us on why we surf. Figured you might have a few stories for her?" He phrases it as a question, which I find unusual, because he obviously does. You don't get the moniker 'godfather of surf' without having a story or two to tell. I detect a certain hesitation in his voice and wonder if something might have soured their relationship, but I'm a sports reporter not a gossip columnist. I'm here to understand what makes people brave the waves, not dive into their personal lives.

On first impression, if you didn't know any better, you'd think Guy was a retired cowboy. He's sporting a faded leather waistcoat over bare skin criss-crossed with little white scars and speckled with liver spots. His face is stretched leather barely distinguishable in its deep brown hues from his waistcoat, except for the scratchy white beard and shock of white hair set in a permanent wave. The familial resemblance is clear except around the eyes, which are a little sadder, a little wiser perhaps. He's sitting - actually, squatting is more like it - on the edge of a tall chair, like he was some ancient ascetic ensconced upon the top of a pole and dispensing hallowed phrases to all who approach his pulpit.

He turns his head slowly toward us, away from the ocean horizon, and regards us both with a gaze hungrier than a basking shark, grey and silent. It's then I realise that Bradley and I are still hand in hand. I shake myself loose, which seems to mollify him a little.

"Tomorrow good enough for ya?" His voice is sing-song, a lilting melody that sounds like it came from a mouth thirty years younger. My eyes open wide in surprise.

"Actually, Madeline has to…"

I cut Bradley off, sharpish.

"Tomorrow will be just fine. It would be an honour." He nods in response, his mind clearly elsewhere as he swivels back, this time picking up a pair of binoculars which had been perched over an arm of the chair. I wonder what he's looking at and try to follow his gaze. There's something out there, for sure, something glinting over where the coral reefs used to be before things got so hot. Whatever it is that's captivated him, it's clear that I'm not going to get anything from him today. I just hope he remembers about tomorrow.

Of course, we didn't know then what a different day tomorrow would be.

***

It's the darkest of summer nights, with the faintest sliver of a moon. In the local folklore of the island, it represents a period of lightlessness in the otherwise long and glorious summer, a time when demons arise from the underworld. Part of me wants to believe that old tale, to take comfort in the folklore of a proud people, rather than admit that humanity was ultimately responsible for what happened next. Until then, I am caught up in the splendour of the local festival - being chased by giggling, enthusiastic children dressed as demons - a celebration I didn't know about but that I am picked up by and carried along with, before it deposits me back on the empty beach where I'd conducted the interviews that morning.

It's easier to see it in the silvery moonlight than in the harsh light of day. I don't doubt this is what Guy saw too, what had spooked him. A thin red line, bobbing in the distant waters beyond the cove, but being carried inexorably closer, closer, on every wave and the incoming nighttime tide, inching its way from the far reaches of the ocean to break with the surf against the rocky shoreline. There's a word for that; a word my dad taught me long ago: moonglade. A line of moonlight reflected on a body of water. Except this moonglade only starts with a sliver of silver. With every passing roll of the waves, it becomes redder and redder, hues of scarlet and crimson churned by the grey-white of the surf. Bradley and I, exhausted from the festival but not tired enough to retire for the night, stare out at it, minds lost in the wonder of the spectacle.

"Just beautiful." I half murmur, turning my head to where Bradley sits next to me. He smiles, unsure if I'm talking about him or the red tide.

"Dangerous is what it is." A voice behind us. It's Venus. For a moment I resent the intrusion. Then I can see the seriousness writ large over her face in what is a frown, not a scowl. She couldn't care less about what we're doing together on the beach. She's come to look at the sea.

Bradley turns his head, but he turns it to me, not her.

"What is it?" He's looking at me but talking to her.

"HAB49." We both turn our heads to her now, we have no idea what she's just said. The puzzlement must be clear on our faces.

"My bad. I sometimes forget to switch back to layman. It's a harmful algal bloom, a red tide. Not a phenomenon that's been seen in these parts before, but they're common enough in the world, worse luck." She takes a slug from a personalised reusable bottle patterned with clam shells and a cartoon crab, then adds an explanation. "I'm the resident marine biologist. I only took up surfing as a hobby. Came here fresh out of the research lab to catalogue what was left of the reef, then stuck around for the waves."

"Sorry, I didn't realise." I'd taken her for just another thrill-seeker, someone with just a love of adventure and the ocean but it seemed I'd underestimated.

"No reason you should!" She smiled back, the comment crashing gently against the towering cliff of her ego. "It's all surf and no reef these days. We wouldn't have these breakers if the reef was still there. Probably wouldn't be seeing a red tide either." She scratches the back of her neck with her left hand and takes another slug. "So, basically, here's the lowdown. Don't eat any fresh fish that have come from that." She jerks her thumb over at the sea. "Which, admittedly, limits our diet considerably. I'll alert the hotel; they shouldn't be serving any surf with their turf for a week at least. Also, stay away from dead sea life until it clears. I wouldn't recommend eating that either. Man, the chef's gonna be pissed. That's probably half his stock he'll need to throw out, and there are no good options as to where to dispose of it..." She scratches her neck again, mentally ticking off all the things she'll have to tell people and who needs to know what. "Oh, and keep out of the water. Obviously. Otherwise, you may end up with severe respiratory problems. Capice?"

"Wow. Like, that's a big ask." Bradley doesn't hold back, saying the first thing on his mind. And I get it. It's the reason they're all here, and therefore the reason I'm here too. The surf here has become legendary since the reef broke up, but there's still a fresh, unspoilt vibe to the place, as if it's resisting the encroachment of all the bustle its new fame entails.

"Yeah, I get it. There's gonna be a whole load of pissed off surfers stuck in a hotel with little to eat or drink except bananas and sports drinks. Look, I know it's disappointing. Hell, I'm disappointed too. Look, these things can fade out in a couple of weeks once the algae have eaten all the available nutrients and run out of food. There will need to be one hell of a clean-up, but we'll be back on track for next season." She shrugs apologetically rather than having to say the word 'sorry' out loud.

Bradley stands up, sliding his hand out of mine. "Two weeks? That's the whole championship blown out of the water. Man, that sucks." I try to sympathise, but he's just flipped from lover boy to obsessed surfer jock in a matter of moments without even looking back at me.

"Two weeks. Minimum. Look, I'm not here to explain the whole eutrophication cycle -" The relief on Bradley's face is palpable - "but I will if I need to. We fucked up the reef real good, now we've fucked up the surf. Deal with it." Venus turns her back and strides off, evidently in a snit herself at what she thought might be an easy audience to convince. Bradley just stares after her, then back at the cove, head lowered like a little lost puppy. I want to offer a shoulder to cry on, but I stare instead back out into the bay, assuming he'll make the first move. That shoulder goes untouched, just getting colder and colder until I realise he's paced off up the beach back to the hotel and I have to cover it with my woollen shawl to keep warm. I sit alone for another hour, taking some video footage of the slow creep of the scarlet tide. Then, stifling a yawn, I make my own way back up the rickety wooden stairs from the beach to my balcony.

***

The next day, the dawn is a soft, muffled pink, brought on not by the rising sun or the wispy clouds but by the suffused glow from what remains of the red tide, tangled seaweed dotted with algae washed up on the beach along with hundreds of tiny dead fish. Gulls and mollymawks begin to peck at them, keen to enjoy a free feast, but immediately realise their mistake. Living tendrils of vibrant red weeds lash out at the flocks as soon as they land, and, while many take off in time, the remainder are soon pulled under by the swarming masses of fronds which litter the sand where it touches the sea, They unfurl like long, thin scarlet snakes, wrapping their coils around whatever comes close. Once they cease struggling to take flight and succumb to the pestilential vegetation, they're consumed and then released, not singly but in a weird, erratic mass of beaks and wings that resembles something from our worst nightmares. The sight is horrific, but the sound is nearly as bad: the cacophonic shrieking of a hundred seabirds trying in vain to wrestle their beaks and wings free before they succumb. As one, we turn our heads in terror and revulsion; all except for Guy, who maintains a grim fascination. He takes several steps forward, gingerly at first, and then with something resembling a stride, oblivious to the calls from his son Bradley and my own hoarse yells to return to some semblance of safety above the high tide mark.

"We have to get a sample! I'll be careful!" His voice promises he'll take care, the spring in his quick step allowing him to hop over any strands that float past as he tries to get closer to a protruding mass of the stuff clinging to a rock in the intertidal zone. Bradley and I both stare on in shock, but occasionally our heads turn away as the waves crash over his bare legs and he inches closer and closer to the seething growths.

The churn of the morning surf now causes a secondary sensation from the bloody blooms. They give off what can only be described as a red mist, rising gently from the growths and moving - mindlessly, malevolently - towards the beach where we stand and watch, dumbfounded and awestruck. We both shout out to Guy to return, but he must not be able to hear us over the crashing of the waves.

He's waist deep now and getting closer, but the red mist is beginning to close all around him, cutting him off from sight. Bradley wants to follow his old man, drag him back, but I manage to stay his hand, despite the anguish on his face. It won't do to lose him, too.

What emerges from the surf a minute later can no longer be called human. Sure, it resembles Guy, but in a way a shadow resembles a person: it's distorted, twisted, out of shape. What we can see of his tanned legs and torso are covered in a thousand cuts, red welts on his skin that bleed continuously onto the white sands as he shuffles and struggles towards us, as if unused to walking. What humanity he retains remains only in those deep, grey eyes which I can make out when I zoom in with the cam, just close enough to see before all hell breaks loose.

People start to run. They run towards Guy to help him, they run away from the red mist now being ushered further upshore by a slight change in the breeze. They run inexplicably into the bay toward the algae, which welcomes their sacrifice with open arms as tendrils shoot out and grab them, carrying them underwater and away, away from the beach and out into the sea. Some of them briefly manage to surface and scream, their arms flailing uselessly as they're dragged under the water. Those that have the good sense to run away from the danger don't have the good sense not to trample each other on the way. It's hysteria like I've never seen it before and I'm torn between trying to help Bradley deal with what's left of his old man, swinging the camera round to record the phenomenon and joining in the obvious flight reaction that so many of the others are preoccupied with. I remember nothing of the next hour except for people shouting at me, past me, around me, instructions and directions that seem to elude everyone. Whatever is happening, it's no mere algal bloom. I walk past rows of stretchers somewhere, I think it's the hotel lobby, each occupied by a surfer I'd met only a day earlier, a day which now seems like a lifetime ago.

The next thing I know that happens, amid the madness and the screaming and the agony, is being offered coffee while sitting on the edge of a makeshift hospital bed in a hotel conference room with just Venus and Bradley for company. Bradley looks devastated. Venus looks cool and competent, a veneer of bravery clearly masking the confusion that lurks just beneath. Her manner is that of someone who is clearly used to working with whatever information is at hand but just as clearly wants to know more as soon as its humanly possible. For the first time, she looks like somebody you actually want to be in a scrape with, both her former hippy vibes and angry ecologist persona now washed away in torrents of anguish. Zen-like calm, just as she said to camera yesterday.

She puts my camera back in my shaky hand - I've no idea how I got here - and points me at the window with words that are intended to reassure, though they are tinged with just a degree of exasperation.

"We've got to get the news out. We've got to warn others, show them what's happening.

Madeline?" She snaps her fingers at me. It seems to work. "Are you with us?"

I look out the first-floor window across the beach. The red mass has slowly crept its way along the shoreline. There is no longer any white sand, just a slick, red, wound oozing and writhing in the light of the morning sun, basking in its light. Beneath it, among it, I can just make out the remains of people who were too slow to run. Dear God, some of them are still alive, clearly crawling toward us through the hellscape, their arms outstretched, and faces contorted into silent screams, hands raised in supplication but relentlessly, repeatedly, being pulled back to the ground by sticky red tendrils until they're too enveloped to move. I steady my hand and try not to retch. Try not to cry. Try not to panic. Then I recognise a shape, head and shoulders above the tide of red surf crashing onto the rocks. It's Guy! How can he still be alive?

"Bradley! Bradley, look!"

I can hear him behind me, padding up to the window. If circumstances were different, he'd be putting his tanned arm around my waist right about now, kissing the rear of my neck perhaps, telling me everything was going to be OK. Instead, his bloodshot eyes stare wide at the spectacle of his father making his way up the sand, faster now, seemingly undeterred by all the bodies or parts of bodies, just emerging from the sea as he must have done a thousand times before.

"Control of your body. Being fearless."

I divert my gaze, and the camera with it. Bradley is standing there, his arms limp at his sides, his eyes still wide open, but now swelling with pride.

"That's what he would have told you. That's what he used to tell me. What attracted him to surfing. He's a survivor."

I admit to a certain scepticism, given what we'd seen of him before the chaos, but I couldn't deny my eyes.

"Let's bring him in. He won't know where we are."

"Go. I'll take care of things here." Venus reappears, this time with an armful of clean hotel sheets and a pair of scissors. "I can play nurse for a bit. You go be heroes."

***

Once outside the hotel, the path down to the beach is pretty quick and clear. The hotel itself is built on the cliff edge and there are a series of several struts designed to shore it up, years of increasingly desperate precautions against the inevitable collapse of the cliff on which it hangs. There's one rickety staircase down direct to the beach at the side of the building: in truth it's just a ladder in at least three places. We take the broader path, with bamboo handrails guiding the way down worn stones and white sand, which zigzags its way down to the shore. The heat is somehow unbearable, stifling, even though it can't be much hotter than it was yesterday. What wind there is reeks of seaweed and the rotting remains of the fish that have now sunk beneath the waves as the red tide approaches, slowly and inexorably, encroaching on the edges of the beach, beginning to reach out feelers toward the dune grasses and the line of palms which line the upper shoreline. The detritus of the horror of the ocean assaults our eyes and our nostrils, but not our ears. Everything is deathly quiet except for the soft undulating noise of gently lapping surf.

Guy appears to be waiting for us. He's sitting where he was yesterday, like nothing in the world had changed. Bradley starts to run across the grassy dunes at the edge of the beach to greet him, but there's something distinctly fishy now about this whole affair and I call out to him in an effort to bring him back to reality. It's not that I'm unhappy to see Guy is still alive, it's more that I don't think this is Guy. I think this is what's left of him. I can just about make out a thin red stretch of tendril reaching out from the bottom of his chair down to the ocean. It's mostly covered in sand, but it's there, and I spot it, and Bradley doesn't. That's one of the benefits, I guess, of having a trained eye, not that it's any consolement to me at this point, not when Bradley is rushing headlong into a trap, not when I find myself running after him anyway, not when every other fibre of my being is screaming at me to run in the other direction.

He reaches his old man, or at least what he thinks is his old man. He's too fast for me to keep up: I'm fit, but I'm not champion-surfer-running-along-a-beach-fit. I pause to catch my breath, bending over with hands on my hips, when I hear him shout. When I straighten myself back up, still retching internally from the sweet, sickly scent of death carried on the ocean breeze, I've somehow managed to be cool and professional again, at least for a moment: my camcorder is in my hands, and my hands aren't even shaking. Much. I don't know what's about to happen, but I do know - I've a dim recollection of Venus telling me as much even if that was only twenty minutes ago - that I need to capture this, that others will need to know what we're experiencing. Especially, and I baulk at the presentiment even as I think it, if we don't make it out alive.

"Madeline!" He's standing beneath the chair on the point where we were yesterday, where his father is now hunched over in the same position, binoculars hanging limply around his neck. I pick up my pace, still feeling the need to warn him that everything isn't as it seems, but drawn inexorably to the pair of them, dragged along by the undercurrents of life, unable to resist that promised interview.

As I draw close, I stop walking and zoom in, starting at the base of the lifeguard chair and panning up to Guy's face. Compared to his appearance earlier on, he's in good shape, and that's what's disturbing me the most. There are no scratch marks or bloodstains on his legs or torso. None. Nada. It's like this morning didn't happen at all. Maybe I was hallucinating earlier, or maybe I am now, and neither of those sits well with me. Bradley seems unconcerned. Perhaps he really believes in the legend of the godfather of surf, or perhaps he's just overjoyed to see his father fit and well again.

Regardless, he begins asking questions that the old man doesn't seem to respond to. Then, as I gradually draw in a little nearer, slowly, quietly, camera in hand, Guy turns his attention to me, looks me straight in the eye (or rather, straight to the lens) and says "Reconnecting with nature. That's what it's really about." His eyes are still grey pools, there's no hint that he's under any coercion supernatural or otherwise, but his voice sounds distant somehow, like it's not really his voice, or at least not all his. This theory echoes a few seconds later when he speaks again and this time Bradley jumps back too. A number of voices speak at one, all using his mouth. "Get back to nature." It's like a chorus repeating the lines just spoken by their lead, but somehow all issuing from the same throat. I stagger, trying not to drop the camera because I have a feeling at the back of my own throat, the apprehension that something awful is about to happen, but that it's my job to document it rather than run and hide. There's another reverb, more voices this time and I realise with horror that I heard some of these voices only yesterday, that recently they belonged to living, breathing, young people, full of life and vigour, but now they're mutated by virtue of issuing from a strange throat, from someone who by all accounts should be dead. I can see them, now, reflected in the pools that are his eyes, their faces once smiling but now contorted with pain and rage, no zen or calm at all. "Back to nature." The voices repeat that phrase like a chant: a gently rolling lullaby that once may have tempted sailors to leap off boats onto rocks. Bradley looks intensely scared, but clearly still believes there's a connection there he can make, that there's something of the godfather of surf that somehow remains among that wrecked and mutilated body.

"Come back with us. Back to the hotel. Dad, there's nothing you can do here. It's dangerous. Please?" Desperation grows in his voice with each phrase: his intonation rising to fever pitch as he extends a helping hand. Guy ignores him, maintaining his pose in what still looks like a vigil he's keeping over the bay.

"Bradley?" One last attempt to get through to him. I want to get us both back in one piece, thank you very much.

Bradley turns, and in that moment it happens. Guy lunges forward suddenly, his arms exploding into a mass of red tendrils, each lashing out with full fury, slashing the air before each of us. We both panic and start to run. I manage to keep my hands on the camera, at least: it's tied round my wrist now, its weight barely slowing me down. Bradley manages to get clear to the treeline and I manage to get halfway back up the beach to the hotel before either of us realises we're not together. Guy's body has gone completely limp by now, toppling from its perch to lay prostrate in the wet red sand where even now little fronds begin to cover its prone form, caressing him gently with saltwater as each successive lapping wave helps the fronds drag it back down the shore to the sea. I look over at Bradley by the palms, hoping to share a moment of solidarity in sadness, but he's not there. Then I spot him halfway up one of the trees and wonder just what's come over him. We need to get back to Venus, need to warn the others, need to survive…

I drag the camera back up and zoom in. Several red fronds of kelp have reached the base of the treeline with the incoming tide and play around the base of the tree he's been forced to climb. He's trapped. He looks over - he can tell I'm looking back - gives a little wave and then blows me a kiss. I think both of those gestures are meant to indicate goodbye, but it's hard to tell because I've started screaming now, the camera back at my side, calling him to escape even though I can't see a way. He makes a futile effort to jump to the branch of a nearby tree, but despite his physique he's not a natural jumper. Perhaps panic has fully taken over from adrenalin. Perhaps he's given in to the call of the wild, echoing the first words he spoke to me before I even raised the camera to record him: *A passionate and intimate connection to the sea.* Regardless of the reason, he falls short and plummets to the shore, then briefly struggles to his feet on what looks like a sprained ankle. The coils of kelp begin to tangle themselves around him, working their way up from his bare feet to his knees and drag him down into their mass. The last I see of Bradley is his torso go limp and then disappear into a sucking pit of red weed beneath the beach. I stand horrified, then tearful, then angry, then fearful. He didn't deserve that. Nobody deserves that. And, if we don't find a way to stop the encroaching red tide, that's the end it has in store for all of us. Without a moment to lose, I rush back up to the hotel to tell Venus.

Venus is still set up in the conference room. She's distilled all her knowledge onto two whiteboards, one of which is a diagram of the seabed with scientific annotations: lost on me, but there were a few others gathered around it chatting animatedly. The other was a repetition of the rules she'd iterated to us the night before. Though it was clear that the situation we were facing had no historical parallels, there seemed to be a method to her madness: control what you can control. I slump, exhausted and grief-stricken, into a plastic lobby chair near the long windows which take up the whole of one wall, but face inside. I can't bring myself to gaze out of them onto the beach, not now. On seeing me, Venus excuses herself from the chattering group and comes over immediately. It can't have escaped her notice that I've come back alone.

We don't speak, not straight away. One look at my face, one glance back up at her, tells her what had happened. I guess she's been hoping Bradley and Guy have returned but gone elsewhere, but after that glance we exchanged it was clear that isn't the case. She stands still in shock, allowing a single tear to roll down her cheek and hit the polished floor. Then she reaches out to me, a hand to hold, a shoulder to cry on.

"It was horrible." Those are the only words I am capable of uttering right now. I try to explain what happened, but I can only do so in staccato bursts interspersed with bouts of unrestrained tears. Unperturbed, she takes the camera from me and watches the video I'd recorded. I don't know how she can do this without flinching, without crying, but she manages it with the clinical detachment of a scientific observer. Then someone else arrives with a coffee for each of us and I begin to recover some of my humanity.

"What can we do?" That's the first question I ask. Not dwelling on the past but trying to understand the present and survive into the future.

"You know what? I've no idea."

Those aren't the words I want to hear. I want reassurance, explanation, not the truth. My mind reels and then races back to a previous interview two days ago before I met Bradley and Venus. A tanned surf dude, almost indistinguishable from the throng of other tanned surf dudes, is opining on why he loves the surfing life. "It's about the challenge of trying to predict nature."

"This isn't something natural." My first genuinely held belief, stuttered out almost in defiance.

"I don't believe in things that aren't natural. There has to be an explanation. Some combination of factors that could lead to what we've seen. HAB49 for sure, as a surface reading. Perhaps an additional complication of toxoplasma gondii, that might explain some of the behaviour." I raise an uncomprehending eye. "It's a virus. It can cause cognitive impairment, poor impulse control, even suicidal ideation." She's clearly guessing but at least trying to make educated guesses. I was about to turn back to the window - what fresh hell might await us there? - and leave her to it, but suddenly she swears.

"If it is, it's going to piggyback on peoples' brains, make them bolder, drive them to break the rules…" We both look over at the whiteboard.

AVOID EATING FRESH FISH
STAY AWAY FROM DEAD SEA LIFE
STAY AWAY FROM THE WATER

There is still a group of people gathered round the boards, involved in what sounds like a friendly but heated discussion and we both have the same thought. It's all very well clearly indicating the rules for survival right up to the point where you're infected by a brain worm that makes you want to break them in a drive for self-extinction. Then it just becomes a challenge bucket list, and these adrenalin junkies love a challenge. Whatever's causing this, and I'm not wholly sold on a scientific explanation, it's going to be a whole lot harder than we thought just to keep everyone alive once they're infected. We all ate fresh seafood yesterday, for example, it's just about the only thing to eat except for coconut milk. Any one of us might start showing symptoms, even those that managed to avoid the horrific carnivorous algal blooms on the beach.

It doesn't bear thinking about, but that's exactly what we have to do to get out of this alive.

I turn away, dejected and despondent, and find myself once again gazing out of the windows. At least there's nobody on the beach at the moment, not that there's much of a beach anymore. Those thin red feelers that had reached out to Guy and Bradley have gotten thicker and sprouted other branches. The whole shoreline now looks like a medical map of blood vessels, reaching and feeling into every area short of the treeline and starting to creep up the base of the staircase to the hotel. At this rate they'll be at the door by - quick calculation - sunset? Maybe earlier? It's hard to tell because they're not expanding uniformly. I let the camera drop again - I don't even remember having started recording in the first place - and turn back to Venus, but there's no need. She's staring out of the window too, she's seen what I've seen and understands it just as well.

"Remain calm." I hear the voice and think it's Venus, but it's not. Where I've put the camera down, it's automatically clicked back through to the first of my interviews: a young wahine with long black hair and a bright green wetsuit. "You need to practise your calm. Let the waves wash over you. Stay in the zone. Otherwise…"

"We've got trouble." That is Venus' voice this time, whispering conspiratorially in my ear. "Don't look now." The impulse to do exactly the opposite is almost overwhelming, but I manage to resist. "The chef just came in. He's clearly not happy, which I totally get, but there's something else. See?" I press record again and angle the camera up so I can see him without looking directly at him. I can't make it out straight away, but when Venus points it out, it's unmistakable.

"His hands!"

"Exactly."

The chef is impressively built, a great advertisement for the hotel in that he clearly enjoys eating food as much as he enjoys cooking it. He's staring at the whiteboard and curling his mouth into a snarl. His hands, though, tell a different story than the grumpy chef trope we were expecting. They're bright red. Not in the manner of someone who's been exposed to the water or the cold for too long: his fingernails are the colour of fresh wounds and week-old bruises, and his palms discoloured with what you'd ordinarily imagine are stains from food dye. If he's noticed this, he doesn't show it.

Venus jumps up and shouts a warning back to me. "He's been handling the fish. We need to keep him away from the others." Then she's bounding over to the group and trying to head off the chef at the same time and I realise that she means for me to help. I stand and follow.

"You!" The mottled face of an angry chef bellows at Venus as she approaches. Thankfully, the others back off immediately, not wanting to be this close to a confrontation. They throng at the entrance door, hesitant to leave but unwilling to intervene. I recognise one of them from yesterday: he's 'escape day to day stress'. Figures.

"Move with the flow and strength of the ocean". An admirable phrase for a surfer to utter on camera, a ridiculous way to attempt to take down an irate chef who you daren't touch because there's a chance he's infected with a dangerous virus. I'm not sure what Venus intends as she heads over, but it doesn't look like the encounter is going to be

civil, so I kick things off by heaving a plastic chair at him. This draws looks of incredulity from both Venus and the chef even as the latter deflects it effortlessly. As he does, though, he raises his hands in defence and the crowd sees them, great red welts and all. Panic sets in and the resultant scene sees him flailing as they join in with the furniture hurling and then capitulating as he is soon buried under a pile of conference room fittings, including one of the whiteboards. We now have a mad, infected chef, dazed and trapped under a pile of furniture. Everyone takes it as a win - there are high fives all round - but nobody has a clue what to do next. Two of the crowd are staff: they confirm our worst fears - communications are down across the island and there's no way of getting our plight known by the world. One of the surfers - let's call him Doom Boy - reckons it's already gone global, that every coastal community is engaged in the same battle as us. This causes another round of panic. Venus looks over at me to check I'm OK and it's at that point I realise we may be the only two truly sane people left in the building.

Outside, the red tide continues to draw closer. It's already halfway up the stairs to the hotel. I check the other passage to the beach and destroy the ladder that leads down. It feels good to be helpful even though I don't know whether it will be of any benefit or not. None of us are in a good place and, as the sun sets, we gradually realise that whatever is happening in the rest of the world, none of us are going to get out alive.

We dine in majestic style on the contents of two vending machines and the complimentary fruit baskets laid out in the luxury suites. We daren't touch anything in the kitchen. The red blooms have fully encroached on the treeline by now and I instinctively film it even though the chance of anyone else ever being in a position to view it seems dashingly small. Every vine, every root and branch in the first five rows of palms now throbs as one with the seething red mass on the shore. There's some talk of burning to stop the inevitable by making a fire break, but that dies a sudden death when Venus points out we can't actually get close enough to try. A hush then descends over the reception room where we're gathered - there are only ten of us left, apparently - and that hush lasts well into the night as, one by one, we drift off into sleep on piles of pillows as each of us in turn keeps watch over the others.

During the night, the sea starts singing. I can hear its lullaby as I'm sitting there watching the others sleep and I've no doubt given their erratic movements that they can hear it too in their dreams. When it comes my turn to rest, I wave Venus off and tell her to go back to sleep. I've no intention or inclination to let my guard down now. It's early morning before I move again, but during that time the familiar voices call to me from across the bay and beneath the waves. I hear Bradley first and loudest, then Guy, then a number of others I recognise from my interviews but can't quite put a name to. They all say the same thing, whispered on waves and carried by the sickly-sweet breezes: Join us. Be at one with nature.

I need to stretch my legs, so I take a quick break - five minutes, maximum, but when I get back two people are missing. I can barely register it among the tears. The others wake, one by one, to the sound of crying and the soft, almost purring, call of the ocean.

***

The next morning holds no more surprises. We all talk a little about the voices we heard in the night, but it creeps us out so much that the conversation dies down naturally after only a few minutes. We have fruit for breakfast, check what's left so we can ration ourselves and try and decide whether or not we think the fresh water in the hotel is safe and decide against risking it until we have to. We're all exhausted, I'm blaming myself for the loss of - damn, what are their names? Joel and Russ? - and nobody wants to talk about tomorrow.

Venus tries to workshop ideas about how we can stop or hold back the red tide, which is now battering against the front door of the hotel. I can see the creepers feel their way up the glass of the doors and windows, searching, probing, seeking an entrance. Fire might work. Salt might work. At this stage, it seems anything might work. The others - myself included - are more geared toward pure survival and the hope of rescue. If we can just last until the red scare is over…but we don't know when or if it might recede. There's a general air of despondency mixed with waves of panic, fear, grief and anger. It's as poisonous as the air outside.

Two of the staff are the first to crack. I never learned their names. Never recorded their thoughts for posterity. One of them - a young waiter - shouts "this is bullshit!" and rushes to the door. We immediately try to head him off but he's expecting it, and his suicidal ideation drives him straight to the long pane of windows that overlook the bay. We watch in horror as he catapults himself through one with an almighty crash and then plummets. We rush over in the distant hope that we can still do something, but his body is visible on the beach and the creepers are already at work, covering him completely until there's nothing left of him to be seen. I get to work trying to board up the window - the kelp is already making tentative moves to reach around the sills and establish itself inside - while Venus and two of the others try to beat them back with a table leg. It's a losing battle, so eventually we withdraw from that room too. Another beachhead lost to the enemy. That's when we realise that the receptionist has also gone missing. The front door is wide open - another reason to abandon the room - and a single blue plastic sandal is all that remains of her.

We're on the first floor now, it's all bedrooms and laundry cupboards. We eat the little food we had left that someone thoughtfully picked up from the reception room, but there are no other sources of sustenance on this floor that the remaining staff member knows of. Luckily, as a maid, she has keys to all the rooms so we spend a good part of the morning fruitlessly scavenging for any food and medication that might be amongst the guests' effects. There's little to our haul, just a few protein drinks and vitamin pills. Then we hear a shout: one of the surfers has decided to try the tap water. At least we can confirm now that the water isn't safe either: he lurches from one of the rooms, foaming pink at the mouth, his hands grasping his temples in pain as his face explodes in a profusion of tiny vermillion fronds and a red mist of his own blood.

We scream. We run. Now we're on the second floor and fresh out of everything so we have to search all over again, but this time we do it together, which is easier because there are so few of us left. It's only a matter of time before the creepers reach us here too...

Or maybe not. When I venture to look outside again, the tides have changed. Red feelers and fronds still litter the shoreline, but they're no longer interspersed with rotting fish and dead friends. Fresh flowers blaze brightly along the bay, a haphazard mix of jungle flora and seaweeds. The tide seems to be carrying everything back out to sea, withdrawing slowly. Vines no longer press at the corners of every door and window. Venus postulates that it may be satiated, that maybe if we can just last another day...but she trails off. She stops pretending that she knows what's going on, stops trying to analyse everything scientifically. I want to believe her, but it's hard when she clearly doesn't believe herself. Nothing about this is rational and there's no point in trying to predict what might happen next. *Live in the moment.*

I start to feel the effects of being up all night. The adrenalin begins to wear off and I collapse into a fitful sleep as the others sit in silence on the sofa at the far end of the suite we've barricaded ourselves into.

When I wake, it's evening and I'm alone. I call out to Venus, but there's no answer. There's nothing in the room to indicate a struggle and nothing in the corridor to indicate where they've gone. I try to concentrate on staying put, half-huddled under the duvet, shivering with grief and shock. I do the only thing that comes to mind at that moment: I start recording myself. For over an hour, I try to recollect the events of the last few days, mustering what strength and will I have left. Beyond the curtains, through the windows and over the balcony, the crimson coast calls and I can no longer refuse it.

***

And then, on that final night, alone with the sand and the stars and the moon and the sea, the tears come. They come to wash away the pain of sudden, recent loss; the fear of what the future might bring; the ennui and dull aches simmering under the surface of a whole life, the decline of a whole species. I cry until I laugh and then I cry again. The camera loops back to a previous interview with a so-called 'poet surfer', looping the same lines over and over, the words distorted and distraught:

Nature, red in tooth and claw
Calls us to her undying maw
And here, upon this scarlet shore,
Her cry, her scream, is 'nevermore'.

Then, utterly spent, exhausted beyond tears, I drop the camera on the shore and step forward into the waiting, pulsing glow of those troubled waters, letting it swallow me, swaddle me, through, through to the new dawn and beyond.

Where once had bloomed a thousand flowers, there was now only one.

Wipeout.

A Change of Tune
The falcon cannot hear the falconer

The spring was silent that year, as I'm sure many of you remember. In any other year, the first signs of spring would have people shedding their winter coats on the first warm day and then determinedly continuing that trend even during March winds and April showers. Free from our self-imposed hibernations, hunkering down as winter winds and freezing rain batter doors and rattle psyches, humanity undergoes a natural resurgence, emerging from their flats and houses with spring in their step - a little warmer, a little happier, glad to have seen the back of the colder, darker months.

Not so in 2020. As the world watched the progress of the virus on our televisions and social media with invested terror and made tentative dawn raids on neighbourhood shops for dry pasta and toilet roll, few initially noticed that the skies were quieter than normal. Different. Since fewer of us were outside and otherwise preoccupied learning how to use Zoom properly or deal directly with a deadly plague and its immediate consequences for our species, few wondered what the birds were doing. Or rather, what they weren't doing.

Eleanor Swann noticed. But then, Eleanor Swann didn't have anyone else to pay attention to, or anyone to pay attention to her. There are Eleanors everywhere, if you look. But of course nobody does.

While that spring might have been silent for traffic, for humanity, it was a riot for new birdsong, if you knew what to listen to. Eleanor knew. She had, perhaps, always known, deep inside, something deep and primal in her soul, knowledge subconsciously acquired from exposure, secrets of birdsong and movement acquired from sources that the rest of the world has chosen to tune out, kept alive now only by a select few. It would be incorrect to state that these individuals guarded these secrets assiduously. You don't need to work to keep secrets if nobody ever gives you a second glance or pays the remotest attention to what you say.

Eleanor was ninety-three years old; she dressed and behaved as if she had always been that age: what soft white down remained on her head was combed and preened until it conformed to a bun held in place with a twig of willow. Her many cardigans were threadbare to the extent that one might be able to fashion a single working woollen garment between them, though she often wore all four of them at once well into summer without seeming to ever get warm. On the rare occasion that anyone glanced at her for more than a moment, they would instantly assume that she was an elderly spinster, probably a retired librarian, a pioneer of cottagecore before it was ever named as a trend. Certainly not the herald of the end of the world as we know it.

When they no longer had to shout to hear each other over traffic, the birds began to sing differently. More confidently. Their vocal performances reverted to previous frequencies before we built roads and towns and cities and drowned them out in our morning flurries of commutes and school runs, before we erected walls and skyscrapers to disrupt their flight paths and migration patterns. Eleanor awoke every day before dawn and made her way to the garden of her remote little cottage, sat in her wicker chair with a pot of strong coffee balanced precariously on the edge of the stone sundial and listened to their morning prayers as they gathered together around the birdbath and the various feeders dotted throughout the trees and hedgerows. She'd always loved this time of day, these moments of so-called solitude. Should anyone have been passing by at that moment, which they weren't, and rarely did even in the glorious summers that visited that lonely valley, they would have seen a woman alone, enjoying the dawn chorus. A little eccentric perhaps. But then it was a time when many eccentricities were born of isolation and desperation and fear.

What people didn't know, couldn't possibly know, is that Eleanor couldn't just hear the birds, she could understand them. If she attuned her mind correctly, she could zone in on just one particular mating call among the avian soundscape. She'd tuned out the gulls years ago - horrid creatures, really - whose calls were rude and jarring. She preferred the delicate songs and calls of her other visitors - the soft familiar coo of the wood pigeon, the haunting hoots of owls, the twittering of blackbirds, greenfinches, chaffinches, robins, tits and starlings…each of them was music to her ears, especially when they began singing a new symphony.

It had something to do with the birdbath, she was sure of that. Just touching its cold, grey stone sent shivers through her but seemed to open up new songs for her to listen to. There was some sort of marker on the top which looks like it should have once occupied the centre of the sundial. If she turned it, as she repeatedly did now after she had once nudged it by accident, she found she was able to listen to birdsong from further away. Songs which couldn't possibly have been sung in an English garden, at frequencies human ears should not have been able to hear. Mexican hummingbirds flitting about as they searched for nectar. Penguins squawking as they marched across the arctic. It's perhaps worth noting that Eleanor didn't mention this to anyone. Even if she'd had anyone in which to confide, it was unlikely that she'd have been believed. Just another 'there, there, dear' and a subliminal, background suggestion that maybe she needed to see someone. Perhaps she needed help? Perhaps that residential home in the town nearby might be better suited to her than a life of loneliness wandering round in fluffy slippers feeding colourful old Mr. Lombard in his little cage in the front room and picking up his moulting feathers. Oh, no, that wouldn't do. Eleanor was perfectly happy where she was, thank you, in her own little world of birds. She barely needed human beings at all.

So little, in fact, that she managed to tune other people out completely. She was so rarely interested in what humanity had to say, especially compared with the chatter of birds, that she found she didn't miss it. She never cared what people said about her anyway. Now she didn't have to listen at all. One species less to bother about.

There were, on occasion, odd or unexpected visitors to her garden. Birds that were just passing through as if breaking up their regular migration patterns for a quick break in her garden before carrying on. Some of them she knew were arriving earlier year by year, trying to reach their feeding grounds earlier because warmer winters meant early budding flowers. Their songs were tinged with longing for those places, a melancholy so profound it nearly made poor Eleanor's heart break.

She might have stopped, once. Might have heard people driving past, one of her closer neighbours knocking at the cottage door, her phone ringing off its hook as a distant relation craved contact. But Eleanor couldn't hear human made sounds anymore, even if she wanted to. By attuning herself to the birdbath, the price she paid was to forego those sounds forever. It only ever occurred to her once that this might have been a possibility, and that was when her wireless stopped working. She did so love that wireless.

One morning, she was roused before dawn by an unusual sound. Not the familiar pitter-patter of the raven knocking on her chamber door, but a gentle bump and thud at the windowsill. She awoke with a start which fluttered her heart and caused her no end of consternation as she tried to rise to take her morning medication: a herbal remedy which she had prepared herself for years (I don't trust them doctors, you know, she would say to Mr. Lombard, there's something queer about the way they talk to you). Then she ventured gingerly over to the window in her fluffy slippers and threadbare nightie, all stubby and brown, threw them open to let in some fresh air and gazed down at the poor, wounded robin on the sill below her. She reached out, tentatively, to determine the nature and extent of its injuries. To see what she might be able to do, before it's too late.

She shrieked, suddenly, and then almost instantly covered her mouth as if embarrassed by the piercing sound that had seemingly come from her own throat. For it was not a sound that had been made before by a human, no voice that could be discerned and understood as speech by any that cared to listen, even if there were anyone that could have heard her.

Eleanor had changed. Whether in that moment, reaching out to another wounded bird with a desire to nurture, or in a moment of despair and rage at those who might have inflicted such a wound, something had changed inside her, she remained ignorant. Eleanor herself became the change, the catalyst, the harbinger of all the doom that was to come, the change she thought she needed to see in the world.

She reached out her arms, now festooned with thick covers of black feathers that were pushing their way painfully through her pale, hairless skin. In doing so, most of the knickknacks she kept about the place were knocked over as she extended and retracted powerful wings. In the few moments that followed, it was all she could do to force herself out of the window, to allow herself a moment of imbalance on the sill as she changed in size and stature, first plummeting to the garden below and then, at the last opportunity, landing gracefully in the little pond. She gazed down at herself, then, seeing the transformation for the first time, and let out another shriek. Not of embarrassment or surprise, this time, not even of pain. It was a shriek of victory from a blood-tinged beak at the end of a long, elegant neck. It was the last sound she uttered from her throat before she took off and all the sound that could be heard in her garden was silenced, dwarfed by the noise made by the flapping of her gigantic black wings.

Nothing in the past, in the sum of human experiences, could have conceivably pointed to this possibility. No patterns of behaviour for scientists to track, no folklore to fall back on as a guide to future behaviour.

Unlike the global environmental breakdowns, unlike the progress of viruses, for which there have been a plethora of clues should anyone cared to have looked, there are no patterns, no precedent.

I know, I know. This isn't how stories are supposed to end. There's supposed to be a realisation after the comeuppance, a time when whoever is left will realise what it is they've all done wrong and maybe learn, just in time, what they can do to correct it.

Because of the nature and meaning of the threat, that time had already passed. Any other bird chosen would have had its own observable patterns used against it, its own folklore that might have brought its own downfall. A raven leaving the Tower of London would have been front page news for doom scrollers. A dead cock robin might have invoked nostalgia about old childrens' rhymes, tapping into an environmental message which might have reached receptive and sympathetic ears as a call to action. Not so the black swan. We behave as if we live in a world where unknowns and uncertainty don't exist. Even if and when we take pains to infer that an immensely unlikely event is going to change the course of history, we will never know what that might be.

As the black swan took wing and scattered, vultures began to descend on a doomed species, destined to never again hold so much power over the planet they had so recklessly wrecked.

Fashion Victims
Things fall apart: the centre cannot hold

Louis, a mere spindle of a young man with no more than a day's growth on his chin after a week, has three problems. The first problem coalesces into two distinct forms: his flatmates Viktor and Christophe. It is his misfortune to share lodgings with them while they are all students at the Centre for Experimental Fashion and Textile Design in Paris. The second problem is that he is weeks behind on his graduation project: his ideas are apparently 'pedestrian' and 'derivative'. In his desire for perfection, he has discarded many not-so-innovative-ideas to the cutting room floor. The third problem, by far the most pressing in his mind, is the location of his precious fabric scissors.

Louis is close to what you might call obsessive-compulsive - though not for certain, not without a proper clinical diagnosis. Let us say merely that he has a strong preference for order rather than chaos. A place for everything and everything in its place is Louis's motto. This is not something that can be said for those who he resides with. Chaos reigns among these two of his fellows, whose lackadaisical attitude to tidiness and cleanliness frequently leaves Louis teetering on the brink of despondency.

Until, one day, he falls from that brink, headlong into chaos itself.

"Where the fuck are my fabric scissors?" Louis stomps into the kitchen from their lounge, startling

Viktor, who is fully engaged in rolling a joint for breakfast. "If I've told you once, I've told you a thousand times, don't use them for anything other than fabric." Viktor has the temerity to not even look guilty: what he looks is stoned with a touch of hungover because that's how he always looks. Viktor looks like an artist's impression of a hipster yeti. He works mainly with barbed wire and modelling clay. He hasn't even bothered to dress this morning so his sweaty, hairy bulk combines with the reek of marijuana and stale beer to make **Louis** twitch. **Louis** believes kitchens should smell like kitchens, not brothels.

"Not me, bro. Think I saw Christophe with them last night? He was doing something complicated with plastic sheeting for some project." Viktor doesn't even look up when Christophe walks in, tanned and toned with nothing on but his tatty dressing gown and a smile.

"Nope. Haven't seen them. Jesus, you need to relax a bit, **Louis**. Stop snipping at us all the time." Christophe removes the newly rolled joint from Viktor's stained fingers and takes a long puff, then offers it to **Louis** on the off chance this is the one time **Louis** takes them up on it.

He doesn't.

"For fucks sake, I swear I'm gonna bloody murder the both of you one of these days! Look at the state of this place! If those scissors aren't back on my desk by the end of today, there'll be hell to pay!" He storms out, leaving the other two in a haze of blue smoke and the aroma of strong coffee. His flatmates sigh, shrug, and get on with their day.

They're usually pretty laid-back, except when it comes to paying their rent, because their bugbear with Louis is that in a desire to impress, he spends all his money on boutique fabrics and rarely stumps up his share. Still, live and let live.

Louis walks through Montmartre, tries to calm down. He can't think clearly when he's in this state and it's thinking he needs to do. He has to come up with that one single idea that will transform the fashion industry and catapult him to fame. He simply has to. There is no alternative.

He hasn't really been paying attention to where he's walking though - he soon finds himself on a little cobbled street somewhere past the Square Louise Michel, a place he doesn't recognise. Ivy grows up the wall that lines one side of this road, scooters putt past with a flurry of horns; a group of young people sit chatting outside a local patisserie, sipping their coffees in the chill of the spring morning. It's picture-postcard perfect Montmartre and he wonders why he's never stopped here before. Then he spots something else: a pavement A-frame spinning in the breeze which reads FABRIC EMPORIUM NOW OPEN. A red arrow points to an entrance down a shady alley where he can see a beaded curtain covering an open doorway. Curious, he moves towards it. He thought he knew all the fabric fairs in this part of the city. Could this be something new? Could it be *the* thing he's been looking for? Is his quest over, his salvation close at hand? Barely able to contain his excitement, he pushes aside the curtain, which elicits the tinkling of a small bell as he crosses the threshold into this realm of promise and reward.

It's strangely warm inside, especially compared to the spring air. Swathes of many-hued fabric hang everywhere, not laid out in bolts on the table as in other shops but draped vertically over screens and from ceiling beams, overlapping each other and pierced through with obscure images like some Dadaist nightmare. There's nobody here, so Louis spends a while browsing. The cloying smell of jasmine permeates the air, rising from unseen censers to dance in swirling motes of light which accentuate some of the more bizarre fabrics on display: a long, thin red and yellow ribbon flapping in the breeze, a deep reddish brown cloth rolled into a ball and hung from a lamp. If he wasn't so curious, so desperate, he'd leave at this point because the displays are getting more bizarre as he pushes aside some of the drapes and reveals little rooms devoted to particular colours and designs. At one point he pushes aside a bolt of brilliant blue to reveal a doorway on which is pinned a single piece of fabric painted with a crude depiction of an eye.

He's committed now, so he reaches forward and opens the door. Nothing but darkness. Nevertheless, he's in too deep, lost in a maze of fabric with no choice but to go ahead. He steps in and two lights flicker into life overhead as he moves forward into the back room.

"Can we help you, young man?"

"Yes, can we help you? I'm sure we can. It's not often people find their way here. You must be very special. Yes, very special indeed."

Two men emerge, one from beneath each of the bulbs overhead, which have been carefully shaded so as to make the effect kaleidoscopic and more than a bit trippy. Louis blinks. Their features are so alike they must be brothers, maybe twins: balding, bespectacled, little round eyes, delicate twirly moustaches decorating their upper lips. They wear identical suits of a deep crimson velvet. They both look on, clearly waiting for his response.

"Oh, I...I'm looking for something rather special." Louis feels a little unnerved by their presence. He'd rather leave and carry on browsing on his own.

"Oh, we do have something special, don't we?" The man on the right looks over at the other with a wry smile.

"Oh, yes. I think we can accommodate the young gentleman. What is it you desire?"

Louis runs his fingers through his hair. "I need something people will pay attention to. Something nobody has ever seen. Something to make me famous. To shock and awe the fashion world. It's just that…"

The man on the right interrupts him. "Oh, you have definitely come to the right place, young man! Do we have a treat for you!"

"Yes, indeed!" The other nods vigorously and reaches under the counter of a little desk Louis has only just noticed in the strange semi-darkness and ever-swirling colours of this bizarre and disturbing little room.

What he retrieves is a bolt of fabric so sheer that Louis struggles at first to see what it is beyond the gleam upon it from the lanterns. "Here, see what you think of this. Come forward, feel the cut of the cloth, don't be afraid!"

Louis reaches forward eagerly. His hand brushes the cloth. It feels a little rough to the touch and he can see close up that it resembles stretched and tanned leather, though it's practically see-through. He turns it over in his hand, caressing it gently between his fingers. It feels somewhat damp but cooling on one side, crinkled and dry on the other. It's like nothing he's ever handled before. He's sold. It's altogether the most remarkable bolt of cloth that he has ever seen.

"How much?" Louis can pay, whatever it is, the rent will just have to wait, or maybe Christophe can stump up his share this month.

"Well, we only have this one bolt…"

Louis' heart sinks. There's barely enough there for a single outfit. He'll have to be pretty creative.

"I tell you what. Just because you're a *special* customer."

"Very special!"

"Yes, very special!" They begin nodding at each other again. "We'll let you have this one bolt for a knock-down price. What's more, we'll show you how to make this cloth. All we ask is that you tell people where you got it from. Understood?"

Louis can't believe it. His dream is turning over in his mind now - so close to fruition he can already see his face on the cover of magazines. "Deal."

"Excellent! Now, follow these instructions to the letter. There will be hell to pay if you get them wrong. What you'll need to make this yourself is a pair of exceptional fabric scissors…"

When Louis finally gets home, it's late and both of his flatmates seem to have retired to their rooms. **He** turns on the light in the lounge and instantly his shoulders slump. There's a mass of washing up to be done, which should by all rights at least be stacked in the kitchen, not the lounge, if not actually taken care of properly. There are also little smears of modelling clay with Viktor's fingerprints in them on the doorknob and on the wall by the light switch.

His precious scissors are there on the table. He sighs in momentary relief but as he gets closer, he can see that someone has encased them in a block of clay like some mock-Arthurian sword in the stone. Then he spots red paint on them. His face voids of that relief and turns instead to a shade of stark scarlet.

Louis finally cracks. Drawing the scissors from the clay, he turns them over and over in his shaking hands as they glisten under the dim light of the single bare bulb. He admires their sharpness, their desire to be used to make the most exquisite garments. Gripping them tightly, Louis wields them as an implement of rage. He wasn't joking when he said he'd bloody murder them.

He decides to take care of Christophe first. As he suspected, Christophe is so out of it he doesn't see or hear him coming. Louis doesn't hesitate. He lifts the scissors over his head and brings them down with all his strength on Christophe's prone, naked form. It's surprising how easy and quick it is.

The scissors sever a major artery and blood spurts forth from one, single, fatal, wound in Christophe's neck. There's a gurgling noise mixed in with Louis' own heavy panting. His head is filled with that noise, his clothes are covered with blood. It doesn't take him long to dispatch Viktor either. It's all surprisingly easy and extremely satisfying.

There's plenty of plastic sheeting in Christophe's room which helps keep the scene clean.

Now Louis only has two problems. He picks up his scissors and begins cutting, slowly and steadily at first but then faster, faster, frenzied, unrepentant. Blood and sweat, blood and sweat. He keeps repeating the phrase over and over, the phrase he learned from the tailors as he prepares a dye bath to dip the strips of skin in. That's the first problem solved. The second problem is this: what will people think?

Louis's entry into the fashion show draws shock but wide acclaim. How daring! How visionary! "Skin on Skin" is an instant hit. They don't need to know how accurate a term that is for his new creation. Some of them, though, are literally dying to find out. He conveniently forgets he was supposed to send people to the strange fabric emporium. The two old men aren't exactly in a position to do anything about it anyway, or so he reckons. He doesn't think they've left that shop in many, many, years. Besides, he's busy, so busy. Instantly catapulted to fame, he's in demand everywhere all the time. At night though, he sews new clothes from those who have come too close to discovering his secret. He sleeps fitfully, frantic, exhausted, but with no attendant guilt or shame. That's just not who he is any more.

It comes as a surprise to Louis when he sees the two tailors in the front row beside the catwalk at his breakout show. They stand out from the rest of the press because they're still dressed in red velvet and rather than applauding with the rest of the crowd, their heads are slightly bowed and shaking violently in disapproval. Then one of them raises his voice and cries out. "It's flesh! It's just flesh and blood!"

The crowd goes quiet. Even the cameras stop flashing. They all stand there, murmuring and pointing. Louis is horrified. His secret is out! What will they do? What should he do? The eyes of the crowd turn to the two tailors, then back to Louis, then back at the tailors. Disbelief is suspended in the air, thick and cloying, choking him. He has one moment to react and wastes it looking for an escape route. Then the crowd is upon him. Not because he's a disgusting, loathsome killer, but because he wouldn't reveal his secrets. He stumbles and falls on the catwalk. His scissors fall out of his pocket and clutter to the ground beside him.

Now Louis only has one problem, which is that everyone wants a piece of him. He struggles and writhes under the mass of bodies each towering down on him, raining blows down as he raises his hands feebly to cover his face and cries out in desperation to the two tailors, begging their forgiveness. The last thing he sees is a pair of scissors, gleaming with inner light, descending at breakneck speed toward his neck. Then Louis has no problems at all, and everyone walks away with a Louis original.

Sign of the Times
Mere anarchy is loosed upon the world

\<Click\>

\<Click\> \<Click\> \<Click\>

Mickey_G! is getting pretty desperate. Only half an hour til his livestream *"Celebrities Unmasked!"* and he doesn't have enough content.

He won't just make things up, his subscribers wouldn't buy it. They're as discerning in their trash content as he is. So, he clicks.

\<Click\> \<Click\> \<Click\>

Mickey_G! clicks on the bait so you don't have to: his weekly roundup shows his fans all the celebrity gossip they didn't have time to consume themselves. He's somehow accumulated over a hundred thousand followers: many of his more devoted fans are other influencers.

To his left - out of camera shot, obviously, is a large stack of pizza boxes. To his right - likewise out of shot so that his livestream followers only see the good bits of his flat - is a heap of discarded energy drink cans. Between his lips - always, it seems - is his trademark vape mod which continuously bellows forth a noxiously sweet cloud of strawberry bubble-gum smoke.

All is right in Mickey_G!'s world, if only he can find something else worth reporting on in the next half an hour.

\<Click\>

Secrets of the Stars! 12 celebrity tattoos you didn't know about! Number 12 will really get under your skin!

Now Mickey_G! isn't really into ink himself - he just has the one tattoo of a hooded cobra on his arm - but the bait works. He's hooked. He's aware that he's the fish in every clickbait scenario, but he hopes to find a bigger fish at the end of this line: something to draw his followers in just as it has drawn him in.

<Click>

He's clicked enough to know how these work. The first few will be people he hasn't heard of, uninspiring minor reality show stars that everyone has already forgotten. It's the last few photos that will count. It's the anticipation that works up the dopamine, it's the background adverts that pay for this drivel.

<Click>

Just as he expected. Who in the heck is Phaisyle? That's a pretty distinctive name but he has no recollection of it. If he had more time, he'd fall down a research rabbit hole that might last for hours. That's where the pizza and the energy drinks come in and that's also why the discarded relics of his high-octane online life still litter the periphery of his workspace.

<Click>

More utter unknowns. Coronis, Phaedo, Eudora, Cleeia. They don't even have tattoos that are that odd or interesting. He's still holding out for an A-lister on the last page. Preferably with one of those Japanese kanji tattoos that they think means 'peace and harmony' but actually means 'superficial wanker'. That ought to get a good enough laugh from his devoted followers. Hell, at this late stage he'll settle for a Z-lister. These people so far aren't even in the celebrity alphabet.

<Click>

He doesn't find that, though. What he finds is much more interesting. If he wasn't so hyper focused, he'd have noticed something else too. There's no advertising on this site surrounding the lines of text and the pictures of these nobodies with their roses and their tigers and their hearts decorating their flawless skin. The right third of the screen - usually devoted to them - shows only a dark void where black stars are rising through the artwork or moons are circling over alien skies.

Stranger still!

It's a welcome change from the ubiquitous 'next' sign, he'll give it that. Not that he's seen anything particularly strange thus far.

<Click>

Haita Shepherd!

He has no idea who that is, but that doesn't seem important now because wow, just look at that kooky tattoo design. He's never seen anything like it. It's presented as an animated gif rather than a photograph, focused heavily on the design: it doesn't show the celebrity's face or even much of the surrounding skin. So much for *Celebrities Unmasked!* It has a vague resemblance to a biohazard sign - which would be a heck of a statement as a tattoo now he thinks about it - but it's only half the pattern. It rotates vaguely as he watches it, rapt with interest, a little one way and then back, as if the flesh it's tattooed on is undulating, flexing…it's impossible to tell what part of the body it's on but it feels instinctively like it's on a chest, over the heart. It's hard to tell because the yellow of the design doesn't really work with the cream of the flesh, except that it kind of does stand out, mainly by virtue of it being unusual rather than purely from the contrast of palette choices.

It's exquisite. It's singular. It's unique. He leans in closer to the screen, hypnotised by its intricacy. Even as a static image, it's remarkably unsettling for reasons which he can't quite fathom, but which prick continuously at his subconscious, igniting neural pathways deep within his brain that have so far been gathering metaphorical dust.

Neurons fire and synapses fry as Mickey_G! experiences a hundred thousand sensations all at once. His ears fill with a low ringing sound. His pupils are so wide you could drive a bus through his eyes right into his grey matter. The saccharine sensation of his vape mod merges with the coppery tang of blood in his mouth as his taste buds overload and pop in a mass of tiny explosions. Mickey_G! barely notices. He feels alive. So alive. Ecstatic, elated, euphoric: he's simultaneously blissed out and hyperactive. This is life as it was meant to be lived. This is ASMR taken to the max. It's better than any drug he's ever taken, and he's taken them all, often with celebrities he's later exposed as addicts.

The first thing he thinks is this: if that's the sensation he gets just from looking at it, imagine what it would be like to feel like this all the time by having it emblazoned in his flesh. The second thing he thinks is this: other people need to see this, feel this. Everyone deserves to feel this high.

He has ten minutes before he goes live. Slurp. Suck. Puff. Deep breath. He knows what to do now. He knows how to really wow his followers and get more besides. Maybe this will be the break he needs. Go viral. Start bringing in the big bucks. He types in the teaser title for the upcoming stream:

"You'll never believe this weird tattoo design I found! Watch me ink it live! Midnight tonight! Be there!"

That should draw the crowd in.

***

DevilDonna666 is first to show up on his feed, as she usually is, bang on the stroke of midnight. From what Mickey_G! can gather, she's some kind of graphic designer. She's shared some amazing pictures on Insta and DeviantArt. She's one of only a few of his followers whose content he actively follows back. She's been tuning in since the early days and has never missed a livestream. He can see her raise a pierced eyebrow as she sees his topless torso amid the vape haze. Good. Let them wonder. Hopefully, with her background, she might be able to offer some insight into the strange design of this tattoo, but that can wait until his masterpiece was over.

Next up is GangreneGoat, another old hand who is a bass guitarist in a Norwegian deathcore metal band. Mickey_G! tried listening to their debut album once. Pretty good technically, but the garbled and grunted lyrics were incomprehensible and would have been even if they were in English. Not his style, but he appreciates the craft.

Then a few other of his regulars tune in: he glimpses down at the ticker showing the number of current live viewers, while trying to maintain professionalism and mystery in front of the camera and dealing with a quickening pulse and blood slowly dribbling from his nose, ears and the corners of his mouth. He'll wait until he has a few more. In the meantime, he's enjoying the comments in the live chat, not that he will get round to addressing or responding to them.

The ticker clocks over to 1000. Not bad for the start of a livestream. Figures always increase as people tune in later. FOMO is the best clickbait.

It's showtime.

Mickey_G! aims for an enigmatic smile for his audience, but what they actually get is the biggest shit-eating grin the internet has ever seen. It's all he can do to speak a few introductory words without speaking too fast or slurring.

"Hello, helllloooo, hello, it's your main man Mickey Gee here with some amazing content for you tonight. Guaranteed to blow your mind!" He manages a knowing wink. This is his usual intro, but this is one of the rare instances when he totally believes his own hype. His viewers can tell: they're absolutely lapping this up because they know he's genuine. Their faces are lined with anticipatory intrigue and their eyes filled with worshipful wonder.

They ain't seen nothing yet.

Mickey_G! doesn't own a tattoo gun: he's improvising. What he does have - as previously mentioned - is a growing pile of greasy mostly-empty pizza boxes, a similar pile of energy drink cans and his signature monster vape mod. He's convinced - utterly convinced - that this is all he needs.

"So, people, have I got a treat for you tonight! Your man Mickey Gee has been surfing on the stranger shores of the web this week! Braving the cloud waves! I found the weirdest thing! Y'all need to see this! I'd show you the image, honestly, I would, but this is going to be so much better. Trust me." He sounds vastly more excited than he normally does. There are no looks of concern among those faces of his audience that he can see on his second screen, only rapt attention.

Mickey_G! picks up one of the empty cans and rips it in half with his bare hands. He smiles at the camera and through it to the multitude in the world beyond, then casually discards one half of the can over his shoulder, leaving a jagged silvered edge jutting from the fist formed from his now-bleeding right hand as he raises it aloft in triumph before lowering it to the waiting flesh of his perfect, tanned, hairless chest. Then, without hesitation, he starts cutting away, outlining the lines of the tattoo into his own skin, going deep to make the design visible to his viewers even as he struggles to

60

maintain focus with his mind blurring and his hand bleeding and his arm shaking and his heart pumping and his pulse racing. The serrated edge of the improvised blade glistens under the harsh glow of his lamp with silvery reflected light and the deep red of his own heartblood. He imagines it looks just like the most extreme of Gangrene Goat's videos.

He nearly passes out. A glimpse shows his audience figures are soaring by the second as he finishes the markings and brings the secondary camera in for a close up to reveal the full impact of the sign upon his raw flesh, continuously wiping away blood so that they can gaze upon its full glory.

To crown off his achievement, Mickey_G! picks at the tiny bundles of hard leftover cheese which have coalesced on their own greasy stains on the box lid of his most recent pepperoni feast, coaxing them into a quasi-molten state using the subpar heat from his supercharged vape mod. It's difficult to maintain concentration, what with his senses roaring from both pain and pleasure, but eventually he manages to drip enough hot yellow-grey cheese onto his gaping chest wounds. There's no additional pain from this move: he has at this stage felt everything he's ever going to feel. He'd love to see what the reactions are at this point, but something thicker than his vape haze is blocking his view. Dark stars beckon at the periphery of his vision, reeling his senses further and promising death and disaster.

For one brief moment, he hesitates, but it's way too late now. The design is complete.

Mickey_G! slumps back into his designer red and white ergonomic chair, barely conscious and rapidly losing blood. His viewing numbers have rocketed to over thirty thousand, the shares and comments coming in faster than his bloodshot eyes can keep up with. He smiles one last enigmatic smile at those who have watched his disquieting transfiguration and his eyes close with a painful serenity as he passes into oblivion. The camera remains live, focused on the sign emblazoned on his breast where flap the tatters of his ragged flesh.

***

That's the end of the story for Mickey_G! Unfortunately, it's only the beginning of the end of the real story.

"*Bizarre horrifying death streamed by YouTuber!*"

<Click>

"*This is what happens if you take things too far!*"

<Click>

"*12 homemade tattoos gone wrong! Number 12 will drive you insane!*"

<Click>

"*Like and share!*"

<Click>

"*OMG! Have you seen this?*"

<Click>

Rat Race

The blood-dimmed tide is loose and everywhere

There was one half of a dead rat in the deli kitchen and Barbara was not happy. A living rat was bad enough but could be chased away. A dead rat, well, that could be carefully disposed of: an unpleasant task, to be sure, but one that could be carried out swiftly. Half a rat? That meant an unsightly and unhealthy blemish: fur matted with blood, glistening entrails already swarming with maggots twisting across the floor. It also meant there was something else nearby that had fought and killed that rat, which basically meant only one thing: a bigger, smarter, faster rat, lurking somewhere out of sight in the shadows or among the cracks in the wall, watching her every move with beady eyes until it saw its chance to wreak more havoc in her larder.

There are somewhere near two million rats in New York, and despite it only being half seven in the morning, Barbara's whole day was already ruined by half of one of them. She sighed heavily, snapped on a pair of disposable gloves and heaved the blooded corpse into a white plastic bag, wincing and retching the whole time. It would take at least an hour to get this place fully cleaned up to code and she'd be late opening again and miss the morning rush. Some vital spark in her gave out, her shoulders slumped, and she allowed herself to sit down on the chair in the corner - just for a moment -

head in her hands, tears in her eyes, a curse on her lips. More than anything, she wanted this day to be already over. She wished that there could be just one day of not having to do extra just to keep up, one day where she still had energy at the end of her shift. If she'd known then what was about to happen, she might have wished for something entirely different.

***

Jakob wasn't having any better day than Barbara, but that's because he hadn't managed to get any sleep. He'd been homeless for over a year now, eking out whatever living he could manage, but always getting moved on in the end. Few people showed him any degree of kindness, but thankfully Barbara was one of them. Unfortunately, her little deli with the red and white striped canopy still looked closed as he pressed his pocked face against the glass. She was always open by now. That's probably why, instead of tucking into a free breakfast reuben, he was staring up at a makeshift mission manufactured from mud, brick, blood, sweat, tears and broken dreams, a sanctuary for the most desperate and downtrodden souls the city had ever met. They had probably seen him coming from six blocks away. Like always recognises like. He rooted around in his pockets for the remains of a cigarette he'd blagged earlier and tried lighting it, cradling it between his mittened, shaking fingers as he fumbled for his last, damp match. Then, having failed, he grasped the railing with all the strength he could muster and climbed the nine stairs up to the door. Behind him on the sidewalk, chittering and watching him curiously, was a large, brown rat. As his hand closed round the doorknob, the rat shrieked and ran off into a nearby sewer grate.

***

Saul and Audrey, by contrast, began the day in better spirits. Audrey was standing in a red and white striped tent at an intersection just around the corner from Barbara's deli and the mission, tracing a line over a blueprint on top of a pile of many similar blueprints. Occasionally, without looking, she'd reach down with her left hand and take a bite out of a sandwich wrapped in brown paper and tied up with a little piece of string attached to which was a thoughtful note which read 'I love you', the sort of gift her partner had lovingly prepared for her every working day in the year since they'd been married. Saul was standing patiently outside on the sidewalk waiting for instructions, his blue hard hat firmly in place and hiding his impressive ginger monobrow, but not his equally impressive sideburns. Any minute now she'd tell them where to dig and he'd whistle to the team to get working. Hard work, sure. Dangerous too, sometimes. But feeling like he was part of the city was something he always found rewarding and every moment of heavy drilling was flushed with civic pride. He looked back from his crew to Audrey in the tent and, in a moment of shock and panic, nearly jumped out of his skin. Then, seemingly recovered, he whipped his cell from the pocket of his hi-vis jacket and started recording a video.

Audrey reached down to her sandwich only to find it wasn't there. Her movement was so automatic that it took her a moment to register its absence. When she looked over, she could see the shit-eating grin on Saul's face as he raised his cell phone to start recording and followed the reach of his extending finger as he pointed down at the floor. There on the concrete was the hugest rat she'd ever seen, tugging away at her sandwich, dragging it over to the street outside. It was one of the boldest moves she'd ever seen. She managed to suppress both her shock and her fear and just began to watch as the rodent pushed and pulled at it with claws and teeth, until it turned the corner of the little tent and vanished out of sight. Saul followed, still filming, until the rat disappeared down a crack in the pavement, sandwich still in tow. The attendant brown paper fluttered whimsically away on the breeze, darting down the road until it too vanished down a nearby alley. They both watched it for a while, still flabbergasted at the audacious rat. The wind picked up briefly and, just for a second, the street seemed to go silent.

Then everybody's world fell apart.

***

Later, when the dust began to clear, those at street level weren't quite sure what had happened. There was now a gigantic crack in the middle of the road, which had become littered at its periphery

66

with the debris of street furniture and the remains of cars and bikes that had been chewed up and then partially regurgitated onto the sidewalk. Along the full length of a block and a half, the tarmac looked like it had been ripped open by a giant pair of hands which had extended prying fingers beneath the surface as if to uncover some precious, lost heirloom. The whole scene was a mass of spraying hydrants, a chorus of clashing car alarms, clouds of errant brick dust, blinking lights, collapsed streetlights, and two small fires. The power grid was down, and emergency services vehicles would soon arrive to block out the limits of the damage, encouraging people to maintain a safe distance whilst letting them get on with the vital work of checking for survivors. These phenomena in themselves, even without the additional problems created by the massive fissure in the middle of the street, would suffice to fill the city's news cycle for several days. People would say it was a miracle that nobody had died or been seriously injured. Earnest news anchors would claim that surely 'somebody would have to answer for the mess' and that 'power should be held accountable for the failings evident at the scene of devastation'. All that was apparent to those at street level. But Audrey, Saul, Barbara and Jakob weren't at street level. Not anymore.

***

Jakob woke first, unsure of his surroundings or how he'd got here. If your every waking day can turn into a nightmare at any moment, you tend to take everything in your stride or give in to the new bad completely. Jakob placed himself firmly in that first category, always had. That's how he survived. He tried to stand, then regretted it when he hit his head on something in the surrounding darkness. Cursing, he tried to work out what it was. Smooth, cold, metallic, with a diameter just too big for a clenched fist. He reached down into his coat pocket and fumbled again for that last match in the hope of it offering him even the vaguest clue of what had happened. Then he heard another voice behind him, a voice that sounded quite familiar.

Barbara's leg was coated in something wet and sticky, which, after a brief clutch at her calf with a bruised hand, she realised must be her own blood. Given how much of it she could feel, it felt strange that she wasn't in more pain. She couldn't see anything, but remembered the rattling and crashing noises the pots and pans in the kitchen had made, then the smashing noises as crockery was let loose from walls and tables, then the floor giving way under her to swallow her up. At that point she'd lost her footing and tumbled to the ground, only to find it wasn't there to tumble onto. She kept falling, cascading through a giant hole beneath her now-wrecked deli, passing pipes at strange angles which hissed out jets of steam, followed by a great intersection of larger pipes which clearly held sewage, evident to Barbara's nose even as she continued to fall. The commitment of gravity to facilitate her downward progress was hindered at every opportunity by the further indignities the fall inflicted on her body: hair tangles, minor bruises, the loss of some of the utensils she kept in her pinafore. Finally, after what seemed like an interminable time, she emerged head-first into a cooler, wetter place, swathed in darkness, and landed unceremoniously with a splash in an inch and a half of what she prayed was merely mud. She was disappointed not to find herself in Wonderland but counted herself lucky to still be mostly in one piece.

"What just happened?" Barbara was used to talking to herself, or to her cats when she was at home. (No cats in the deli. City code rules. No doubt the rats were delighted)

"The road caved in. Don't you try and stand up. 'T'ain't safe." A hoarse, raspy, voice. An older voice. A familiar voice.

"Jakob? That you?"

"Well, it ain't Mel Brooks."

"Where are you? I can't see anything."

"Reckon I'm about ten feet to your left and two feet up."

"You OK?"

"Yeah, sure. Top of the world. Heh-heh."

As they began to edge closer to each other, a good deal of rubble began to fall close by, inches away from Barbara's face but close enough to Jakob's that some of the dust made him cough and a stray brick hit him on his bare left foot. There was a good deal of swearing and cursing at that moment and then another voice interrupted. This time it wasn't one either of them recognised.

***

69

From the first expansion of that tiny crack the rat had crawled into, Audrey and Saul had guessed at once what might be coming. That didn't help at all when the ground gave way under the tent. Their downward spiral was similar to the others, but their experience of it was vastly different given their more apparent familiarity with the city's underpinning foundations. The depth and consistency of the often eccentric infrastructure constructed or found beneath Manhattan is recorded roughly as follows in great blue filing cabinets in far-flung offices at the rear of City Hall, and, despite the tragedy that was befalling them, was recorded by their two pairs of eyes as they began a joint, ungainly descent. It goes like this:

Immediate: cellars and basement apartments

6 feet under: steam pipes used in heating and cooling buildings

7 feet: a small boarded up room with walls and ceilings covered in mirrors

8 feet: sewage pipes

10 to 180 feet: subway tunnels, depth depending on the line and station

15 feet: a 92 feet long shipwreck, in an area which used to be shallow water

20 feet: a warren of small tunnels under Chinatown, once used by gangsters to transport bootleg liquor

50 feet: several hundred feet of highway built in the 1960s

Etc, etc. Basically, it's a lot busier and weirder than most people think, a real slice of New York's long history. But Audrey and Saul aren't most people. It's not the weirdness that bothers or surprises them, it's the fact that these weirder finds were reported from all over Manhattan island and beyond by centuries of public works engineers digging merrily beneath the city's roads to lay more cables, clear out slums, create more subway routes and generally conduct routine maintenance on the more common elements of the city's underground infrastructure. When they do so, they consult colossal meticulously kept blueprints of what's already there, because nobody wants to drill through a thick electric cable or suddenly find sewer water overflowing in the street because someone took a pick to the wrong section of wall at the wrong depth at the wrong intersection. It had been copies of these prints that Audrey had been consulting when the street had swallowed them up.

To get back to the point here: they shouldn't be passing by all of these in one fall back in time through the city's history; these finds were scattered around all five boroughs. So what occurs to them both, apart from 'ouch', is 'huh?'

***

They started arguing almost the instant they hit the ground, Audrey just managing to avoid landing on top of Saul by virtue of twisting herself at the last moment and spraining her ankle in the process. Strangely, it only occurred to them later that neither of them should have survived such an extraordinary fall through so much gravel and mud and sewage and cable and flagstone and bedrock and history. What happened between them once they landed was the same dance that always happens between overseer and worker when something catastrophic happens. It's called the blame game.

"Christ, I'm gonna lose my job over this! Why on earth didn't your crew wait until I'd given the all clear?"

"Don't you start on me! We hadn't even marked a dig site. We'd have started earlier if you'd just…"

"Excuse me?!" That didn't come from either of them.

"Isn't there something better to do than argue about which of you got us into this mess? Like, how exactly do you intend to get us out?"

They both turned to greet the new voice. Saul fumbled in a pocket for a big torch which he shook into life with a flick of his wrist.

"Hey, watch where you're shining that! Can't a fella just enjoy the dark once in a while? Heh-heh."

"Who the hell are you two?"

"Wow, friendly greetings to you too. Most days, I make your sandwiches. You never even noticed me? I'm swelling with pride here."

"That's Barbara from the deli, and I'm Jakob from…around." He shrugged. "I guess you're the lucky crew that got the swanky assignment marking ground for a new subway line? Pleased to meet ya." He extended a hand so caked in blood and dust that nobody wanted to shake it, so he instantly withdrew the offer and instead thrust it deep in one of his many pockets.

There was a silence between them all which nobody seemed to want to break, so nobody did. In that hush a new noise emerged, one which started low and distant, but which heightened in pitch, intensity and volume as it drew gradually closer to them. It wasn't a noise any of them had heard before, nor one they even wanted to hear again. It was the chittering of hundreds of rats. The collapse of the road, it seemed, was only going to be the first of their worries.

***

Rats have been chomping away at the Big Apple since the first boats arrived in the port: the wretched refuse of foreign shores, huddled masses yearning to break free. As numerous as they once were, they have never been more aggressive, more ferocious, more adaptable. New Yorkers, no strangers to adaptation themselves, have come up with many ingenious ways to kill them: with poison, with dogs, with extreme prejudice, with rat czars. The fittest survive, though, and breed…and breed…and breed. Take one statistic by means of example: The count of rats killed is roughly 100 brown rats to 10 black rats to 1 alexandrian rat. You might extrapolate from that data and assume that was roughly the division of population in the three types of rat common in the city, but that ain't necessarily the case. Perhaps there were ten times more brown than black rats; perhaps the black rats were ten times sneakier at avoiding capture. Being a rather unpleasant sort of statistic, it's not something regular New Yorkers spend a great deal of time or energy contemplating, and our four protagonists are nothing if not regular New Yorkers. They looked on in a mix of disgust, fear and plain horror as a carpet of brown fur, glistening with muck and sewer water, rounded a nearby corner, occupying every inch of ground and three inches of the tunnel wall as the hundreds of rats that composed it raced toward them, hungry and unafraid. Barbara, still in her rage-hate state against her earlier intruder, overcame her revulsion first and began throwing things at them in a futile attempt to stem the ravenous tide. Despite everything she hurled at them - a saucepan, three knives, two rocks and even her right sneaker (for good measure), none of them so much as flinched. Jakob froze in place, flexing in a manner that indicated he hadn't decided whether fight or flight was the more effective response, especially when neither seemed possible. Audrey shrieked and tried to clamber up a nearby rusty ladder, which almost immediately gave way and deposited her, still on that sprained ankle, back in the mire and grime of the tunnel. Saul, with the benefit of having a light already to hand, managed to shine it at full power directly into the oncoming rodent rush. This did nothing except to highlight the extent of their peril as the torchlight glinted equally off dark matted fur, beady black eyes and even glimpses of sharp yellow-white teeth. With no means of escape, they bundled together for whatever comfort they might find in what was left of their shared humanity, even though each of them secretly hoped that their position in the group would ensure they were the last to be attacked. There still remained among them a glimmer of hope that they might still avoid the particularly horrific fate that apparently awaited them, a glimmer that briefly sputtered into full flame as the parade surrounded them, circling and eyeing their huddling forms with soulless gazes, until they stopped, all standing at once on hind legs, their rancid claws scrambling at the air before them as if fighting off an unseen flow.

Yet this apparent moratorium on their mortality was appalling in itself, in that this is not the sort of thing that rats do. Still, with no apparent means of extricating themselves from danger, it was Jakob who took the first step forward toward the throng of small, furry bodies that had them trapped. No tentative movements here: a full lurch which might have startled a starling but made no impression on their tiny captors. Three were felled beneath his right boot with a sickening crunch before the others reacted.

They swarmed over Jakob - a few at first, then tens, then finally hundreds - snickering and chittering away, gnawing with tiny teeth and grinding with tiny jaws. Before Barbara could get to him, they covered every part of his long, thin frame, covering him in a carpet of slick, putrid velvet even as he kicked and punched back, sending many of them reeling and fleeing back into the open sewer, but eventually returning to take part in their malodorous massacre. The howls and screeches from Jakob's throat were horrific to hear, but soon drowned out by the continuous skittering noises as more rats swam and ran toward them, covering all parts of the tunnel now, eager to partake in the grisly feast. Audrey and Barbara recoiled into each other's arms to seek sanctuary in solidarity; Saul averted his eyes but not his torch, incapable of any action other than illuminating the ghoulish scene for the edification of the two women who would, at this stage, rather be coddled in the comfort of darkness. Then, after an interval measured only in heartbeats, silence once again descended. The screams that followed it this time weren't because of the rats, but at what had become of Jakob as the throng receded from his still-twitching corpse.

Four rats, working diligently together, had chewed through each of his arms and were tugging at the tendons and sinews until they were without his body and stretched upon the slag heap. Three more had worked their way inside what remained of his mouth and throat. Yet more, tearing through the bare sinews with purpose and vigour, then carried one end of those threads to the ceiling. Jakob's body twitched back into a semblance of life and he began to walk forward down the dank corridor ahead of them, trailing blood in the thick sludge as the rats moved him as a puppeteer might move a marionette, their shadowed forms barely visible on the tunnel ceiling only because that was where the glistening sinews ended and rat teeth began.

His jaw opened, mouth still full of rat, and the horrid dead form of Jakob spoke to them, a muffled sound but one that only needed to convey one instruction.

"Follow us."

***

The rats, led now by the ambulatory mockery of Jakob's dead body, directed the others through a series of tunnels, twisting and turning so that not even Saul could tell where in the city they might be beneath. It was not just the rats that teemed down here, but the millions of tons of refuse the city generated every year, the billions of gallons of wastewater. Everything the city didn't want ended up on these underground shores. Finally, there was light ahead. Not the bright light of day, nor even the diffused neon and stars of a city night. The light came from the rubble around them; the profusion of broken glass which had once lit city streets and comfortable homes but now glowed and glowered at them from the darkness and stillness of what could only be a great cistern.

Water - if, at this stage of its evolution through the city's waste pipes, it could even be called that - trickled and poured into this chamber through a hundred apertures. It oozed through tiny fissures in the slime-decked walls. It cascaded in lively, gushing torrents from dark tunnels which Barbara never knew existed, Audrey knew shouldn't exist and Saul knew couldn't exist. The steady flow of excrement continued to bob around them. Each of them tried to hold their nose and close their mouths to keep nausea at bay, but it overcame them anyway. There was a small, rock-like platform onto

77

which the parade of rodents deposited them. On a similar plinth across the chamber, lit by a single shaft of light from the ceiling, there was another rat, fatter and meaner than the rest. That would have been enough of a sight in itself were it not for the thousands of other rats which now surrounded them, each chittering away in supplication to what appeared to Barbara to be some sort of rat queen. Partly, her supposition was a hunch based on the way the rats behaved toward her and partly it was because this rat had managed to slip inside - and then grow inside - what appeared in the strange half-light of the cistern to be a discarded ballerina pointe shoe. Even in its dishevelled state, Barbara could make out the delicate shape of it: pink satin stained brown with muck, ribbon laces trailing behind it as if it were the train of a wedding dress.

If what had happened thus far was not enough to convince the three of them that they were living in a nightmare, what happened next was the clincher.

The rat queen spoke.

***

Barbara screamed. At this stage, it was the only possible and appropriate reaction. Audrey looked away, burying her head straight into Saul's shoulder, but then turned her head back, hoping everything had changed again, that Barbara's scream had pierced the walls of this unreality and sent them hurtling back upward to the familiar rattle and hum of New York above.

Saul blinked. His hand went instinctively to his phone. People had to see this… then he dropped the cell in pain, sploshing down into the depths of the canal of effluence, forever beyond his reach. He brought his hand up to see what had happened and found a great rat still clinging to it fiercely with sharp teeth piercing the back of his great, hairy hand as if it had been starved since breakfast. It was the same rat that he'd tried to video earlier. He threw his hand around in agony, trying to dislodge it, but it continued chomping. He bellowed in pain, adding his voice to Barbara's in the weird echo of the fetid chamber.

Then Jakob spoke.

"Pray silence! Silence for Vagabond Shoe! Silence for the herald of the Mother of Exiles! Here at our sewage-washed sluice gates she stands!"

Now, with lips finally silent, the rat spoke again: a hoarse, raspy voice, but one which still sounded undeniably feminine.

"What have thou brought me?"

Audrey was about to speak, though she was not convinced she could at this moment. Then she realised that it was not her that was being addressed.

"More wretched refuse, o colossus of rats. Witnesses to our numbers, testimonies to our strength." Jakob's slack jaw opened and closed as baby rats crawled in and out of it while others gnawed furiously through his larynx and lungs to operate his speech.

The rat queen turned to Jakob to thank him, then back to the others. "Too long has the city ignored us. Too long has it ignored many. Liberty is forgotten. Life is cheap. Corruption is rife. We shall show it true liberty. The unfettered, famished liberty of my teeming hordes, each eager for a life undreamed of. New York will be ours! You stand before us now, but you can stand alongside us or with us, should you wish. You know this city like the back of your clammy hands. You know its hunger, its belly, its veins, its blood. I see my scouts chose well."

"We will never support you!" That was Audrey, her voice found at last. "You're an abomination!"

The queen laughed. Pray you never live long enough to hear a rat laugh. It's the single most unpleasant sound you will ever hear.

"You have done nothing but support me. Hundreds of miles of new tunnels! The discarded remains of thousands of breakfasts! And we thank you. Now, it is time to claim what is rightfully ours. This audience is only a courtesy. Flee, now, if you wish. Your warnings will not matter. All will be swept aside in the coming storm. You have been temporary custodians, at best. It is time for the Mother of Exiles to walk the streets above. I've always wanted to stray there. And there is little you can do to stop me."

She turned away from them and spoke to her army of rats. "Tell them all. We start now."

They ran, then. How far, they do not recall. For how long, they do not know. When they finally emerged, bruised and blinking back in the city they once knew, the rats had gotten there first. Right to the very heart of it.

The Last Resort
The ceremony of innocence is drowned

It is not easy writing this message. I have lived a life of privilege, free of guilt, free of consequence. It is only in the events of the last few hours that each of these has caught up with me and forced me to witness the true horrors of my actions.

I do not seek forgiveness, for I know now that is beyond me. I know my fate. My only hope is that whosoever should find this will learn from the error of my ways and therefore that my death may have more meaning than my life. I go now willingly, but not before I pen this dire warning to those of a similar calling or possessed of like ideas. You will bring this place, all places, to utter ruin and destruction in your futile pursuits. Stop now before it is too late.

If that warning is insufficient, if you demand evidence, then allow me to attach a name and a story to it so that the world may come to understand the folly of my life and the manner of my execution. Read on and weep, by all means, but take heed of the lessons within. These lessons are for us all.

I am known to the world as 'Captain' Yiannis Xiphias, shipping magnate, owner of fleets of commercial ships and ocean liners. It is typical among us monied folk to indicate that our wealth is a well-deserved reward for a lifetime of hard work. My own life differs considerably from this narrative, and I make no claim to it: it is common enough knowledge in the biographies in glossy magazines that I was a jobbing deckhand who just happened to be close enough to save a drowning heiress from a watery grave. When romance ensued from gratitude, her father cared not that I was poor, only that I was clearly a man of the sea.

Thus, catapulted into both fame and fortune, my life changed immeasurably for the better. Previous friends were treated with the professional aloofness befitting my new status as their ultimate boss. The crew I'd served with became distant and in their place the yachting set embraced me with open arms. I moved in different circles, learning the old man's business with his daughter on my arm. I expanded the operations rapidly and confidently. Our cruise liners were packed with eager sightseers, swooping on every Mediterranean port, flocking to bazaars and churches, museums and galleries, keen to have a quick fix of cultures they could take home and place on their mantelpieces as mementos. I latched onto each new venture with the arrogant swagger of someone who had it all but always wants more and will do anything to get it.

It was early February when my yacht Helen's Joy rounded the coast and drew close to the haunting beauty of La Serenissima, that ancient and marvellous city of Venice where I had hoped to meet with like-minded company to enjoy the celebrations of the annual carnival. I should have noticed first that something was amiss, when the air and the waters alike were enveloped in a low, lingering fog rather than the brilliance of the late winter sunshine which habitually greeted us at this time of year. The light in Venice always visits twice: first from the sun and then from boundless reflections on the canals which have lent a quiet beauty and elegance to the city from time immemorial.

We drew in toward the docks which came up before us in eerie silence. I could spot masked figures waiting for us at the quayside, cowled and cloaked, but with none of the exuberance of carnivale partygoers. A great shadow loomed to our left and squinting through the mist I could make out a few lights and the distant, sputtering thrums of motors. As we drew nearer, I was shocked to see the name of one of our liners, the Tyche, now a rusted hulk, rammed against the debris of a customs-house at the dock edge. As I looked on in horror, familiar but forgotten voices raised themselves from behind those masks and began a mournful shanty I remembered from my early days at sea:

"And one more day ashore we'll go.
Leave her, Johnny, leave her."

My crew! My first crew! But what a greeting! I ran across the deck to return the refrain, but after a single line their chorus was drowned out by the relentless drone of a foghorn, so loud that its volume knocked me to the deck where I lay prostrated, hands over my ears in agony, until the waters rose so far that I was washed overboard and carried by the waves to be dumped unceremoniously at their feet. Not my most auspicious entrance.

I stood, sodden and shaken, water sloshing around my ankles. No. Not water. Blood, thick and red, swirling around my ankles, blood in the puddles and in the canals, lending an eerie red glow to the evening light. I brushed myself down, mask lost in the crimson tide at my feet. Wherever I was, this wasn't Venice, couldn't be Venice, at least not the one I knew from my many visits.

A lone gondola approached, the fog parting reverently around it as the gondolier, cloaked in heavy raiment of shimmering black velvet, drew up to the nearest mooring post. What face lay hidden in the depths of his night-black hood I have only now begun to guess. At that juncture, I was still grimly transfixed by the novelty of the experience and when a single, crooked finger emerged from the long robe and beckoned me approach, I felt helpless to resist.

"Now the rats have gone and we the crew."

We progressed in total silence except for the slow movement of the oar through the waters and that haunting melody whispered through the darkness by the chorus of my first crew. From the cruise ship docks at Santa Chiara through the length of the Canale Grande, we passed under the covered bridge at Rialto. Here the gulls swirled in their hundreds, diving in ones or twos into the deep waters and emerging with cries of victory at the trinkets borne in their beaks, carrying them home to decorate distant nests. It was a disturbing and disgusting site to witness as they fought over meaningless trifles found in the foulest waters, pecking and plucking at the corpse of the city. My cowled gondolier said nothing, and it was clear he would not or could not answer any of the questions burning in my throat. We continued, the solitary travellers on this maritime highway, until he began to slow down at the Salute docks at the stairs of the Basilica di Santa Maria Della Salute, our Lady of Health. I scrambled to my feet, still full of questions, but eager to escape the macabre and unsettling clutches of the ferryman.

The Basilica was submerged in the low, thick smog which I had first encountered on docking. Here, though, the hue of it was a sickly yellow-tan and it clung to the crumbling church like ancient ivy. Beneath that fog the waters had risen so precariously that they encroached over the top of the steps, just visible in the scarlet-hued waters beneath us. I raised a hand to my mouth in a vain attempt to hold back the sickly sulphurous smog as I clambered out of the gondola, still knee-deep in swirling waters and waist-deep in settled fog and made my way to the altar.

Votive candles commemorating the dead of the plagues which had been visited upon the city lay scattered in this once-holy place, now as forgotten and neglected as the Canal Grande itself. I reached up to find one I could still light, but those that remained were sodden and would not succumb to a flame.

"Where you wish to Christ you'd never been born."

Beneath this great dome, the inhabitants of the city had seemed to make a last stand of sorts. A vigil held in candlelit prayer; a ceremony of innocence now drowned. Now it was teeming with bloated, inundated dead, skeletal hands reaching out of the waters in desperate supplication, hoping for rescue from those on land - who had long forgotten them - and upward to the heavens who seemed to have done likewise. These sepulchral intrusions grabbed at my ankles beneath the surface, trying to drag me down with them to a watery grave. I managed to knock some of them away with a candelabra and scrambled up onto the relative safety of the altar, where my panic subsided and my panting gave way to a wracking, consuming cough. The pollutive mix of the smog, heavy with sulphur and nitrous oxides, fought its way into my mouth in an attempt to do to me what it had done to the building. Limestone statues of the saints had been heavily corroded, so much so that their faces were no longer recognisable. As I spluttered and wheezed and struggled to breathe, the only salvation came in the person of my gondolier. His finger was no longer beckoning but wagging in accusation. I struggled back to the gondola, and we departed in the same silence we had entered as we drifted slowly across to Piazza San Marco.

"Oh the work was hard and the voyage was long."

Every column in those fabled colonnades bore the enduring marks of the Acqua Alta: a succession of stains showing the height at which the spring waters had finally ceased their assault. I baulked when I saw that the topmost of these marks was a full arm's length over my head. Pinned to one column in the piazza, flapping audibly in the breeze

86

above the quietly dripping tears of a lost city, was a single flyer, seemingly oblivious to the destruction about it. Roughly translated, it indicated a place where the residents had made a last attempt to hold out against the rising tide, a place on higher ground where the desperate might find shelter. I took it with me, eager to leave this desolation behind and find out what had become of its final inhabitants. I left just as the Acqua Alta sirens began to sound and followed the directions on the flyer, each step taking me to higher ground, lest I become immersed in a tidal flow of blood, salt and water.

The flyer in my hand had almost disintegrated in the damp air by the time I reached the place marked on it. I looked up at the inauspicious building with its faded grandeur, cracked tiles and bust drainpipes. A rivulet of sludge navigated the slick cobbles at my feet. I looked down at the flyer again, making sure I had the address right, squinting at the smudged pulp in the night gloom. Devastated, dejected, disconsolate, I sat on the doorstep, my head in my hands, deciding what to do next. Then I looked up across the muddied gangplanks over the sludge- and trash-strewn alleyway to the low row of buildings opposite.

"In one more day, why we'll go too."

In the fog-choked darkness of the narrow passage, the row of squalid, huddled tenements loomed like a spectral bluff. Not a sound broke the brooding silence save for the screeching of gulls - those verminous vultures of the sea - far overhead in the gloom. Rain beat against the windows and against the roofs, where there were still roofs to beat upon and windows to beat against. It came down in hissing roars, then in whispers, then in loud shishes like sandpaper rubbed on a deck.

Human beings shouldn't have to enter such doors, shouldn't have to stay behind them. No sun or moon ever entered there, no stars, no anything at all. They were worse than the grave, for in the grave is the promise of closure, of or rebirth and another life. Providence orders the grave for all of us; but providence did not order such lodgings as these rat-fat alleys teeming with refuse and the grim, mould-slick halls within which wretched souls are forced to dwell.

I stepped through that threshold. Huddled there against the walls were those last few living inhabitants of this doomed city, rag-clad and cheerless, their red eyes rimmed with sorrow and loss. They looked up, pleading, desperate, until the glimmer of recognition reached the watery grey of their eyes, and I realised with horror that they knew who I was.

If the city was doomed, it was I who had doomed it, and in doing so also doomed myself. Those doomed souls, driven to a semblance of life in this abject hovel, knew the architect of their destruction. Sorrow gave way to anger, grief to wrath. One hand raised a fist in fury, then others took up that call and began pelting me with the contents of that beleaguered ruin: broken Murano glassware, rubble groaning with the weight of history and rotted vegetables from the markets of Mestre. I stood in silence and let myself undergo this onslaught with the last scrap of dignity I could muster until, their rage spent, they withdrew to the upper floors in a mindless, pitiless procession of shuffling feet and murmured curses.

I don't know how long I then spent meandering, lost in the depths of the sinking city and my own thoughts. The next thing I recalled is that I was back on that same gondola, passing under the Ponte dei Sospiri.

The Bridge of Sighs was a sorry sight, evocative now of not even a murmur. There was no beauty here any more to offer a condemned man his last, fleeting glimpse of La Serenissima. Its Istrian limestone, which had once glistened so white as to elicit such sighs from prisoners on their way to judgement, was pocked with grey splotches of shadowed mould which in combination with the moon-specked blood of the Rio del Palazzo, gave the impression of entering Hell itself. Blackened, tattered banners hung from its barred windows, wherein I spied a single figure, staring back out at me. I recoiled instantly but then turned back to face that irrevocable fate of an unmasked reflection of myself, in procession to the palace of the Doge. In an instant I was with him in that place, and I stared through the stone bars as my ferryman waited for me on the cool waters as the chorus ushered me forward. Only then did I allow myself a sigh, a single sigh for the lost beauty of the place and another, deeper sigh for the formal trial I knew was about to come.

"And it's time for us to leave her."

Inside the palace a makeshift throne had been crudely fashioned from the rubble and here sat a figure masquerading as Aeacus, he who was famed for his justice in life and now holds court to judge the dead.

Surrounding him were many other figures. My first crew continued their role as tragic chorus while I stared into the faces of my later crews, haggard through overwork and underappreciated, whose gaze I could now barely meet. Along the stone parapets and atop crumbling columns sat the gulls. Voracious yet still aggrieved, fleecing those tourists was my second egregious sin. Neither of these compared to the legion of drowned dead who now stood arrayed to one side of the courtyard, blood lapping at their feet, their number too numerous to count, no longer able to give voice themselves but seemingly content that Aeacus would do it for them.

He did this with a single gesture, a shake of the head which indicated disappointment so extreme it is rarely seen except upon the face of a parent.

My crew picked up the last refrain of their shanty and the remainder of the crowd carried the chorus until the choice of words finally came crashing down on me like Hokusai's great wave.

"It's time for us to leave her
Leave her, Johnny, leave her
For the voyage is done and the winds won't
blow."

Leave her. Not the sea, not the ship, not even the city, but life itself. I'd overstayed my welcome. I begged humbly for one final attempt at contrition which, in their leniency, they granted. It is this last, anguished endeavour that you hold in your hands.

I leave this message in a bottle and consign it to the ocean in the vain hope that benevolent currents carry its confessions and lamentations to the ears of those who need to hear it. One final journey awaits me, one we must all take, one whose ferryman has now been paid in full: in blood and horror, in tumultuous waters and rotting terrors, in life and death. I see it drawing close now through these dark waters, its prow low, its gondolier as silent as the grave itself. The waves withdraw from that ship of endings as it approaches and gather again in its wake, out of respect and sheer terror both. I offer my wretched soul as passage to the infernal ferryman Charon and to the eternal punishments of the underworld that lie beyond the lagoon and across the murky waters of the Styx.

A Design for Life

The best lack all conviction, while the worst

I was in an underground cocktail bar in a cellar beneath a bridge when the bells rang to tell me that the end of the world had started. That's the kind of thing we did back then, the kind of place there was before it happened.

I was halfway back to my branded budget hotel, cursing my timing, my age and my fitness (though not strictly in that order) when I became aware that I was being followed. How they'd found me so quickly I didn't know. I'd deliberately kept a low, off-grid profile in those last, desperate days - the very essence of incommunicado. There were seven bridges back across the river - there's only the one now, of course - and I was between two of them, in the sort of place normally inhabited on an autumn evening by dog walkers and young lovers. It reminded me, whimsically, of Paris in the old days, of meandering along the banks of the Seine arm in arm with Michel, sharing a headset back and forth as we listened to the latest jazz tracks. It was that moment of whimsy that ultimately cost me.

It takes me two circuits to really get the feel of any city; it's a handy skill I've acquired. One trip in the daytime with the sun overhead and the streets clean with fresh early morning rain and one after dark, lit by the pin pricks of a hundred streetlights and the fevered prospects of a hundred revellers. Which roads have all the bars and restaurants?

They'll be full of people on a summer evening, less so in the winter. Where do the local kids hang out? That's discernible even in their absence by the bins full of discarded things - cans, cigarette ends, needles, condoms, hopes, dreams. Where is the open ground? Plazas and gardens set as an antidote to steel and stone, cobbles slick with winter frost or strewn with crisp autumn leaves. Westgate, Oldgate, Eastgate, North Street, South Street, Station Road... every old city has at least one of them and they're all pretty much where you expect.

You pick these things up as a spook, whether you're hunter or hunted. Before I got drafted into the counter-occult services, though, I was a town planner who had asked too many questions. That's how they got me. They told me the secrets that would change my life. That we weren't alone. That we'd already been invaded twice but that threat had been seen off. That they were expecting another incursion - another test of the waters to gauge our reaction. That they needed my help and contacts specifically. They flattered me and I fell for it. If they hadn't, it's likely they'd have threatened me instead. The end justifies the means when that end is preventing an apocalypse.

I brought up a mental map of the town I was in and its local landmarks. They were usually obvious and well signposted; churches, abbeys and spires that have been there longer than half the town; magnificent civic edifices of grey slate and white marble that form the heart of any old European city - a town hall, a church, a museum, a gallery. It's sometimes unexpected what you find near them though; rows of little huts lined up along the edge in preparation for a christmas market, giant umbrellas and wooden benches for outdoor eating. Imagine! In those days we wasted both heat and light energy on outdoor street dining in this part of the world, even in the winter, even in the rain. I always thought rising energy prices or climate change would put paid to that, but that played second fiddle to another horseman of the apocalypse, then another, until it was too late. Our plans began to unravel and then the liminal made their move.

They came from a between-space we had termed the interstitial, for want of a more precise nomenclature. A place between realities. What other realities lay beyond we had only been able to guess at. If anyone had visited those alternate realities and returned, we didn't know of them - and believe me we had people looking. The liminal came into our world from the shadows. Literally. Every human shadow (we'd never encountered a liminal non-human) had the potential to take on a life of its own, infused with the life-force of a liminal spirit. That's why there was so much insistence within the counter-occult community on well-lit outdoor spaces. That's why we hoped people would gather together, even without discernible purpose. Where shadows merged with one another, or fell in the shadow of tall buildings, it made it much harder for the liminal to get through. That's what we were relying on. They focused on latching on to the shadows of those alone. You were safer in the light. You were safer in complete darkness too, but that was much harder to engineer and maintain in any increasingly packed metropolis and somewhat detrimental to regular human existence.

I looked down on the town from the vantage point of a bridge. You could tell who'd heard the news and who hadn't. There wasn't a grand outpouring of fear and anger and desperation. People didn't take to the streets. They gathered in place, mostly, in dimly lit living rooms, behind closed doors of cocktail bars in cages of neon and gin, in front of giant TVs in sports bars. News passed through crowds in a wave, but there were still smatterings of the uninformed, drinking and eating their merry way through our last evening of freedom.

Someone in the unit had had the bright idea to ring the cathedral and church bells as the first sign. Where they were present and understood, we latched onto existing protocols for wars gone by when our enemies were easier to pinpoint and easier to defeat. Perhaps it was some old, half-forgotten protocol done in deference to a dusty rulebook which had sat in a cupboard labelled IN CASE OF EMERGENCY, like it was a fire that could be put out if one just followed the rules and had rudimentary plans. But the third incursion - what would be briefly known as the Great Incursion until labelling things was rendered pointless - was anything but rudimentary.

Everyone knew what the bells meant; nobody knew what the bells meant. In those precious moments after the peals began, the exodus started, and the streets thrummed with the crowd of bodies and the heady scents of panic and confusion. People hugged and cried and held their heads. They rushed to their loved ones and where that wasn't possible physically, they tried it digitally. Mobile networks were overwhelmed in a matter of minutes. That was what we wanted them to do. That's how our research had indicated we could combat the liminal. For a while, it worked.

I'd rushed to this bridge but then paused to take in my surroundings, which was foolish of me because there were now two of them in front of me and as well as two more behind and I was stuck between them. At least I was trapped over water, which our research said was helpful even if we didn't understand exactly why. It seemed to have to do with the way ripples on the water broke up the form of the human shadow. It would have been difficult for a lay person to notice the liminal in those days. Later, of course, it was much easier. They were the ones still walking.

They'd singled me out. They knew who I was. Or at least, what I used to be. Whether they still thought I was a threat that needed eliminating or whether it was revenge for the experimental procedures the units had inflicted on any of them we'd managed to briefly capture, I didn't know. I'd been out of the intelligence loop for a couple of years by that point. I'd been more afraid that my former colleagues would catch up with me than I was about the looming liminal threat. Clearly, that had been a misplaced fear on my part. One that I was about to pay for.

I made to dive into the river. Cold as it was, they couldn't get me there, I was sure. No shadows under water. If I made it, I could survive there for a few minutes while thinking over my next move. Unfortunately, they got to me first. Four men, seemingly deliberately selected for their large size, bound by their own shadows, bore down on me. I thought that would be the end of me, almost welcomed it in that frozen moment of time when there was no movement and no direction, nowhere to go and nowhere to hide. One of them pulled out a flashlight. That was a new tactic. They were learning, adapting. We would be too late to respond. They flashed the torch - not into my eyes, but at my feet as I'd feared. My own shadow lengthened, then contorted and shrunk again back into me. I watched, unable to stop anything that would happen next, screaming silently behind now unfamiliar eyes. I never made it far enough to see if the incursion was local, national or global, or to check back in somehow and warn anyone else that would listen. They had me in their umbral grasp and I was unable to struggle. I heard a few plaintive cries from outlying streets, then more and more, with increasing urgency and proximity. Three people ran across one of the other bridges, silhouetted in the moonlight, then one by one they succumbed to the inevitable.

In the days that were to come, I saw that a lot.

They made me watch.

They made me watch it all.

Given the entire span of urban history, permanent street lighting to the extent that we had engineered it was quite a recent phenomenon. Light was good, darkness was bad, therefore what we needed was more light. Criminality thrived in unlit alleys and on the edges, in the shadows where there was more darkness than light. It used to be that nightwatchmen patrolled the streets, keeping a watchful eye on the darkness and shining a light into the darkest corners of humanity. Nocturnal travellers were few and far between and always regarded with suspicion, even then many carried candles, rushlights, oil lanterns, torches. Unless you didn't want to be seen, of course. Then you fumbled in the dark, slowly, deliberately, obviously up to no good.

Gradually, the night became lighter. Houses and shops on main streets were required to hang lanterns outside after night. Then gas lamps came, and finally electric street lighting. All of this done with the best of intentions. Sometimes those intentions were nudged by counter-occult teams; these really took off in the late Victorian and early Edwardian eras. Minor incursions from the liminal were dealt with summarily, then covered up. We carried on fighting, carried on recruiting, but it was a war we thought we'd won.

We were wrong.

Standing here, in the heart of the city, under this streetlight, I saw it all. I saw it from behind my own eyes as my shadow self stood, arms folded, smiling from my mouth and indignant to my silent pleas from a voice now hidden deep inside a form I was both unfamiliar and familiar with.

Then, I did the unthinkable in pursuit of the impossible. I reached out, forcing my mind into a mental conversation with the liminal that possessed me.

There was only one question to ask. The answer to it had eluded the counter-liminal unit during its entire history. I'd never found the answer in any of the extensive literature amassed in our libraries, nor in any of the brief excursions into the liminal realms or in interrogation of shadow prisoners. Perhaps it wasn't a question we had asked very often. We knew we were in a secret war with them. We just had to win.

"Why?"

I could feel my own brain reeling at the question. Then there was a painful wrenching feeling from my gut which forced me to the ground, shivering and retching. I was beginning to regret those earlier cocktails.

The shadow moved out of me, then away from me. As his fellows took the fight to those around us, as the city fell, it manifested eyes in the darkness - tiny slits where my own would be, questioning, probing. It was forcing itself to do that, at no considerable expense to its own existence, or so I wagered given the pain evident in those eyes, mirrors of mine own, staring down at me.

Exhausted, beyond contempt and almost beyond caring, I dared to find that answer if it was the last thing I did, which I imagined it probably would be. I resorted to anger.

"Why? Why do you do this? Why invade our world when you have one of your own? When our own plane of existence seems to make you uncomfortable in the extreme? Tell me!"

"Why?" I swore it raised an eyebrow, though it possessed nothing of the sort, only a pair of luminous, vacuous spots of formless emptiness in a vague, amorphous, umbral shape which now only vaguely resembled my own. "Because."

I had tried to stand, to steady myself against the streetlight, but failed and sat back down hard.

"We oppose you because you oppose us. We occupy your space to make it more like ours. Soon, it will be." Its voice was odd, as if it had trouble forming words, but hours of interrogating these before had prepared me for this jarring speech, this low, uncomfortable drone, this monotone of madness.

"You're evil! You must be destroyed. You're a threat to our civilization!"

He rounded on me as I tried to stand a second time. "Must all threats to your civilization be so destroyed? And who's civilization are you talking about? And are all those threats evil?" It looked right at me, no - I thought - right through me. I shuddered but managed to find my feet. It moved closer, slowly at first then suddenly leaping to clutch at my neck. What passed for its hands were icy cold as it attempted what I thought must be a stranglehold, but being made of shadowstuff, it was a threat easy to counter. To them, I thought, we must be evil. We must be wrong. Perhaps they were even right. That hadn't occurred to me before.

Perhaps there was still a chance, for peace talks, for reconciliation… It seemed to understand what I was thinking. A residual effect, perhaps, of taking my form, or of its recent possession of my body and mind.

"You have it wrong, human. We are not evil. Neither are you good."

It took a moment for this to sink in. Its demeanour seemed to relax a little as it regarded my puzzled expression, perhaps, just perhaps, in the hope that expressions might transform into one of understanding. Under that umbral gaze, though, I felt no sudden conversion, only vehement defiance.

"You want to end our world, to put a stop to what we've created. You're instruments of destruction. That makes evil, in my book."

"Ah. Your book. What book might that be?" I staggered to a standing posture as my mind reeled. Had it taken my statement literally?

"Your books, your holy texts…the authors of those I think understood what the true nature of the conflict is. It's not about good and evil. It never was. It's about creation and destruction. Either of those forces might be used for what you call good, or what you term evil."

It seemed to be enjoying this monologue. Since I'd managed to stand and fumble for my mobile phone in my jacket pocket, I was recording it all. In that way, I was enjoying the monologue as well. In falling prey to a classic villain trap, it was about to broadcast something to the world without realising, as soon as I reached into my pocket again and sent that recording back to the unit. I wasn't sure that was strictly necessary either, to be honest. If I was them, I'd have been looking for me. Chances are I was already bugged. I earnestly hoped that they could hear everything, understand the context. It might be our last, best chance of survival.

"Creation gives things a form. It imposes law on the underlying chaos of the cosmos. Your earliest mythologies and sacred texts understood this as the central theme. Creator deities of all stripes impose form and structure. Heroes rail against the chaos of their time, become rulers, fight for order over disorder. Bandits are driven out to the wilderness and then even that wilderness is tamed. Crime thrives best in the shadows, so you bring light. Yet, you have it wrong. So wrong."

Darkness seemed to ooze out of its snarl, hissing and spitting as it hit the dark cobbles beneath our feet. I idly toyed with the idea of legging it back to the bridge, making a dive into the river, but I felt attached to this spot, attached to this shadow of mine as we both stood beneath the streetlight. What if I broke that light? Plunged the area around me into darkness? Would that work? I gazed around for anything I could find within range to throw at it but came up empty. The liminal seemed to regard me with a kind of pity - it wasn't in its eyes so much as a vague emotion emanating from its umbral form. My form. That still spooked me, it was the first time it had happened to me, and I wish I'd read more of what to do next while I was still in the unit. My brain struggled to recall anything pertinent while it simultaneously juddered under the onslaught of monologue.

"Every hero venerated, every epic told, has tipped the scales on these fundamental truths. That nature, as you understand it, abhors a vacuum. That something is better than nothing. That every system, in the end of all things, tends towards entropy. That every action has an equal and opposite reaction. Every work undertaken, every time you decide you know what's best and impose your will, tips the balance in favour of order and against us. We are only the inevitable ending, the elastic band snapping back after being pulled, the extended rope suddenly snapping when its cut."

My best hope, I realised, was my worst fear less than an hour ago. That I hadn't been incommunicado. That the unit had been tracking me, after all, but had decided not to do anything. That didn't give me agency, though, only a desperate inner cry for a deus ex machina.

"You oppose us. Your very presence, everything you do, is anathema to our kind. In framing the debate as good against evil, you tragically lost sight of what the battle was supposed to be about, what it has always been about."

So that was it. There was no way to break free of this stalemate, this battle between the two of us, equal and opposites. The problem was in part that I agreed. We had over-engineered and over-planned. We'd brought in too much creation as well as too much light. The very thing that attracted their attention. I myself had always been drawn to those quirky neighbourhoods that we hadn't flooded with identikit chain stores, those thriving, busy, family-run cafes, those underground cocktail bars...

I managed one last gesture which I thought may well be futile. I launched my mobile phone from my pocket and shone the light from its torch app at his feet. That gave me one moment of disconnect as my shadow recoiled backward and a second as it lurched forward again. As it did so, I threw the device full-tilt at the streetlight. It shattered into a hundred tiny pieces, each miniature fragment crashing to the street, suddenly plunged into darkness.

I'll never forget what happened next. We both uttered the exact same phrase, alike in meaning but wholly separate in intent.

"What goes up must come down."

Then, my shadow lurched forward again and vanished from sight. Not back inside me, but back where it came from. Somewhere out there, back there, in the liminal. In the formless chaos that existed before life, before civilisation, and would again when it was all over.

In what little light there was available to me, proffered from sources such as stars and streetlights, I saw only chaos. I looked around at what was left of the town, devoid of life, love and community.

We'd made every town familiar, every street identical. Forced every public place into the same form, repeating blueprints for what we thought was our best hope against them. In doing so we had made the city - and by extension every city - was soulless. Thanks to us, it now belonged to the soulless. We hadn't designed for life. We'd designed for death.

Eat the Rich
Are full of passionate intensity

"Look, I haven't got much time. They're after me... I've had to go into hiding. Oh God, where to start. There's a dangerous conspiracy. As far as I've been able to trace it, it goes right to the heart of governments. I'm onto something big, for sure. Might need some backup...but it'll be dangerous. If they find out that I know, I'm toast, I'm telling ya, toast. Gotta go now, there's someone I need to hook up with. I'll be back in touch when I can."

"That was the last we heard from him."

I chewed on my last stick of nicotine gum, making a little ball of mint flavour in my mouth. It wasn't as good as I remembered cigarettes being - it still gave me a kick, but that kick was somehow unfamiliar.

"That's not much to go on, Mr. Edgely." I'd take the case anyway, but he didn't know that. Never let a potential client know you're more desperate than them. They thirst for justice, you just thirst. Those are two different appetites.

Edgely nodded and adjusted his ample behind on the flimsy office chair I'd bought at the thrift store. It squeaked in protest. I looked up while still looking downcast. My eyes were bleary and my brow was weary. I'm not sure what visitor I'd been expecting, but this was a new level of unusual. I reached across the desk and pressed a button on the ancient answerphone, shutting it off just as the recording gave way to white noise. I looked up at Edgely to try and ascertain the mark of the man. He dressed in the manner of many men of modernity, which is to say that, having digested the dubious wisdom that looking fashionable and feeling comfortable were two styles in direct competition, he had opted firmly for the latter and would brook no argument as to the finality of his decision. I started the interrogation the way I always have.

"You say your correspondent has been missing for three days now. Why not come to me before? Come to that, why come to me at all? Why not go straight to the cops?" I knew the answer to the first. Noone came to me unless they'd already exhausted all the other options. It gave me what I like to call, in moments of odd optimism, an exclusive clientele. Edgely ran a website imaginatively called 'The Edge', which was basically a two-bit version of the National Enquirer. I'd never even so much as glanced at it before - hell there was enough fake news in the lamestream media without delving into this trash heap - but I knew its reputation. He did seem to actually give two fucks for his missing guy, though, which said something.

"Really, you're my last hope." Edgely reached one fat ring-drenched hand down to his hip. I shrugged. I was everyone's last hope these days. It had been far too long since I was anyone's *first* hope. Then I saw the size of the billfold he'd just placed on the table and tried not to show how wide my eyes opened. Damn, that just came fresh from his suit pocket. Not even tucked away in a wallet.

"I'll take it. First, though, I'll need more info on what your man was looking into and what he found out. I'll have to start somewhere. Oh, and forward me any more messages you get from him."

Edgely sat back in his seat, visibly relaxed though still clinging on to the billfold with the tips of his chubby fingers and proceeded to tell me what he knew.

There wasn't much to go on. Edgely set up a divert so that I'd get any more messages incoming from his guy, whose name was Abe. I tried ringing the number back - I'm no rookie - but every time I did it was unobtainable. All I had was whatever voice notes he forwarded to his boss and the name Walker, who Edgely indicated Abe had been trying to hook up with. Looks like I would be doing a lot of walking myself before this gig was over. Luckily, I had an advance that was more than generous when it came to the cost of shoe leather.

***

Walker was sitting at a bar, washing down the last of his bourbon with the last of his cash, when an unexpected visitor arrived.

Hurtling through the bar door, the newcomer nearly tripped on the welcome mat. This guy weren't no regular, he was running from someone and Walker thought he knew why.

The stranger took one look around, eyes wide, breath short. It didn't take a genius to spot either the blood spatter on his crisp white shirt or the look of fear on his face. He eyed the sign and made his way to the restroom, his footfalls heavy on the cracked floor tiles.

Roztok glanced over at Walker.

"Looks like we got ourselves a fugitive. Maybe some cash in that for you." He spoke like he was being altruistic, like he didn't know that cash would be going straight back into his till before the evening was out.

Walker wondered who or what he was running from, wondered if it mattered to him, decided it didn't. He stood and followed him into the gents' lavatory where the newcomer stood shirtless and scrubbing, then looked up in alarm at Walker's intrusion on his privacy.

"Throw us fifty and we'll change shirts. Then, get lost."

The visitor complied eagerly, hastily, then legged it while Walker did his laundry.

You can remove a stain on a shirt. A stain on your character, that was harder. Water generally does a good job of washing away bloodstains. What it doesn't wash away are tears and regret. Even time has trouble with those. But blood? Blood comes out. To Walker and his kind, it wasn't thicker than water, it was just another resource to be negotiated over.

Back in the saloon bar, Walker drank deep from his bourbon, emptying the glass. Then he pressed his already mangled flesh hard against the glass, shattering it. Roztok sighed. Glasses weren't cheap these days - heck nothing was cheap these days - but didn't dare say anything. He knew Walker would cover it. What he didn't know is why Walker didn't bleed red.

Truth was, neither did Walker. He'd not bled red since he'd reawakened in this body just three weeks ago. It didn't bother him as much as it should. Looking up at his distorted reflection in the broken glass though, he saw something that did bother him. In each facet, a hideous, grinning face pressed forth, all false smiles and rows of sharp, sharp teeth, as if trapped there and struggling to escape. There were precious little avenues to escape the living nightmare of what he'd become. He drank, and hoped that someone would come looking for him, and that when they did, he'll still have enough of his former humanity to act appropriately.

One nod to Roztok and there was a new glass, a new path to oblivion. Then the phone rang, knocking Walker back into the world of the living, at least for a time.

Roztok picked it up, then handed it over.

"It's for you."

***

They're...they're not human. Dear God, they're something else entirely. I've seen one, underneath the human skin they wear, I've seen what they really look like. I don't expect you to believe me. I need to get more evidence, get a picture of one. Blow the whole thing wide open. People gotta know. We gotta tell 'em, dammit, before it's too late. First, though I gotta..."

Then there was a loud clanking noise, and the message cut off. I spent a good ten minutes replaying the end of that message, trying to work out what that noise was. The closest I could think of was that it was something metallic and heavy dropping onto something else, likely also metal.

I'd made a few discreet enquiries - the sort that didn't come with shiners or nosebleeds but did come at a price. While Edgely was paying, I didn't mind, but there was one caveat I'd forgotten. People weren't used to seeing me flash cash to get my way. And some of those people that saw, they might tell some other people I owed money to. And those people, well they weren't exactly nice. So, whilst I maintained the delusion that my discretion was entirely for my patron's benefit, that weren't necessarily so.

Those enquiries told me a little about this Walker guy. He was, apparently, a small-time fixer and full-time barfly over in what was left of the theatre district. In other words, a classic loser taking whatever he could from the world and trying to make it his business. In more other words, he was my kinda guy. I prepared myself for an evening visiting all the bars in that part of the city. Normally, I'd do that anyways, except somewhere cheaper and less glitzy. Things were starting to look up in my world.

***

I've got a list! It's...oh my god, the names on this list. They're all super rich. Like, billionaire

110

*playboy rich, investment banker rich, oligarch rich.,
royalty rich, rock star rich. Mostly guys looking at
the names (*the sound of pages rustling) *but I don't
know them all. Need a better wifi connection to…
then I can… just need to find a way out of ….* (an
uncomfortable sounding progression of puffs and
wheezes, then a cry of pain*). Damn this place, it's
like a maze!*

This message cut off with a further collection
of puffing noises, then clattering noises and finally a
plop. Context suggested it was the sound of a fat
man running and dropping his mobile phone into a
pool of water while climbing a ladder. Pretty good,
huh? That's why I occasionally do get paid the big
bucks - my father used to work as a foley artist for
the movies and he'd practise all these ambient
sounds around the house when we were kids. It was
the one talent I could really boast, and I owed it all
to a mean son of a bitch who'd made my childhood
a living hell.

I got bored after three identical-looking bars
with identical-looking staff. It takes a lot for me to
get bored in a bar, let me tell you. But I had what I
needed: the number of a bar where Walker was
apparently laying low. I decided to give him a call.
He agreed to meet up with me. Dude sounded way
more wasted than I was and that takes something.
First though, he wanted me to check on someone he
thought had been following him, someone he'd like
to avoid.

We all have those people, so I agreed. He gave
me the descrip and I went back over it with him to
make sure I hadn't left anything out. Though I

doubted there were many cute redheads on crutches in the city. Then I set off to this bar, Roztok's, in the hope I'd find him and nobody else.

***

Between the red ribbon of the setting sun and the surging white foam on the layered blues of the ocean, the boat nudged at the docks and disgorged a swarm of folk like so many flies, all buzzing around the marina eager for a first glimpse of the city. Magnus was among them. There was nothing notable about him, except a slight contrast between the gaiety of his clothes and the gravity of his face. The outfit he wore consisted of a long deep red coat with black trim - a little dusty but serviceable - and a cheap two-piece in shades of grey flecked with scarlet motes. Atop his head he wore a well-worn felt fedora, also in red, from which escaped several locks of curly dark hair. Hands in pockets, he wandered unobtrusively through the throng, clearly expecting someone to be here to meet him.

"Surprised that you'd answer the call. Feeling the heat back home?"

He turned at the sound of that puckish voice, his mouth contorted between grin and grimace.

"Nataly! If I'd known you were here, I'd have gone elsewhere!" Marcus liked the taste of shade in the evening.

Nataly, still grinning, replied. "Aww, I love you too Marcus! We'd better get right to it, I'm afraid. We still have the advantage of being undetected here but that won't last. Now that the call has gone out, all manner of friendly folk are gonna start showing up. We've rented a disused theatre in the civic district…here, follow me. We can talk on the way."

Marcus sighed. He'd have liked to get to know the place first, check out some choice joints, but hell, they'd own them soon enough. He didn't expect any problems with the plan, but Nataly is the local lead so he paid attention for now. They walked together, away from the quay up a stone ramp and through a series of trash-strewn alleys. There was little noise in this part of the city except the distant hum of police sirens and the clack-clack of Nataly's crutches on the cobbles. Few people looked out from locked houses, shop doors were boarded or chained, walls were covered in the red and white tags of gangs long gone. Had it been anyone else he was anyone else he was following; he'd have figured it for a trap. But, despite their history, he knew Nataly was loyal. She'd tell him who and where to focus their attention on, he'd provide the necessary ground troops. Bikers, he thought. He'd always had a thing for bikers.

***

"None of them are truly human. Most of them never were. They still live in our cities, occasionally pulling strings behind the scenes. Controlling our lives to make things more convenient for them. Sometimes, just for the sheer fun of it, the sort of playful attention a cat gives a mouse. Of course, what's sauce for the goose isn't always sauce for

113

the gander. Did I say sauce? You know what I mean. Blood. Life. Knowledge. Power."

The throng of humanity is largely ignorant of who really holds the reins of power in the world. They're unaware of these inhuman imposters and their inhumane plans. If they found out...

I'd made it into Roztok's easy enough. Nobody following me and nobody waiting outside for our man Walker. Honestly, though, this guy was a flake at best, a patsy at worst. I got the feeling there was something he wasn't letting on, even as he let me buy him a good half bottle of sipping whisky between us. He seemed to be eyeing me up to see how much he could trust me. Little late for that. The one thing I did want out of him was where Abe might be, or any other clues as to what was happening to him. I was getting increasingly irritated and concerned about the paranoid yet vague messages I was receiving. If I ever found this guy, I concluded, he'd need sobering up more than I ever had.

***

"We appear to have company." Ramone looked up from his binoculars, passing them to his companion though the cord was still around his thick, tanned neck. "Wasn't expecting them this early." He leaned heavily on the handrail at the water's edge.

Hannah peered through the instrument briefly to confirm her colleague's words and nodded curtly. "You think they're going to be a problem?" Her

114

hand went to a talisman hanging from the pocket watch in her waistcoat pocket. She muttered a minor incantation.

"If it's just those two, maybe not. But that new arrival's got a mean streak a mile wide. I heard what he tried to do in Davos. Still, he's only one person, and so's our old friend Nataly. We can handle them."

"Good. Hannah withdrew a pair of long, thin, off-white gloves from the pocket of her waistcoat and dragged them over her long fingers. "Anyone else here yet? I expected this place to be a hotbed of activity once the word got out."

"Three more came in on the ferry yesterday evening, glamour down even in the twilight. We tracked them to a local strip club. Haven't had eyes on their true form yet to confirm if they're known faces."

Hannah winced. Ostensibly they were all on the same side now; at least that was the point of the upcoming conference. That didn't mean they would agree on everything. In fact, their different families rarely agreed on anything, mainly because so few of them had any active agendas. That was also the point of the conference.

"Good work, Ramone. Please stay here and continue surveillance. I'm needed back at the university laboratory; we have a new batch of drugs that need testing before we release them onto the streets."

"Yeah, will do. Ain't no boats due in until tomorrow morning, so I reckon it'll be a quiet night."

Hannah looked over at him. "Oh, I don't imagine they'll all arrive on boats. Not at all. Keep your eye on the tides, Ramone. You'll know it when you see it. Lucas will replace you at dawn."

Hannah strode off along the seafront, then turned back to watch the crowd still disembarking. Somewhere among them, there might be other new recruits for them or new rivals among the arrivals. She'd have to bribe someone to get her a copy of the manifest and passenger log. Yes, today might turn out to be lucrative after all. She checked her makeup briefly in her compact and then disappeared into an underground carpark.

***

There are plenty of places of interest in the city. How interesting are they, and to who? Well, that's the question. Each of these families have places they need to survive. Sources of nourishment, of wealth, of status and power. Behind those walls, they mass and scheme against each other. Ultimately, for them, it would be best if only one family was calling the shots. Consolidated power. Especially if it's your family. Especially if you're the one that put them there. Got it?

Walker and I were getting along famously. Between his enemies and mine, it seemed we were avoiding about half the city in our search for Abe. He jumped at every shadow, including his own at least twice. He said he was leading me to where Abe was hiding, but didn't want to tell me where that was. They must be a great pair at parties.

We'd turned down so many side streets at this point I had no clue as to where we were. The shop signs were unvarying in their invitations: vape shops, pawn shops, porn shops, candy shops. The only thing that varied was the amount and smell of the trash heaps in the bins beside each. Walker didn't seem to tire, didn't seem to want to talk, so I just shuffled along beside him, wondering just what we were walking into and whether or not I'd be ready.

**

Gyala had been watching Ramone watching Marcus, but now she turned her attention back to the newly berthed vessel.

She made her way gingerly across the quay, unburdened by any baggage, and then sat on a mooring post at the end of the dockyard in the shadow of the harbour gates, watching carefully as the remaining passengers disperse into the nearby city streets. Only when the last of them had vanished did she allow herself a little smile of triumph.

It was about to get very interesting here, very quickly. When nobody was looking, she hopped off the mooring post, ran down the pier and dived straight into the water, leaving her coat on the beach as she swam back to the far end of the pier where she hoped her brothers had managed to catch some raw fish for their supper. Then, once they've fed, they'd arrange some unfortunate drowning accidents to ensure their people were in the right positions of power. Soon it would be time to harvest the kelp pods they'd been cultivating. Soon after that, they'd release their strange fruits onto the street. Humanity wouldn't know what hit them.

***

Mostly, they hate doing the work themselves. It must have taken something big for them to decide to call this meeting, let alone for every family to actually send people to the table. Mostly, they recruit us - humans, that is - to do the dirty work for them. Give them the newbie spiel. Welcome to your new life. Such as it is. The five families that have their fingers on every pulse demand respect, value loyalty, brook no dissent, reward success, and punish failure. If we didn't know this before, we were about to find out the hard way. There would be some tough choices ahead.

Walker made no comment as I played the latest of Abe's voice notes, even though it was clear to me that he did want to say something. Perhaps he wanted to wait until we were alone. Perhaps he already thought I knew more than I was letting on. I decided not to ask him any questions. Well, just one question.

"Why is Abe hiding in the sewers?"

Walker looked back at me, eyes raised, impressed, but just shrugged a "you'll see" which didn't answer anything. For the first time, I noticed something about him that someone in my occupation should have noticed a good nine streets back. What I noticed was that - despite the light snowfall and the chill wind that had my hands thrust deep in my pockets and my coat lapels up to protect my neck - Walker's breath didn't show at all. Mine was like a fine white cloud, albeit this time without the tell-tale stale smoke smell, his just wasn't there. When I caught up and offered him my hipflask, I took a long, hard, look at our Walker.

He wasn't breathing at all. By all accounts Walker was dead as a doornail.

Huh. I've seen a lotta things in my line of work, but nothing that made my skin crawl quite like Walker at that moment.

Of course, the night was still young.

***

Ishab squatted on a small pile of skulls. Above them, the rain came down in drips, each echoing as it sploshes into the foetid water beneath.

They know it has started again. They could feel the pulse of the city down here in the sewer, every dreg of humanity flushed away, carefully sifted through, and analysed. The last investigator had finally left not two weeks before. Thankfully, he hadn't thought of looking down here, beneath the streets in the bowels of the city. Nobody came looking down here for anything. Ishab had been able to ride it out, just, down here in their little kingdom with only the tittering rats and roaches for company. But without a change of strategy, they were likely to fade into obscurity again, an obscurity which served their needs well but which some of the more gregarious types might not survive. Depending on who won the arguments at the upcoming meeting, there could well be a new wave of sabre-rattling or - perish the thought - actual action, which would no doubt be accompanied by fresh violence among the humans who lived here, washing what remained of their humanity straight down the toilet. Luckily, that meant it all flowed past them. They hadn't planned on going topside again but there didn't seem to be much of a choice when they'd all been invited to a pow-wow. All five families. What a world.

A screech - their screech - echoed eerily round the chamber as they called forth their own and began to make plans with them. The city above had largely forgotten about Ishab. They were about to make sure the city remembered. In response to their cry, hordes of vermin issue forth from every leaky pipe and cracked wall. Swarm after swarm of roaches, fresh from their nests, made their way topside. They knew which restaurants had the best pickings and waited only for Ishab's word to begin a new feast of frenzied feeding.

**

They're psychopaths, the whole bunch of them. Utter narcissists. I've been watching them for a while now without them knowing. They're masters of deception, all fake smiles and fake tans. On the surface, they're alluring, charming even. Under the skin, however, they're vicious, callous, ruthless. No empathy, you see? They're not human, they don't feel like us, don't care like us...

120

They don't want to rule the world. That's what Walker told me. They just want to sit comfy on their fat piles of cash and watch us try and rule ourselves. But we've wrecked it. The world, I mean. That's why they're all coming here. I need to find out where this meeting is, try and find a way in... the dark hearts are gathering in secret to lay down their plans. They must be stopped.

Three figures moved across the busy road in front of us, clearly trying to corral us. Whatever it was we'd done, we'd clearly upset someone.

"Walker, run." He at least had the sense to know what was good for him. I guess the survival instinct was still strong in him even though he was technically dead. It had been so long for me I'd forgotten.

We turned a brisk right into a broader street which I hoped was still busy at this hour. Losing ourselves in a crowd would be easier than losing ourselves in a dead-end alley. Lucky for me, I was right.

The rules of being chased are not dissimilar to the rules of tailing someone, which is not surprising since they are equal and opposites, even though they're usually conducted at different speeds.

Rule One: Keep your distance.

Anything you could do to lengthen that distance was good. We'd chosen to weave our way through a throng of early evening shoppers. You could do a lot more with people than you could with more conventional obstacles. Talk to them, distract your pursuers, bribe or coerce them into blocking a route. Get them to lie for you. Or, of course, when those options have run out, you could just throw them in the way of whoever is after you just as you could with a chair or table. You could always apologise later if you felt the need.

Rule Two: Know your enemy.

This is easy if you're tailing and harder if you're the one who is being pursued. Getting to know your enemy is often the whole point of tailing them in the first place. Avoiding them finding out more about you is more subtle and more difficult. Don't run straight for your house or office; if they don't already know where you live and work that's a surefire way to have them find out. Go out of your way, but at the same time try and learn about them. How many were there? Well, three, in this case. What were they like? Are they sprinters or long-distance types? Strength and stamina, dear readers, mean more than lineage. One of ours was already flagging - ah, there see, he's stopped to mop his brow and clutch his sides.

Rule Three: If They Can See You...

The game's up when you get spotted, usually. Sometimes they lead you on a little dance just so you know they know. I was fond of that myself. When it's all done at high speed, it can be tempting to try and get a closer look at just who wants you out of the way. This is normally best avoided if you want to avoid tripping over your own boots. Of course, if you're a seasoned investigator you can combine it with Rule One. We ducked into a nearby alley once we knew there were only two of them left, knocking over a cart as we did. News sheets went flying everywhere as our pursuers hurtled after us. One of them was calling my name. I enjoyed that moment of fame until I realised the invoice for that knocked over cart was going to find its way back to me eventually. Still, it bought us the time to try our next trick. I stopped just at the entry to the alley. I knew it was a dead end, hopefully our pursuers did too, but didn't realise I also did. That false confidence is a great lever. It's a guessing game where you have to be confident in yourself. Luckily, I was. I crouched, tucked in round the corner with a reliable piece of wood held at knee level. Walker was halfway up a wall at the other end to focus their attention.

One of them ran round too fast, as I'd hoped, and was unable to stop herself from going head over heels into the cobbles and trash. Now when I say head over heels, that's not a figure of speech. I mean it. Here was an honest to goodness gymnast. She recovered far too quickly for my liking, but not fast enough to shout warning to her friend who was about to fall prey to the same error.

"Wait!" she shouted. "Stop! We have a message for you." She was barely out of breath, as if the chase had barely begun. "Under the auspices of the current truce," - she spat out the word as if it was something uncomfortable, if not outright distasteful - "we're obliged to invite you both to the parley. Hear us out. Then make up your own mind. We'll even give you Abe back, if you like. He's been our guest for a while now."

I was exhausted after the chase; Walker didn't seem to tire but he wasn't that much to begin with.

I'd take up the offer of a chat even if all it did was clear the waters and buy us time.

***

It was midwinter. Not exactly their favourite time of the year, far from it, but one with a potency, nonetheless. It was also freezing cold. A soot-black cat slinked out of a warm house into a refuse-strewn alley, made one tentative step into the snow, then withdrew back inside. Further up the alley a short fat cook, aproned and puffing, emerged in a cloud of smoke from a restaurant kitchen, whiffed the cold air and gazed yearningly at the sky as though his dreams were up there, much too far away, lost in the clouds and forever beyond his reach. The sky itself was the perpetual grey of thick snow-laden clouds, day and night. The stars themselves hid behind that blanket of ashen gloom, cutting themselves off from what was about to happen.

Just beyond that kitchen door was the entrance to another place entirely. The worn, aged letters written above it once used to read something, used to mean something but that text was mostly lost under thick layers of accumulated dust and grime and a thin dusting of powdery snow. Approaching that door, a number of figures picked their way down the alley from opposite directions. Some of them strode confidently, oblivious to their surroundings, concentrating instead on the other visitors. A few of them made those last steps through the alley more meticulously, taking in every falling snowflake and every discarded bottle, with bright eyes wide open in a manner akin to childlike wonder but which, on closer inspection, might indicate heavy drug use. One of them even smiled at that cook, who immediately fell to his feet and began to weep uncontrollably, as if the stars had finally answered all his dreams with one moment of dazzling beauty. He would never stop crying for the rest of his life, which, it would turn out, would only be about five minutes. Even the cat, gingerly poking its head out for a second time, took a moment to assess the newcomers. Overcome by what it could perceive, it backed away to the wall, hissing and screeching, its back arched.

These figures congregated in silence outside of the door. One of them ran a slender, gloved hand through the dust on the sign which now read 'STAG DOOR.' A second giggled uncontrollably at that seemingly deliberate gesture and continued to do so until a jingling of keys was heard from the interior and the door lurched open. An auburn-haired young woman covered in piercings peered out at the newcomers from within, beckoning them all inside. As they followed the clattering of her crutches down a dilapidated corridor, the last of them closed the door behind them, then touched his thin lips with a slender finger and gestured at the lock. There was the sound of an invisible key turning and the lock clicking back into its rigid place, and then there was silence save for shuffling steps and low whispers.

Outside, a second group of figures approached. Walker, myself, and a trio of unlikely ladies who somehow seemed to surround us, continually circling us like a pack of wolves. More than once, I was convinced I was talking to the cowled figure who had addressed us with the offer of parlay, only to find that the form within that hood was another woman entirely. They looked similar to each other - sisters, perhaps? - but differed enough to know that I was still being played with. It was the strangest game of Find The Lady I'd ever indulged in, but curiously it had helped pass the time as we had picked our way from one alley to another. Mostly, I'd taken it as an intellectual exercise to occupy my mind because I didn't want to dwell on what I'd learned about Walker. The walking dead don't sit right with me, shouldn't sit right with anyone. We passed the laughing chef, weeping tears of joy so hot they burned his face. He was shovelling snow onto them to try and help with the burns. That face still haunts me; not because of its alarming grotesquery of melted flesh, but as a symbol of what they could do if they wanted, not as a stratagem but just on a whim.

They saw me looking and didn't say anything. It was as if they just assumed I was part of their world now, that I should just get used to such surprises until they became as commonplace in my mind as the filth on the streets. One of them began to knock at a dilapidated wooden door, but a second shook her head and instead drew a perfect copy of that door in chalk on the wall next to it. I looked on in wonder as the three of them led us through a portal which only a minute ago had been a graffito sketch in coloured chalk and only two minutes ago had been nothing more than a stray thought in one of their crazed minds. Walker, I noticed, was as much as ill at ease about our surroundings. Perhaps he was like me, a new arrival to this darker and more disturbing world, ill-placed and ill-fated to be part of it without truly understanding.

Inside, we were led down a series of depressing passages which must once have formed the backstage area of a grand theatre. Red rugs dotted the floor, threadbare and riddled with mould which rose in little clouds whenever we trod on them and assaulted my nostrils with their mustiness. The walls were adorned with peeling posters indicative of the faded grandeur of the place - playbills past, stars that hadn't graced the silver screen for many years. Even some of these golden oldies weren't recognisable by their faces, distorted as they had been by damp and disinterest. Eventually, we were ushered onto a well-lit stage at the front of a row of plush red seats occupied by a panoply of different, waiting faces. Squinting into the semi-darkness, I wracked my brain for any semblance of similarity to faces I knew to be active in the local underworld, but nothing struck me. Whoever they were - or whatever, I hadn't forgotten Abe's delusional, vague warnings - they were unknowns to me.

***

Our three companions led me to a chair stage left and Walker to a similar one beside me. The third was occupied by a pot-bellied guy who might have been anywhere from his late thirties to early sixties; he looked old before his time but somehow gave the impression that he'd been young only yesterday. The remnants of a recently removed gag of red silk hung around his neck like a forgotten noose, but he was still tied to the chair by strands of golden rope at his wrists. I figured this was Abe, even though he bore no more than a flicker of resemblance to the one photograph Edgely had of him. He looked up at us both but exchanged glances only with Walker.

Then the real show started.

I don't remember which direction it was she came from, but she was suddenly there, centre-stage and lit up as though she was the only one in the room. That light was no stage light, it was her own inner light, and she used it as part of an intricate dance as her long arms weaved golden rays about the place, wrapping the room in a suffused glow and bringing warmth to the midwinter blues. The red velvet curtains swished back into life; the rot visible in them earlier somehow vanished as if she wouldn't tolerate such things in her presence. Mirrors on the walls of the auditorium uncracked themselves, the better for everyone to see her in all her blinding majesty. Perfect smiles beamed back from all those faces in the playbills on the wall, bygone heroes and heroines given new vigour merely by being in the same place as her.

Her sensuous, full red lips parted, and she spoke with a voice that ordinary folks would call enchanting or bewitching without having any real idea as to what those words actually meant. She was beautiful, sure, the kind of beauty the world hadn't seen since Elton John sang goodbye to Norma Jean, but there was something else to that beauty, something alien. It was fake to the core: As fake as the red velvet curtains and the glitz of the stage lights. It was that old razzle-dazzle that was all style and no substance, smoke and mirrors honed to perfection. It was also utterly beguiling. I was hooked. My body relaxed despite the evident danger and my own protestations not to let my guard down. I was beginning to enjoy the show, even though I knew that was all it was.

***

"Thank you all for coming. I cannot begin to imagine how difficult some of you found this journey, literal or metaphorical. It has been a while since we all met up. Since we at least tried all to sing from the same sheet."

"I must first address our three visitors. Walker is…now one of us, of a sort, whether he knows it or not. The others show potential for the future. But I'll get to that. I suspect they would like to know the truth of who we are, at least as far as I speak of it."

Heels clicking, she strode across the stage, her own limelight following her, and stood straight in front of us, simultaneously towering over us with gathered illusion and presenting herself at a height of what must have been four feet, tops.

"Who are we? We're the Chelsea Hotel, darling. We're Studio 54. We're the Moulin Fucking Rouge. We're the scandal in Bohemia. We're the actors that Pinocchio ran off with. We're everything your parents warned you about and more." She turned her attention then solely to Abe, who was visibly melting under her gaze. "We're not vampires. We're not lizards, or ancient serpent people, or aliens. Honestly." She looked disappointed in him.

"We're fairies. The original little green men if you will. We've been around a lot longer than you. Largely, as your friend here found out, we leave you to your own devices. Maybe we nudge a few things in directions that help us, but generally we just sit back, watch and eat popcorn." She leaned in close over me and batted her lashes. "You're as fascinating to us as we are to you."

Moving back centre stage, her long gown leaving nothing to the imagination, she addressed the front row of the theatre again.

"Humanity has no humanity left. They're increasingly intent on turning on each other as we once did" - she parsed this as if it was at once both a distant memory and a fresh wound - "and so we act. I thank you for submitting all your schemes. Most excellent and devious! You are to be commended, each and every one of you. I have, however, chosen a winner. This is the scheme we shall follow to bring us back into true power so that we can properly manipulate the masses, to maintain our masquerade and keep ourselves entertained.

"We will eat the rich."

There was a gasp: a single, garbled, gasp, immediately hushed by a round of applause that gathers strength until it reaches a standing ovation.

She bowed, then turned to us. Walker's eyes were glowing with the zeal of a true convert, his fists balled so tight that I could see what might once have been blood begin to dribble down his sleeves. Abe just fainted dead away. It was hard to tell, but the word faint may have been unnecessary there. Dead, most likely. Away? Seems like he'd been away with the fairies for some time now.

"What you choose to do for us, Saul, well that's up to you. I'll help you decide. Help you make the most of what gifts we offer. New freedoms, new pleasures."

"There's no turning back now, Saul. So, what are you going to do? Once you're in, you're in. One door may have closed, but others open. Opportunities arise to gather power for yourself, or fame if that's your thing, or fortune. Your past life? Forget it. Was it really that much of a life anyway?"

"Are you in? Or out?"

I took only one look - my last look - at the world outside, at the meagre pickings of my former life, and made a decision. There's no business like sidhe business.

I closed the door behind me.

*****

I met Edgely one last time, briefly, over breakfast in The Dionysus Bar N Grill.

"So, there's nothing to report?

"There's nothing to report. He made it all up for a good story, faked his own disappearance and made off with the advance you sent him. He could be anywhere in the world by now, living under any name you care to mention."

Edgely looked disappointed. "It was all a lie?"

"Every last word of it. Gotta hand it to his imagination."

"Dammit. I really thought he was onto something big this time." Edgely sighed, then pushed the remains of his grill plate to the middle of the table. "Finish it off if you like. Seems like I've lost my appetite."

I smiled at him. A big smile. Lots of teeth.

"No thanks. I just ate."

Eve of Destruction
Surely some revelation is at hand

"So, from tomorrow it basically belongs to us, right? What happens to it after?" The voice was muffled behind the N95 mask and the voluminous hood it emanated from.

"Beats me, I'm just here to tear it up. Maybe his nibs will know." This speaker was tall and broad-shouldered, muscles rippling under the hi-viz jacket, luminous in the drizzle and the near-dark. He leant heavily on a shovel. "You don't have to wear that mask outside, you know."

A groan and a shrug. "I'm not an idiot."

"Oh, and that means I am, I suppose?"

"Now, now, no fighting." They both turned to see a young woman picking her way across the wasteland. She moved gingerly on long spindly legs like a rag doll and had long straggly hair to complete the image. "Late again, is he?"

"He usually is. Must be busy at the office again." The first speaker drew back the hood and shook out a frightful mane of platinum blond. From inside a pocket in his frayed greatcoat, he withdrew a long roll of biohazard marking tape. "No reason not to get started though, we know what we're here to do."

The three of them stood together for a moment on a little artificial ridge of rubble consisting largely of discarded tyres interspersed with industrial sand and a few brave green shoots. They gazed out over the wasteland of Lot29, ill lit in turn by flickering neon, rain and dappled moonlight.

"Not much to look at, is it?" It was Shovel who broke the silence.

"Kids like to play in it." Ragdoll thrust her arms into the deep pockets of her raincoat. She shivered despite the uncomfortable heat of the evening and pulled out a bottle of vitamin pills which she opened with shaking hands and then emptied into her mouth without a second thought.

"Well, they shouldn't. I mean look at it. Health hazard, that's what it is. Look at that murky water. May as well be straight from the sewer." Mask began extending the tape between the posts marking the edge of the lot. "If they wanted to keep it safe for the kids, they should've taken better care of it, that's what I say."

"I imagine it's a grand place for an adventure." Shovel took off his bright red hard hat and held it before him as if paying respect. "You could have a great time here still, even if parts of it resemble an apocalyptic wasteland."

"Used to be a community garden, apparently." Ragdoll's voice was quiet, almost pensive. "Must've been lovely to look at once. Lots of fruit trees."

"Yeah, once. Mebbe. I dunno. Looks like there was a building here too, you can still see some of the foundations if you look close." Shovel lit a cigarette and flicked ash onto a nearby tyre. "Whatever. It's useless space now."

"Those things will kill you, you know." A new voice, deep and growling. They all turned round as one, somehow surprised to see him though he'd clearly been expected.

"'Ullo, boss. Just killing time till you got here." Shovel dropped the rest of his smoke and stubbed it out with a heavy boot.

"Been here long?"

Shovel shrugged. "Long enough." He shifted his bulk and stretched.

"Eager to get started? There are some formalities first..."

Ragdoll fished around in her satchel and pulled out a sheaf of paperwork and a clipboard. "Here you go, results of today's town hall meeting. It's all ours, just sign on the dotted line."

The newcomer beamed and puffed himself out, his already ample form stretching the outline of his charcoal suit. With a flourish of plump fingers, he signed a brief name at the bottom of the document having only glanced at it. The print at the top read: 'Council of Parishioners Town Hall Meeting, Lot29.'

"Any trouble?"

"Nah. Half of them didn't bother to show. Of those that did..." She exhaled sharply, her warm breath lingering in the stillness. "Hot air and empty promises. As we thought, the whole thing was a waste of time, just like all the other meetings. A few holdouts, but no one really listened to them. It's not like they haven't already had 29 meetings to discuss this."

"Ah. A tale told by an idiot, full of sound and fury, signifying nothing. That's life, I'm afraid.

Right, we'll call it quits there for tonight. Get some rest while you can, it's going to be a busy day for us tomorrow."

He took a last look over the vacant lot. A muddy puddle swelled with fresh rain and not-so-fresh groundwater. A slow burning fire in an oil drum where a few had apparently gathered for warmth. A gust of wind blew up handfuls of thick, choking dust. From his throat emerged what might have passed as a sigh or what might have been merely a last gasp. Then he turned back to the others.

"Shame, really. I was starting to like the place. Well, looks like things are about to really heat up."

Then he squeezed his bulk inside the driver's side of the van while the others piled in the back. If the van was once white, an onlooker would have trouble recognising that now under layers of grease, dust, and soot. Then they drove off, but they'd be back with a vengeance in the morning. Just another working day for Four Horsemen Property Management.

Poster Girl

Surely the second coming is at hand

"Silent Night..."

Faith slipped out of the church as the choir began singing another carol and quietly closed the door behind her so as not to disturb them in their moment. Packed inside were most of the town of Salvation, Montana, praying for her best friend, Joy. The vigils had been Faith's idea from the start, bringing the community together in this time of profound loss. Rather than celebrating the miracle of the birth of Christ, they were huddled together inside praying for the safe return of one of their own. Nobody had seen Joy in nearly a month. Nobody knew where or why she had gone. There were no leads, no clues, no ransom demands. Search parties returned each day just before dusk, the hills and the woods being too dangerous to search at night. They had found nothing. So, each night, the town of Salvation did what they did best. They prayed.

"Holy Night..."

It was Christmas Eve, so Faith wanted to believe in miracles now more than any other time. She wanted to believe she'd see her friend again tomorrow, safe and well with a story to tell. Instead, the single candle she held in her gloved hands sputtered in the winter wind as snow flurries blew in continuous circles in the car park around her. Catching a moment of silence outside, she looked up at the heavens and, as she wiped a solitary half-frozen tear from her eye, offered a sincere, solitary prayer.

"*All is calm…*"

A thin layer of snow peppered the car park, but the clouds above were thick with the stuff. A fresh layer, deep and crisp and even, would put paid to any hope of the search parties, covering any prints and removing any traces of her friend that might remain. Faith shivered in the chill of the night, but the cold was invigorating, strengthening, somehow, compared with the stifling heat of the crowd. Faith needed a moment alone with God, a pause from the frantic mayhem of the past weeks and the constant attention of the townsfolk's perpetual, penetrating gaze.

"*All is bright…*"

As she was about to turn and rejoin the vigil inside, something in the hills above the town attracted Faith's attention. A procession of lights - bright as stars but lower in the sky - began to dance across the horizon, ducking below the silhouetted treelines on the ridges of the two mountains and then resurfacing. Silvery motes arcing across her vision, beckoning her forth, promising her all would be well. She took three steps gingerly forward, convinced her prayer had been answered but still unwilling to leave her father the Rev. Shepherd to manage the congregation alone.

She hesitated for what seemed like a heartbeat but felt like a lifetime. The modern world being what it is, it would later be simple enough to time that pause properly and ascertain that it lasted precisely nine minutes according to the CCTV footage of the church entrance. At the end of that pause for thought, one light in particular shone very briefly and very brightly and Faith took one more step forward toward the source, raptured by the beauty of that strange glow.

It was to be her final step. Nobody in Salvation ever saw her again. The wind picked up around the chapel, carrying with it flurries of snow that hid her precious last movements and blew an old poster, torn at one edge, onto the church door where it stuck almost in defiance. The poster read: Missing. Joy Carpenter, aged 15. Please contact Sheriff Carpenter in Salvation with any details. Between these sentences was nestled a slightly grainy black and white photo of a young girl, smiling through pearly white teeth, a pair of glasses jammed into a bun of dark hair rather than resting on her nose.

Nobody noticed Faith was missing at first. Not like Joy, whose absence had been picked up and reported almost immediately. There was a singular advantage, after all, in being the daughter of the sheriff, even if that relationship was somewhat strained by the natural problems of bringing her up as a single parent with a busy job, not to mention the nascent rebelliousness of teenage years. The community had brought the three girls up: Joy, Faith and their friend Hope, all daughters of prominent townsfolk. They raised them with good Christian values and a respect for their family and community which would have been the envy of other parents, had Salvation ever had visitors from outside except for the odd hunter or hiker. The three had been inseparable, the loss of Joy had left the others inconsolable.

Without Joy, though, the cracks had started to appear in their otherwise picture-perfect community. While nobody could conceive of a bad word to say against any of the girls, there were others upon whom scrutiny and suspicion fell in equal measure. Accusations of impiety began as mere whispers then rose in volume and frequency with each passing day Joy remained undiscovered.

Sheriff Carpenter, distraught and sleepless at the loss of his only daughter, called a town meeting at which he could barely contain his grief and others, particularly those with youngsters themselves, could barely contain their fear and anger. The Reverend Shepherd urged calm: for the first time in his career, he realised that his loyal congregation weren't listening to him.

"Keep faith," he repeated ad nauseam, "The Lord moves in mysterious ways. Keep faith and we will find Joy again." This offered less comfort than he imagined: he was terrified himself, incensed that something so horrific should happen to Salvation, to the little town where, like so many others around him, he had been born and lived his entire life.

Meanwhile, the lives of the three girls were laid bare. They were constant companions, had no romantic interests they were willing to divulge, had lived blameless, selfless lives helping to cook and deliver food for the elderly. None of them had been in the slightest bit of trouble except for the occasional familial arguments which were always followed with loving reconciliation.

If there was nothing wrong with the town of Salvation, as its population firmly believed, there must be an outside influence. The hotel guest book was scrutinised, every visitor traced and contacted. It all came to nothing.

Missing posters were printed and distributed to other local towns. Unthinkable as it was that Joy might have met her end, it also seemed unthinkable that she might have run away, especially without leaving a note and certainly not without telling her firmest friends. Nothing came of it. It seemed Joy had simply vanished.

Now the same thing had happened to Faith, on Christmas Eve no less. As the vigil continued throughout the night, nobody else left the church until the clear evening had become the dull grey sky of a snowy Montana dawn. When the carolling and prayers ended, the Reverend Shepherd looked frantically for his daughter to help fill the urns of tea and coffee and offer blankets to those who were shivering. When he couldn't find her, he began to call her name over and over, the congregation gradually hushing as their leader became more fraught in his plaintive cries. Sheriff Carpenter went to his side and began to ask the questions that nobody wanted to hear again, questions they could not answer even though in their hearts they all believed somebody must know.

"Is anybody else missing? Who isn't here? When did anyone last see her? Luke, take three others and make an immediate search of the area. Don't worry Reverend, we'll find her. We'll find her."

Thus, the disappearance of Joy ceased to be an isolated incident. If the town was afraid before, it was now in full blown panic, even as they retreated to their own residences to celebrate Christmas. Curfews were imposed in every household. The movements of anyone outside in the snow were scrutinised behind twitching curtains: the switchboard at the Sheriff's office was overwhelmed.

Sheriff Carpenter himself, a stern but fair man with great bearlike arms, listened attentively to young Luke as the search party returned.

"There's no sign of her, Sir. No sign at all. There's only a few footsteps in the snow, just off the porch, and then they vanish into the drift. But there's something up there, you'd best come and see yourself before it gets too blustery."

Following his deputy outside, the Sheriff was certain of two things. Call it a gut instinct underlined with years of police work. Firstly, whatever had happened, the two girls were together somehow. Whether they'd run away or been abducted was something he wasn't sure of - if it was the former there'd be hell to pay - but he was convinced that the same thing had happened to them both. Two missing girls in a town like Salvation couldn't be a coincidence. Secondly, that meant that either their willowy, preppy friend Hope knew something, or she was in danger herself. He'd get to that once he'd taken a look at what his deputy had found.

It was a perfect circle of burnt grass, seared into the ground at the edge of the car park just beyond where Faith's footsteps finally ended. He'd not seen anything like it in his life and had no idea what might have caused it. Luke was busy taking pictures of the scene, as much for his keen interest in the unusual and bizarre as for a record. Sheriff Carpenter nodded to him and asked him to bring Hope to the church as soon as he'd finished.

Back in the church, he found the Reverend seated at a little table in the kitchen, his hands shaking as they gripped a cracked mug of hot coffee, a blanket over his shoulders placed there by his loving wife who stood quietly behind him. They both looked up as the Sheriff entered and shook his head to indicate their lack of progress.

"Who could do this, Sheriff?" The Reverend was openly weeping now. "What manner of evil creature could have taken away our precious girls?"

Removing his hat to reveal a scant growth of greying red hair, the Sheriff shook his head again.

"I must admit, I don't rightly know. We'll find them though, mark my words. We'll find them and make them pay. You have my solemn vow."

They stood there in silence for several minutes until they were interrupted by the face of a young girl, framed with dishevelled golden locks, eyes red and puffy with weeping, standing in the kitchen doorway. It was Hope.

"No one is accusing you of anything." Sheriff Carpenter was doing his best to put her at ease, but it was clear that young Hope was terrified out of her wits and that his attempts to mollify her anxiety were only making things worse.

"I haven't done anything!" Near hysterical, she turned to the Reverend. "What's happened to Faith? Please, tell me? Why won't anyone tell me what's going on?"

It was Mrs Shepherd who answered, her husband's head being firmly buried in his hands.

"She's gone, Hope. Just gone. From right outside the church. Please, if you know something, please let us know." Mrs Shepherd bit a quivering lip to hide her worry, but her pleading words were spoken with a soothing tone.

"These first few hours are usually crucial." The sheriff interrupted. "Luke is organising search teams…"

"I want to join in. I want to help find her."

"Hope, we need to keep you with us."

"You don't understand! She was my best friend! Of course I'm going to help! You can't stop me!" A grim defiance arose from Hope's tearstained face. Only after she spoke did Hope begin to comprehend what the Sheriff actually meant. She spoke again, faltering and stuttering this time.

"Is…is something going to happen to me too? What's happening?" That last question came out as a near-wail, the last, desperate call of distress and loss.

Luke shuffled in, a sheaf of papers in his hand. From the excited look on his face, it would appear he had a lead. He cocked his head at the sheriff and then over at Hope. Sheriff Carpenter stood up from the little wooden chair, dragging it back under the table as he nodded to the Shepherds.

144

"Back in a tick." He closed the door on a room of silent sobbing and fretful finger biting and beckoned his deputy to follow him out of earshot.

"What is it? Have you found something?"

Luke shuffled the papers nervously, almost breathless in his excitement.

"You're not going to believe this, boss. It's aliens."

Sheriff Carpenter sighed and massaged his temples. He could feel a migraine coming on and could do without any of his deputy's dubious theories. In the absence of anything else to go on, though, and out of the need to let Luke's prattle run its course, he waved at him to continue.

"I ran some images of that flattened circle of grass through an image search program on the internet." Luke was eager for acknowledgement, but his revelation was lost on the sheriff, who's knowledge of how tech operated began and ended with the patrol car and the fax machine. Undeterred, he continued. "They're similar to these satellite images of crop circles, there are hundreds of them across the US reported every year."

"And how does that prove it's aliens?" Sheriff Carpenter knew he had to draw this to a conclusion, preferably one that wasn't a long, drawn-out explanation. Thankfully, he didn't believe there was one.

Luke looked perplexed. "There's always aliens where there are crop circles, chief! Everyone knows that. And we know nobody in Salvation could be responsible, right?"

The sheriff knew no such thing, as much as he wanted to believe it.

"How does this help us, Luke? You want me to find their alien spacecraft and issue a search warrant?"

"Reckon it's gotta be lurking around here somewhere. Floating above us. It's probably got a cloaking device so we can't detect it."

"Tell you what, why don't you round up a few people and go looking for signs of it in the hills." Anything to get rid of his annoying deputy before his headache really set in. Besides, that would get his deputy back out searching.

Luke beamed. "Sure thing, chief! We're sure to find something! Maybe some more of these strange signs!" He reached down to speak into his radio as he left the church, leaving the sheriff alone again.

Back in the kitchen, the Reverend and Mrs. Shepherd sat across the table from Hope. They all had something to say, but none of them were quite able to articulate it. Hope spoke first.

"They've found something, haven't they? That's why they left."

"Oh, sweetie." Mrs. Shepherd took her hands from her husband's shoulders and leaned across the table to take Hope's hands in hers. "They'll tell us if they find anything." She sounded reassuring, but there was a lingering doubt. What could they have discovered? She shuddered at the thought.

"I can't just sit here and do nothing. I just can't. If I..." She jumped as the door creaked open and the sheriff returned.

"Luke is leading a search party." He leant heavily on the little table, wishing the world would stop spinning long enough for him to think clearly. "Meanwhile, Hope, I think it's best you stay here. I'll let your mother know."

Hope balled her hands into little fists and stood up, her hair flicking back from her freckled face. "I want to help. I can't just sit here. Please." She cast her eyes round all the adults in the room anticipating that one of them might agree but only met blank stares as they exchanged glances.

"We'll come with you." The reverend's voice echoed unexpectedly in the gloomy air of the tiny church kitchen. He looked over at the others.

"Guess we're all going together then. I'll radio through to Luke, let him know we're about to form a second search team." He fiddled with the dial but met only static. "Maybe it's the weather interfering. I'll go outside and call him. See you there. And wrap up warm, for Heaven's sake, it's freezing out there."

They stood with Luke on the ridge just above the town. The deputy was gesticulating wildly and excitedly about something they couldn't quite make out until he shared his camera with them.

"Look at it with the zoom on. You'll see!"

One by one, they did. They saw it all. Where, on the ground, it had looked like a perfect circle, the scorched ground outside the church looked different from up here. There was a criss-cross of smaller lines inside the circle itself, visible now only because of their vantage point and because snow had settled along those lines while leaving the rest of the burnt ground untouched. Even with the low midday sun barely piercing the clouds, the fine mesh of lines was bathed in its light.

"Tell me that's an accident." Luke was jubilant. "Tell me that's man made."

"What are you talking about?" The reverend was cross, and it only now dawned on the sheriff that Luke was about to share his crackpot theories with the most devout people in the town. He winced.

"These are clear signs of an alien visitation! There are hundreds of websites devoted to UFOs, if I take a photo and share it…"

"Enough, Luke." Sheriff Carpenter's look said, 'I'm going to kill you for doing this'. Reverend Shepherd's said, 'I'm going to pray for your immortal soul.' His wife just looked confused as she held her husband's arm tightly.

Hope gasped as she lowered the camera. "I've seen that sign before. Joy painted it on her backpack. It's exactly the same, I swear to God." That last comment was directed at the good reverend, lest he doubt her. "I…I don't know what it means, but I think Joy did. She was really happy with how well it came out and showed us both. When we asked what it was, she just smiled, that kind of beatific, all-consuming, all-knowing smile she had sometimes." She looked over at the sheriff. "I only just remembered that. It didn't seem important before."

All eyes turned to the sheriff now, who shuffled uncomfortably. "Yeah, I remember. I was upset with her for ruining her school bag. That was the last argument we had, just a week before she went missing. She apologised the next morning. God, how could I have missed that?"

It was Reverend Shepherd's turn to speak. "I don't remember seeing anything like that in Faith's room. I'm sure I'd remember." He looked over at his wife who nodded silently in agreement.

"Chief, I'm going to head back and run this through an image search, see what it brings up. Maybe it'll give us an idea of where to look. I can take a look at Faith's things as well, if that's OK with the Rev.?"

Mrs. Shepherd walked over and handed Luke the keys. "Anything for my Faith."

"I want to keep looking. There might be more of these. There might be other signs. Stay with me?"

It wasn't the way any of them had planned on spending Christmas afternoon, especially the reverend who was worried for his flock. A missing daughter was more important, though, so the four of them spent chilling hours on the outskirts of Salvation, climbing both the local hills to get better vantage points on high to look out on the town as their world lay in solemn stillness with the strife and woe far below them.

As evening drew in and the gentle snowfall of the day gave way to a clear moonlit night, the weary group began to make their way back to Salvation, exhausted and with nothing to show for their efforts. They were about to turn into the pine forest on the hill beneath them when Hope gasped.

"Look! Look over there!" They each turned to where she was pointing, up in the sky on top of the ridge they had just left. Hovering over them, drawing closer as they stared, came a procession of dancing lights, each burning brighter than a thousand stars, lighting up the whole sky now with their brilliance as they flitted toward them in fits and bursts. A mighty dread seized their troubled minds as the glowing orbs grew in size and began to take on a vaguely human shape.

Hope was the first to react. Convinced these strange beings were responsible for taking her friends, she ran toward the lights in a kind of rapt stupor, begging them to take her too so that she might be reunited with them.

Reverend Shepherd, also believing them responsible, fell to his knees even before the aliens reached the clearing and revealed themselves in their full awful phosphorescent presence. "Bring her back! I need her! We all need her! So help me God, bring her back!"

Mrs. Shepherd stood stock still, paralyzed with fear, awestruck at what she was witnessing.

Sheriff Carpenter began to run after Hope, to bring her back to safety, when a burst of static came over the radio. He buzzed it and heard Luke's excited voice.

"Hey Chief, this is Luke. I was wrong, so wrong. It's not aliens. That sign, it's the sign of the archangel Gabriel. Do you know what that means?".

The Sheriff knew but was unable to articulate anything beyond "Oh…my…god."

Before them manifested three beings. Their likeness was broadly humanoid in appearance but atop each of their long, translucent necks there were four heads with twelve eyes apiece, atop torsos that sprouted four sets of slowly beating wings. Each in turn was blinded by their brilliance, except for Hope who wept with joy, tears filling her eyes so that she was shielded from the magnificence of their radiance.

"Be not afraid."

The voice, not meant for human ears, boomed. They were all on their knees now.

"I bring you tidings of Joy."

Thus spake the seraph and forthwith appeared a shining throng. Suddenly a great company of all the heavenly hosts appeared with them.

Glory shone around. The whole town, the whole valley, possibly the whole world now was aglow with their incandescence, their all-seeing luminosity. By the time the group could see again, the visitation was over. The reverend was insensate, irreconcilable. "Take me! By all that is good, it should have been me!"

"Where is she? Where is she?" That was Mrs Shepherd, desperately trying to find Hope. Sheriff Carpenter joined her, frantically searching in the undergrowth near the new burnt circle where the angel had appeared.

It was too late.

The Shepherds returned, glorifying and praising God for all the things they had heard and seen, but their hearts were empty. Why had the angels taken those young girls to the rapture but spared them? Were they not good enough for the kingdom of heaven? They preached, but their words were as empty as their hearts. Salvation was never the same

again as it was after the time they became bereft of
Joy, lost Faith and finally were devoid of Hope.

Burnt Offerings

It's a common enough saying: "Sticks and stones will break my bones, but words can never hurt me."

It's not true. Words have profound effects on us. There are reasons why the pen is mightier than the sword. It used to be that written words would fade over time, but the advent of modern technology has changed that. Everything spoken can be recorded, published, distributed, exchanged, as soon as they are uttered. On days like these, when everyone in the city is already hot and bothered, words are like dynamite.

There's another common saying: "There's no smoke without fire."

That, unfortunately, is true, at least for the purposes of this narrative. Let's take a look at what happens when these two sayings get together.

To illustrate, let's take a little glimpse at the tinderbox that is the mother of parliaments. That's what our two protagonists are doing. Think of them as viewing events through a network of CCTV monitors, if you wish. It's not far from the truth and it's certainly more palatable than the reality, which is that those monitors are the flayed skins of humans stretched ultra-thin above a pit of eternal flame populated with writhing salamanders where unholy sulphurous fumes belch upward to these smoke screens. You don't want to know what they're

153

eating as they watch. It is most definitely not popcorn, though it does have a similar sickly-sweet aroma and a not unfamiliar crunch.

It's hot in the city, hotter than it has ever been. Haze hovers over the sticky tarmac, hopes of any rain in the country synonymous with drizzles and downpours are still a distant dream on this scorching July afternoon.

One journalist stands before a camera, a serious and earnest mien belying the broth which simmers in his soul. *"I don't know why I do this any more. They're all as bad as each other. To hell with the lot of them."* That's not what he says to camera - what he says begins with: "A heated debate in parliament today…"

Ai-Zerai and Balsheputh nod in unison and perform an extraordinary gesture which, were there any onlookers to their activities, would look like a bizarre dance move, perhaps a brief sexual liaison. It is over in a matter of seconds, but for that brief time they are entangled in each other, a mass of limbs, serrated iron and flaccid flesh entwining and then receding.

"The minister's speech, denounced by many commentators as incendiary…" Another reporter, another news crew, another channel. Indistinct from the last save for the colour of his tie, which blazes a brilliant red against grey flannel suit and greyer flagstones. His internal monologue reads like this: *"We just repeat what they say. And what they say is trash. A bin-fire of the vanities. Hey, that's good. Wish I could use that."*

"Fanning the flames of extremism..." A younger correspondent, without the camera crews of traditional media, sits sweating on a low wall nearby, furiously typing in bursts of limited character length into every social media platform he can think of in the hope that someone is actually paying attention.

"The situation in the House of Commons has reached boiling point..." An old-fashioned newshound, an old-fashioned notebook.

"Oh, good choice," chortles Ai-Zerai. "That'll go up very quickly."

Hell learns from mankind's mistakes even if they don't - in fact, especially when they don't. It adapts. It changes tactics, varies its strategy. There are parts of the infernal machine that operate so subtly that they don't even ping on the radar. This is where Ai-Zerai and Balsheputh position themselves. They've found a way to combine their two spheres of influence to greatly inflame the impact of both. A hellhole that is more than the sum of its parts, if you will.

There are no more traditional scenarios where demons possess people, get made vulnerable in the attempt and then get sent screaming back to hell with a flea in their ear when their host rejects them or gets offed by some goody two shoes priest with a bell, book and candle.

The modern hell resembles a modern workplace, which naturally returns the kindness. (There's a good deal of banter in some of the infernal chat rooms as to which actually came first.)

That is to say, it's largely open-plan these days so everyone can see what everyone else is working on - except for the boss, of course, who's still working alone out of the basement. There's still a hierarchy, after all.

Ai-Zerai and Balsheputh technically work for Belial, although since they are alone in the security room more often than not, they're under a lot less scrutiny than those souls being tortured in the cacophony of open-plan hell.

Today is very much the culmination of their plan. Having witnessed humanity for millennia, they've got a pretty good fix on where and when it's going to end. That's why they've brought the not-popcorn.

Here's their unique insight. It's so simple that they've had trouble convincing the boss of its veracity:

They don't really need any help from us anymore. They're now capable of wrecking it all by themselves.

"A fiery rebuttal from the chancellor…" The profusion of commentary fans out beyond the green in front of that gothic edifice, runs in rows of protest to nearby roads and paths, affecting everyone.

Ai-Zerai used to be in charge of heretical rhetoric before their current demotion. They'd influence the thoughts, speech, and acts of anyone who could bring the church down. More often than not, those voices came from inside the church. They've been on official warning since the heyday of the Borgias. There are fewer and fewer souls that care about that anymore.

"There's no smoke without fire, Mike, and these allegations..." A young woman, speaking passionately into a phone held at arm's length to a face unknown and unseen and a viewership beyond that. She's been on the job for a week. She'll burn out within a month.

Balsheputh used to be in the fire department. Obviously, in hell, that means starting fires rather than putting them out. He lost favour when the Gunpowder Plot failed and was shelved completely after the Great Fire of London 'accidentally' ruined the plague department's plans for the end of the world. If a demon could be said to have a soft spot in its heart for anything - and Balsheputh's squishy mass of oily flesh is literally all soft spots but no heart - then theirs is London. Balsheputh likes to think of London as an old flame, one that can be rekindled if it's treated just right, so that's what they're currently looking at today with increasing attention and no small measure of gleeful anticipation. As well as the aforementioned definitely not-popcorn.

"The leader of the opposition, incandescent with rage at recent remarks by the prime minister..."

So, they squat together, these two disgruntled middle-managers, no longer caring about whether they win back the boss's favour. Mostly they watch humanity rather than influence it, though it hasn't escaped their attention that humanity loves the attention of being seen, of being heard.

"Sentiments simmering under the surface...those are sure to flare up again..."

It almost doesn't matter at this point what the scandal is they're all busy discussing. There have been so many that even Hell's accounting department has given up counting.

"Inflammatory rhetoric, indeed, and there may be repercussions for that at the next election..."

Ai-Zerai switches monitors and glances at their compatriot, who is apparently reaching similar conclusions: Why wait until then? Why, when all the circumstances point to something happening right here, right now. Outside the palace of Westminster, in the melting pot that is London, those words and their effects are spreading like wildfire.

That eternal flame, which burns from the very fires of hell, the inferno which never ceases, finally reaches through to the surface and takes hold. Every petty vengeance, every hurtful thought: all touchpaper for the coming conflagration. A different kind of heatwave than the world is currently enduring.

London was burning. Soon, it would be Hell on Earth.

WildOats

When a vast image out of spiritus mundi troubles my spirit

Once upon a time…well, last Wednesday if we're honest…there was a poor little girl who lived alone with her mother, and they no longer had anything to eat. In older times, she might have gone into a nearby forest to find food. But there were no longer any forests. One day, though, she was doom scrolling on her mobile phone when she saw an advert for a new app: WildOats! The advert said that if she installed this app then every day, she could click on it and get free food delivered to their house.

As you can guess, she downloaded the app immediately and clicked on the delivery button. Then, eager to find out what delicious food might be coming (and to check just in case this was too good to be true), she sat on the little wall outside their block of flats and waited for the delivery driver to arrive.

She could track the driver's progress on the app and got very excited when he was near, as you can imagine! When he did, he handed over a small package which smelled delicious! The little girl thanked the driver and left him a 5-star review. Then she ran inside to tell her mother that dinner was ready.

Her mother opened the package to discover that inside there were two tupperware containers full of steaming hot porridge complete with single-use plastic spoons. They both enjoyed the delicious food and agreed that it was very filling. An hour later, though, they were both hungry again. "Never fear!" giggled the little girl. We can just order some more free porridge!" She clicked the button on the app again and sure enough another driver dropped two more cartons of porridge off outside their flat a few minutes later.

The little girl and her mother ate porridge for every meal from that day on. It was not long before other people in their road started to notice. They wanted porridge too! Soon the little girl was ordering porridge for everyone. Drivers would come to her house at all hours, and she shared the oats among everyone until they got round to installing the app on their own. Everyone seemed happy and content for a while.

Now, there are those who say there's no such thing as a free lunch and unfortunately for us - and the rest of the world - those people happen to be right. The first thing that happened to everyone who ate the porridge was that they stopped caring about anything else other than eating porridge, talking about porridge, sharing porridge recipes and ordering more porridge from the app. The second was less noticeable, only because everyone was pretty much in the same boat and not paying attention anymore. Everyone's eyes turned black. Where once an iris might have graced us with tinges of blue or green, there were only empty voids, dark as the pupils within. If eyes were indeed windows to the soul, these windows showed nothing, led nowhere, rarely opened.

With the latest subscription models, WildOats drivers anticipated when people might be hungry and delivered them in advance, for as long as they could.

The problem, ultimately, was that kitchens began to fill with oats faster than people could eat them. Then overstuffed people became overstocked cupboards, which became overflowing rooms, which became flooded neighbourhoods. Eventually, the deliveries stopped being accurate and timely because there was no way to get to many addresses. That's when the drones took over. The drones just dropped oats in every street and home - accuracy wasn't so important when nobody was eating anything else anyway and nobody was paying for it. Streets became overrun with sticky honey flavoured cereal as rivulets of thin gruel carried the surplus into the sewers, the rivers and the oceans.

Among those who were the last to succumb, there was frantic activity to subvert or reverse the process. They noticed other things too. All the WildOats drivers wore visored helmets and full leathers, so that nobody had actually seen what was beneath.

Global logistics and communication had broken down, since nobody was interested in maintaining anything other than a healthy diet of WildOats. There was no need for logistics for anything apart from WildOats anyway, which were universally free and arrived whenever you wanted them. What this meant, though, was that nobody knew how to stop it. Even if they had, there was no way to fight against the rising tide of WildOats.

Dream A Little Dream of Me
Somewhere in sands of desert

I am going to tell you a story. I do hope that you are sitting comfortably. You certainly won't be by the time we have finished, but that's hardly my fault. I should here be honest and indicate up front that the story is unfinished, but then it is the story of my life and that isn't finished either. Yet. Were I my father, you would be reading the first verse of an epic poem right now, no doubt, but what poetry I write or recite I keep for a special audience. Here it is in prose, then. I hope it keeps you on the edge of your seat right up to the final scene and even beyond, leaving you hungry and begging for more. Just call me Scheherazade: the story of my life is a tale that just keeps on giving.

For as long as I care to remember, I have been fascinated by the stars. This interest developed from a young age - I spent many happy evenings as a young girl on my father's knee staring above and beyond the Zagros mountains from our home in Iran as my father pointed at the heavens and recited poetry. I wondered even then what awaited us should we ever reach them. As it happened, we should have concentrated on more earthly predictions. I have very dim memories of the night we fled Shiraz in the early days of the 1979 revolution, but among the fear at every stage of that flight was the very real pain that I would never again see those stars under such a clear sky.

163

Our arrival and life in the US had been very different: jarring, but exhilarating. Now, my parents long deceased, I'd graduated in astronomy and mathematics and drifted into academia as a career. I think part of me wanted to recreate those precious moments shared between my father and I and tell people stories of the stars. Outside of the rigour of the academic year, I had become effectively nocturnal in those times where I wasn't actively lecturing, spending long lonely nights gazing up at those points of light in the unfathomable darkness, peering at them through a variety of increasingly intricate and expensive telescopes and retiring only when the delicate fingers of dawn began to extend their grasp over a very different horizon.

It was because of these all-nighters that I was fast asleep when the planes hit the towers on 9/11 and, on finally waking, found myself in a different world, alien and alienating, terrible and terrifying, fretful and threatening.

It did not take long for my university to decide to review my tenure and ultimately reach the conclusion that my services were no longer required. They cited one particular old paper of mine entitled 'In defence of astrology: what the stars can tell us about our future', with the clear indication that I was not to be considered a serious scientist.

I was escorted from the campus that same day. I sat, rejected and dejected, on the cold grass beneath the steps of my department, my only memento a box of oddments which had adorned my desk. I vowed, eyes swelling with tears, that I would not give up hope. Every day, though, brought familiar frustrations and new disappointments both in my increasingly fruitless search for a new position at work and in the world at large. Once again, I took to the stars and my father's poetry as my sole refuge, hiding from the perils and fragilities of the mundane world in their distant but bright embrace.

It was at this moment, when my patience and sanity were both rock bottom, that I received a most unexpected invitation from an establishment I was unfamiliar with, asking me to consider a post with them which would be part lecturing and part archival, yet still allowing time and scope for my own studies and access to what they described as a considerable research library. I held it gingerly between trembling fingers, daring to hope. My curiosity was piqued but not yet equal to the desperation with which my daily life was fraught. I therefore accepted the interview offer before I began to peer closer at the only portal which stood wide open when all the others had been firmly closed in my face.

There were no glossy brochures advertising its campus with photographs of eager smiling freshers, no indication of what subjects they taught, no alumni praising its programme, nothing. The place seemed to exist only in that single letter of invitation, which I still clung to with my last remaining shreds of my faith as the taxi deposited me in front of imposing gates of rusted iron and the great gothic edifices which loomed behind them. It was a sleepy looking college, forgotten and forlorn, in a quiet New England town. Piles of autumn leaves resplendent in their reds and golds lay strewn across cobbled quads as I meandered my way through mazes of cloistered courtyards, weaving between pillars in search of an unsignposted reception block or simply anyone from whom I might elicit directions. The residential campus was eerily silent in the late summer outside of term time, but I eventually flagged down a pallid, haggard young man who thankfully escorted me to the academic reception rather than present me with a set of jumbled directions. Even then, he took two misturns, scratched his head and uttered a stammered apology. *The stars themselves would be easier to navigate!* I thought frantically, one eye on my watch and the other on the quiet flagstones that surrounded us. When I finally spoke to the receptionist, I was fully a half hour after the appointed time and feared I had blown my chances. He merely indicated that the Dean was expecting me and ushered me along a myriad of identical corridors each panelled in dark wood and poorly lit by tiny lamps in the roof. Finally, he knocked on a large, well-worn oaken door, smiled and nodded at me and returned through the labyrinthine halls back to his watch post. I stood shaking like a leaf, trying to steady my nerves and recite my prepared introduction, in a place I could not hope to escape from without assistance. I nearly jumped out of my skin when a white-maned head peered from around the door and spoke my name.

"Professor Leila Sattani? Please do come in."

Thus began my first introduction to the erudite and esoteric world of Miskatonic University.

I sat opposite a panel of three, each of which I was convinced was scrutinising my every move and word. I began to fidget a little in my seat, an old habit that often repeated when I was nervous. My heart raced; my blood pounded in my ears. I looked up at the three of them - all men - with open, pleading eyes which were entirely at odds with the fire in my belly. I hated having to genuflect to the patriarchy of academia - I always had - but this was almost certainly my last chance of a position so I tried to bite my tongue as I launched into a detailed history of my academic life, frequently interrupted with both pertinent and impertinent questions from the panel which I hoped I answered to their satisfaction.

In addition to the white-maned elderly Dean Jessamy - a mild-mannered, quaint Englishman who I half expected to still be wearing a wig and frock coat - there was a short, lean man with red-brown sideburns whose shirt and waistcoat appeared to be stained with chemicals and whose solid hands, tapping the desk with a pen, spoke of years of practical science. He was introduced to me as Professor Halcyon, who was also apparently the Bursar. The third man on the panel took notes profusely throughout but spoke rarely. On those occasions he did, it was usually to clear his throat in a series of guttural grunts through stained teeth just visible under a black moustache. It was only on departure that I got told his name: Doctor Gülgger.

When the interrogation was finally over, I breathed a sigh of relief internally. I also had a host of unanswered questions which, in my desperation to acquire the position, it had seemed imprudent to ask. Firstly, I was intrigued as to how they had heard of me and then decided to offer me an interview: this was quite the reverse of the usual practice. Secondly, I should have liked to know in much more detail what the post actually entailed. Dean Jessamy had indicated that Miskatonic had a broad curriculum across the liberal arts and sciences and was most keen to inform me that my specialties would be in great demand without really going into depth as to what my specialties actually were. It did not occur to me until I was back at my local guest house that there was a third question I should have asked, namely what had happened to the previous holder of the post I was now being invited to apply for? It turned out, obviously, to be the most important question of all.

By the time I had reached my lodgings, the landlady there had received a message indicating that the university had very much found me greatly to their liking and would like me to start the very next week, if my schedule permitted. My schedule very much permitted. Everything I owned was here at the guest house since I had no alternative lodgings: two huge carpet bags stuffed with clothes, a small collection of books and papers in a sagging cardboard box and the only telescope I hadn't yet sold to make ends meet. Those were the only remaining possessions I had beside one of my father's little book of poems, which remained in the pocket of my suit jacket throughout the interview.

My relief was immediate and palpable: I was torn between a whoop of joy and a sob of relief, so naturally my body attempted both at once. Then, once I had prayed and eaten, I fell into an untroubled, dreamless sleep the likes of which I had not enjoyed since this whole episode of my life had begun, confident at last that a new leaf had finally been turned over, a new chapter ready to experience. I caught myself smiling in the mirror, a rare sight these days. It was as if I had previously forgotten how to be happy, but life had shone just a single ray of sunshine to heighten my countenance and lift my sagging spirits.

I returned to those unhallowed halls of academia the following morning for a longer discussion with the Dean. To my surprise, I had no problem finding the building or the room this time: it was as if the place itself had begun to accept me and stopped confounding me with its confusing extent of gothic architecture. Gargoyles still stared down as I passed but somehow their stances had shifted: they no longer looked poised to pounce but instead seemed to maintain their stoic silence with dignity rather than dread. Now I was operating from a position of strength rather than desperation, my tactics changed back from pleading to bargaining and my nails and lipstick were a matching deep red. Thus armoured, I knocked on the Dean's door and he called me in with a hearty hello.

"Delighted, delighted to see you again!" He began shaking my hand vigorously at my acceptance of the offer and then assured me that I had made the right decision. In return, I was honest and forthcoming about my genuine relief at finding somewhere and even threw in an off-hand reference to my old paper on astrology which had been the apparent sticking point for every other college I had queried where the veneer of politeness was used to cover the naked racism and islamophobia that those august institutions professed to have rid themselves of even while it festered in every syllabus.

"Oh, I most assuredly have read that paper! I confess I find the whole subject fascinating and really rather misunderstood in current scientific culture."

I gently lowered my teacup to the table, knocking the saucer slightly. That was certainly unexpected. "Then you have no concerns about it?"

"Not at all. We were really rather hoping you would teach part of it to some of our select undergraduates." If I hadn't already placed the cup back on the table, it would have clattered to the floor at this point. Dean Jessamy laughed. "I'm afraid you'll find us rather, let us say, different from other places of so-called higher learning. Oh, we have our foibles, as no doubt you will discover yourself, but we're actually much more open to subjects other institutions often consider beyond the pale in terms of science curricula." He lowered his head momentarily, seemingly lost in a haze of nostalgia. "Of course, that often means that we can be rather an academic dead-end, as it were." He looked over at me to see if there were flecks of melancholy in my eyes to match those I saw in his, but in my current wave of heady euphoria, the only things reflected therein were the distant memories of longed-for stars.

Over the course of that morning, and after several pots of tea ceremoniously poured into delicate china cups, we reached an agreement on what subjects I might want to teach and how they would fit into the curriculum. I wish I could say that I'd been a hard negotiator as intended, but every initial suggestion I offered was immediately taken up with firm agreement and genial smiles. In this manner, I had found myself agreeing to teach astronomy, astrology, middle eastern history and written Arabic. It transpired that it had been the Dean himself who had insisted on recruiting a new staff member that understood Arabic. Once the other matters were settled, my curiosity was piqued enough to ask why.

"Oh! Goodness!" He almost sprang from his seat, his old frame evidently still yet spry and limber enough for quick movement. "Do forgive me, I have yet to introduce you to our library. We must rectify this immediately!" As he sped across the office to the door behind us, he added "I expect you will be spending much time there before your teaching slots are finally allocated for the next term. We have many texts in Arabic that we should love you to look at, catalogue and translate where possible. Yes! Many, many texts. Do follow!" He added this last command as I had not yet arisen from the seat, but giving into his infectious boyish enthusiasm and my own growing inquisitiveness I eagerly traversed many of those long corridors and empty quads until we arrived at a remote edifice of old hewn marble draped in ivy. He produced a large silvery key from his waistcoat pocket and deftly opened the imposing doors. It seemed distinctly odd to me that the library did not take pride of place in the middle of the campus where it would be more accessible, even more confusing that such a place of study would be closed and locked with a key held by the Dean. I was about to enquire as to why this might be when I caught my first glimpse of the interior which, despite the room being locked, was already well lit with strip lighting on cords dangling from its vaulted ceilings and shaded wall lamps of gilded iron and green glass.

"It can get rather chilly in here, I'm afraid," he said in an apologetic tone of voice. "Some of the older documents are rather precious and best kept in a temperature-controlled environment. Still, I'm sure you'll be most comfortable." The broadest of smiles arose on his face, simultaneously eliminating those melancholic worry-lines I had noticed were seemingly ever present upon his forehead.

There were more books in this room than I had ever seen in one place. In size and scope, it may have equalled the Library of Congress. Floor to ceiling shelves covered seven of the eight walls and each of them groaned under the weight of ancient musty tomes, crumbling yellowed scrolls and volumes of creaking vellum. In the centre of this paradise of learning were eight long reading tables arranged in a square formation facing a centrepiece which resembled a golden pillar though it was made of cool marble. I could just make out delicate

Arabic writing in jet black script adorning its plinth. I let out an involuntary noise somewhere between a gasp of excitement and a shriek of rapturous elation.

"Such a library! I can hardly believe it!" I managed to stop gushing long enough to regain a professional composure. Looking around at the vast array of literature before me, I asked the Dean where the Arabic section was and where he would like me to begin. He crooked his long neck slightly to the left.

"Oh! Our main library is a much bigger collection, it doesn't all fit into a single room. Luckily, we had a grant made available for us to house this collection separately in this purpose-built library here." He beamed broadly as he spoke, clearly waiting for some response. I must have looked somewhat perplexed as he felt compelled to clarify further. "This room IS our Arabic collection." He looked around again, evidently proud of what the university had assembled. I stood open-mouthed, awestruck for the first time at something that wasn't the night sky and pinching myself to make sure I wasn't dreaming. After a few hushed moments, he shuffled lightly on his long legs. "Well, I shall leave you to get further acquainted. I trust you'll be able to find your way back across campus to make it back home?" I nodded. As far as I was concerned, I was already home.

I deposited my bag on one of the writing desks and removed a slim notebook - too slim, I realised now for the task at hand - and an elegant fountain pen which had been a graduation gift from my mother. Then I set about the room in a flurry: a naive, wide-eyed, keen student wishing to explore and understand everything in her world.

The collection in its entirety would take years to fully catalogue, let alone translate, even were I not also to lecturing undergraduates and tutoring postgraduates. I had clearly landed such a perfect position that it hardly seemed to be real. This dreamlike fugue state continued as I began to explore some of the titles around me, picking each up with white-gloved hands and delicately leafing through one at a time, moving between shelves and cabinets to sample each literary specimen on offer. Here was a perfectly preserved Zij al Sindhind written in 830 by the mathematician Muhammad ibn Musa al-Khwarizmi, who first introduced Ptolemaic concepts into Islamic science and marked a turning point in Islamic astronomy, an astounding work I had never seen before as it was believed lost. The extant corpus of Islamic astronomical texts was estimated to be in the region of ten thousand manuscripts. Either they were all here or that number was far below the mark. I replaced it reverently and took a sheaf of manuscripts from the shelf below, carrying them carefully to the writing table, then drew up a chair, jolting myself into a momentary scare as the noise of dragging it across the marble floor reverberated around the muted walls of the library.

I gazed with wonder at what lay before me: Al-Battani's Movements of the Stars, not even published in Europe until 1537 when the Renaissance had begun to drag them kicking and screaming out of their so-called Dark Ages. Next to it was Al Sufi Abd Al-Rahmen's Book of Fixed Stars, slightly singed but nonetheless a complete catalogue of 1018 stars and their approximate positions, magnitudes and colours. These seemed from the aged parchment to be the original works and for the first time I wondered, with furrowed brow, what journeys of colonial plunder and deceit had finally ended with them being hidden away here, in this most inauspicious of academic establishments. The magnitude of these discoveries, as well as others I would find later in the day, slowly dawned on me and the fact that I was now their willing custodian made me dizzy with power and gasping for breath in the dusty, rarefied air of the Miskatonic Arabic library with its trove of lost manuscripts and its shining central pillar.

It was approaching dusk when I left the place. Even then I could hardly bring myself to do so, but as hungry as I was for knowledge there was another hunger which needed to be satiated. I'd spent three full hours leafing meticulously through Omar Khayyam's Rubaiyat - one of my father's favourite things to read to me on those mountain slopes in a distant memory of a place no longer home. It had sat on the bottom shelf next to a work of his which was lesser-known to the western world: the Treatise on Demonstrations of Problems in Algebra. Nobody but my own family had had such an influence on the way I viewed the world - through lenses both poetic and scientific. I nearly shed a tear when I imagined reading this back to my own father. There were marginalia on this copy too, but too small for me to

175

read effectively. It was this want of a magnifying glass, as well as a good plate of pilaf, that eventually drove me from my seat back outside into the cobbled quadrangles, their doric columns so long-shadowed in the setting sun that they resembled prison bars which my own shadow passed through with slow, deliberate steps as I made my way to the staff quarters.

The journey back across campus, strolling among those umbral colonnades in the first throes of twilight, should have been a simple and uninterrupted journey. I stuck to the paths I knew and did not venture beyond my vision to explore what lay beyond among those brooding cloisters and alleys where the dizzying heights of the tall turrets made one claustrophobic when traversing their narrow walkways. I had done all the exploring I wanted for the day, and in much more salubrious surroundings. I was still reeling from the richness of my earlier discoveries and therefore did not notice at first the sound of distant but encroaching footfalls making their way deliberately and patiently many steps behind me, always out of sight, echoing from deep in the gloom. Maybe if I had paid attention at that point, had turned to confront my nocturnal pursuer, the events of the next few days may have played out very differently. Still, I returned to my lodgings and fell, exhausted and reeling, into a fitful slumber.

***

I sat alone on the edge of a rocky precipice, shuddering at the sudden change in location and shivering at the difference in temperature. Below me, laid out like a fine carpet, were the villages and vales I remembered from my childhood: above me shone distant stars set in a tapestry of midnight blue sky. My heart skipped a beat as I gazed longingly up at those familiar, never-forgotten jewels of my distant childhood. The quiet of the mountain air was unperturbed by traffic or voices, the brilliance of the night sky unimpeded by the polluting lights of the city. I stood and stretched, a layer of mountain dust cascading down my jalabiya and tumbling down the cliffside as I fully oriented myself. There was no doubt I was somewhere in the Zagros mountains, but since I had fallen asleep in New England I contented myself to the realisation that this must be a dream, brought on perhaps by the enormous relief that I had found a new place to call home and the grief of what was happening in my old one.

Then I saw him. A shrouded figure on a nearby peak, long robes swirling in the breeze around his silhouetted form as he surveyed the skies. At first, I resented this intrusion into the very personal experience I had been enjoying, but there was something about this fellow stargazer which piqued my interest, and I continued to watch him as he stood, unmoving, staring up into the night and beyond. Finally, his posture changed, and his gaze descended, realising perhaps for the first time that he, too, had company in these cold, moonlit mountains. Despite the distance, I felt cold eyes

burn into my skin as he acknowledged my presence.
Though he was too far away to recognise any of his
features, he seemed at once familiar to me but
utterly, utterly, terrifying as those eyes coalesced
into two brightly-burning stars and then dimmed,
dissolving into the coldness of the vast expanse of
the heavens.

***

I awoke with a start and a shiver, beneath sky blue blankets in the rooms where I was lodging. Morning had already broken but the sun was hidden beneath a gently rolling fog which looked like it had no intention of burning off as the morning edged toward midday. It took me a moment to reorient myself, to discern what was dream and what was reality. I gave thanks for my new life but could not forget those moments in the night where the stars and the stranger had all felt very real, despite it not even being night in Iran while I slept here in Massachusetts. I rolled out of bed, made myself a pot of jasmine tea and prepared for a second day of discovery in the library. First, though, I had to face my first staff meeting which, it turned out, consisted only of myself and the three professors who had interrogated me at my interview.

"Naturally, our unique funding position allows us to take these matters into ready, ah, 'account', as it were. Bit of bean-counter humour there." The bags under my eyes had either gone undetected or uncommented on. It was clear from their discussion that they weren't used to sharing beyond their long-established trinity which had no doubt held sway over these meetings for more terms than there were galaxies: the easy way in which they finished each other's sentences, the tacit understanding between them of how the university actually functioned. They weren't used to dealing with a newcomer, even one they had deigned to invite beyond the veil, and Gülgger in particular was the sort of academic who had no time for women at all. In terms of structural misogyny, this was nothing new to me and remained a constant frustration. It was just that it had recently given way instead to an underlying structural racism. With the disturbing dream still pressing on the recesses of my mind I was in a mood to confront it head on, but that dismal sleep which I had managed to grab had left me too groggy to reply with the necessary ripostes. At this juncture I would have to resign myself to being thankful at the very least that I hadn't been asked to make the tea or take the minutes. Then the unexpected reserves of strength shone through, and I had a few moments of heated exchange with the Doctor, who - in response to my queries about funding for an orrery - muttered, guffawed and then descended into quoting the most awful doggerel.

"I have seen the dark universe yawning, where the black planets roll without aim...Where they roll in their horror unheeded, without knowledge or lustre or name..."

I responded swiftly. Proceeding to name those planets, and by which means they acquired them, seemed to beat him into submission, but I wasn't done, not when I had something to prove. I remonstrated him fully with a literal finger-wagging as I spoke.

"You forget too easily who it was who named the stars, Doctor Gülgger, and the terms still used to study and measure them. Does the word algorithm mean nothing to you? Or algebra? Or azimuth, nadir, or zenith? Do you have any comprehension of the origin of Deneb, of Altair or Aldebaran?" I was shaking again, though this time in anger more than exhaustion or despair.

The Dean had looked horrified when the Doctor had replied to me thus and I detected a good deal of sympathy within him that I had been treated in such a fashion, even as he recoiled similarly at my rejoinder. The Bursar - who had also seemingly been unnerved by the whole exchange - simply wrung his calloused hands nervously and looked down at the floor as if some answers were to be found in the polished teak of the wooden boards beneath our feet. I slumped back into my chair and the ensuing stony silence indicated that our first staff meeting was over.

I spent the remainder of that week in the library lost in my own thoughts and cataloguing the extensive poetry collection, which I had now rearranged so that it occupied the entirety of the three bottom shelves on the bookcase immediately to the left of the door. Yet every evening on my return to halls, those same footsteps dogged me, forever out of sight yet still alarming. Being stalked on campus was sadly not an unfamiliar concept to me, though on a campus where I had only seen five people during my week here, it beggared belief. I doubled back on myself, hid in deep doorways, laid in wait behind shadow-shrouded pillars, but my pursuer remained elusive. In the apparent absence of any campus security to report this to, I left the library later each day in the expectation that whoever it was proved to be less familiar with the hours of darkness than I was and secure on the knowledge that my rape alarm, loud screaming voice and can of bear spray would prove equal a match to any would be predator.

My days, meanwhile, were full of the passion of poetry. I was familiar with Khayyam, of course, and the works of Nizami (Laili and Majnun being a childhood favourite) but there were other more esoteric works here which I pored over as I indexed their titles: El-safar zahar, Dīwān al-nujūm wa-firdaws al-ḥikma, la salam eabr albawaaba... I didn't stop until I found a copy of my father's own collection - here in English and Persian - The Song of the Mountains, wherein I was lost in nostalgia until I heard a polite cough behind me. It was the Bursar.

It occurred to me that I hadn't spoken to the other faculty since that display at the staff meeting and had hardly spoken to Bursar Halcyon at all except during my interview. It also occurred to me that of those few people I had met and spoken to here, I shared a staffroom with three of them and now shared my own space with just one. Probability dictated one of them was likely to be my secret stalker. I had dubbed the three of them in turn as charming, alarming and disarming: Halcyon was about to live up to the latter.

"Did you come here to discuss my funding request, Bursar?" It was a genuine question, yet I spoke it in an almost playful fashion to elicit a desired response. The Bursar wrung his hands. I could see dark spots on the cuffs of his shirt which seemed likely to be a by-product of careless chemical experimentation.

"After a fashion." His smile was very different to the Dean's: it hardly existed unless you were actively looking for it. "Actually, there may be something you can help me with. I've been looking for a particular text to help with some research. I'm hoping there might be a copy somewhere in here. It would be great news for Miskatonic if there was, it would allow us to make great advances and secure funding for a great deal of upkeep."

I looked seriously at him for the first time, wondering what advances he might be referring to and how they might relate to either chemistry or economic theory. As he spoke the next sentence, I began to understand how it was that my position here and the frankly mouthwatering salary I had been offered had actually been financed.

"It's a collection of works known as the Jabirian corpus. I'm hoping our collection here has some. He's really one of the most original minds on the subject..." He tailed off, somewhat on edge again, as if he was teetering on the brink of a revelation and was unsure exactly how much to tell me.

"Alchemy. You're talking about alchemy." My mind reeled at the possibilities. After all, if I asserted that astrology was a very real science, why not other studies that had been relegated to ridicule?

"Is it The Great Book on Specific Properties that you're after? Or one of the treatises in the One Hundred and Twelve Books?"

Bursar Halcyon almost fell over in relief and smiled enigmatically at my immediate comprehension of the work and my unblinking acceptance that alchemy was a practical and desirable subject.

"I'm afraid I'm not intimately familiar with any of the works. It's one particular avenue I've been keen to explore, to augment my own rather limited successes based largely on the banned works of Isaac Newton." He paused to allow me time to parse that remark and revel in the understanding that, yes, Miskatonic had acquired those too. "Now you're here though…well, it can't hurt to ask." Beneath those pale grey eyes blinking at me amid those works lit by reflections of the golden pillar, I saw a kindred spirit whose academic journey had perhaps not been dissimilar to mine, even if the imminent cause was quite different. I was reminded of that unfinished conversation with the Dean when I'd asked him about why he needed someone who understood Arabic and which had provoked a similar nostalgic feeling. If this place was a dead end academically, I couldn't think at that moment of a better place to be trapped.

I promised the Bursar I'd let him know if I found anything, content to have found a soulmate who had confided a great secret in me without any threat attached to revealing it. If it occurred momentarily to me that I did, after all, have nobody to tell - certainly not anyone who would believe me

- the moment passed as I concluded my cataloguing and made my way back through the deserted campus. No footsteps followed in my wake this time and I retired early, in equal measure too excited and too tired to fully comprehend what any of this might actually mean. On drifting into a fitful sleep, my mind was again interrupted by disturbing visions.

***

I stood on the high ridge of a greyish rocky escarpment overlooking a desolate landscape of burnt orange where the sand whipped around into high dunes around the edge of a flat plain, featureless except for a few clumps of low-lying brush. The moon was full and high in the sky. Even on this windless night, it was bitterly cold, and I wrapped my headscarf tighter as if that would warm me somehow. It did keep a good deal of dust from my eyes, dust which seemed to have never quite settled despite the lack of even the mildest breeze. To be in this sparse sandy wilderness under the midday sun would be to swiftly invite death: to be here in the dead of night was hardly more forgiving.

Once again I appeared to have company: the robed figure whose piercing eyes had previously terrified me. He traversed the valley between the dunes in front of me, this time turning his head in my direction and beckoning me forward with a long finger. Against my better judgement, I found myself following in his footsteps, sand sinking between my bare toes as the dunes parted to reveal a deep, wide depression in the sand ahead. He spoke not a word but waited for me at the edge of that forbidden and foreboding place and then pointed in front of him. I looked up at the sky first to fix my location with the starry wisdom I had always turned to, and then onward in the direction of his finger. There I saw vague shapes looming and shimmering in the distance, miraged minarets from which there issued no call to prayer but rather a forlorn droning which could not have been issued from any instrument or beast under Creation. The vision then departed as soon as it appeared, and those monotonous sounds with it, leaving me with only the low hum of the dunes for company and a burning curiosity to venture forth into that valley between the ridges of sand, to lose myself in that desolate and unforgiving place, to wander its abandoned streets and drink deep of its proscribed wisdom.

My guide had similarly vanished before I could ask him anything or even see his face. My senses reeled and my body shook at those spectral sights which greeted me. For I knew this city from legend and was awestruck by its appearance even as the accursed tendrils of evil which pulsed from it repelled and appalled my very soul. Though others might have thought the city nameless, it was known to me as a place of wickedness, that city called 'many columned Iram' by Scheherazade in the Arabian Nights, described by T E Lawrence as The Atlantis of the Sands and in the Koran as the city destroyed by Allah when the tribe of Ad transgressed.

***

I lay half-awake and half-asleep, drenched in sweat as I recalled that fearful dream. It seemed that Khayyam had spoken too soon when he wrote that "Iram indeed is gone with all its rose". I retained enough of a memory of that starry sky from my nightmare, the remnants of its stars still burnt into my retinas, that I was able to make a very quick sketch of the positions of them in the sky. Once I had prayed and eaten, I headed to the library to ascertain whether my hypothesis was correct. I decided not to share this unnerving experience with any of the faculty until I had more information than two nights of bad dreams to base a theory upon.

It was simple enough yet alarmingly took all morning in my drowsy state to painstakingly leaf through available historic star charts and compare them to what I had seen. It would be quite an achievement to publish a paper on the discovery of Iram via retro-engineered stargazing.

I knew what the poets said of the place, but nobody knew its location or its exact fate. In some accounts, the sins of the Ad were idolatry, in others hubris. In all, the city was wiped from the face of the earth and had never been seen again. Whether its inhabitants had been men, jinn, giants, or nephilim was still a matter of debate. If it could be found, if that mystery could be uncovered… I dwelt for a while on the possibilities. It seems that moment, snatched in the early afternoon with heavily drooping eyelids brought on by poor sleep and worsened by a lack of food, was enough. I must have closed my eyes at that moment and drifted off.

***

The city drew me into its innermost streets, and I scrambled through the two landscapes superimposed on my feeble uncomprehending brain. First was the city as it now stood - a ruined remnant of hubris and debauch buried or lost beneath the shifting sands of the Rub al Khali, brought low by the wrath of Allah. Secondly there stood the city as it once was, a sinful yet wondrous place of shining pillars and white marbled domes. Whilst this second city was still devoid of life, it ignited all the senses: pungent night-blooming jasmine blew on nocturnal breezes, the heady tastes of rosewater and red wine tickled my throat, drums beat frenetically in distant districts. Above all, that same distorted drone buzzed forth from every minaret, drowning me in a cacophony of perverted prayer. Of my earlier guide there was no sign, but I plodded through courtyard and thoroughfare until I spied him at the entrance of what must have been a great temple, though at the periphery of my vision I could see that not only did this monstrous, stuccoed edifice lie in repugnant ruin, but appeared to be the very epicentre of whatever blast had finally destroyed blasphemous Iram. Even knowing this, my feet carried me forever forward until I stood at its very threshold, gazing down into a pit of unfathomed depths.

***

When I awoke, I shrieked in a temporary fit of disorientation and panic, accidentally scattering scrolls to the floor. Thankfully, there was nobody nearby to hear or see this ungainly episode. I glanced over at the clock and was surprised it was already evening. Had I really been asleep for that long? Had my meanderings through the lost city actually taken place in real time somehow? My body bore no signs of the journey: no sand between my toes, no lingering scents in my nostrils, no acoustic remnants of the droning. I recalled every moment of it though, in exacting detail, and if I were artistically inclined, I might have managed some rather fine sketches of the place.

I resolved to take the Bursar, at least, into my confidence and broach the subject of these dreams as soon as feasible. There was something spectacularly wrong going on here which I didn't think I could fathom on my own. Perhaps, as someone clearly initiated into whatever world I had been drawn into, he might be able to offer some advice, or at least a sensitive ear for my troubled soul to whisper into.

I carefully picked up the scrolls I'd inadvertently strewn over the library floor and inspected each for any sign of damage. Nothing. I sighed in relief: that would be one less thing I'd have to explain to the rest of the staff. Sweeping my pen and notebook lazily into my tote bag, I left the library behind and picked my way through the dimly lit campus until I came upon a walled garden I hadn't noticed before. Despite myself, I sat down on a bench there in that academic pairidaēza, far from the worries of reality and dream both, and gathered my thoughts. I decided to address the triumvirate of professors all together in tomorrow's staff meeting, to gauge the reaction of each and ascertain friend from foe. I already had questions I was burning to ask about the provenance of the collection I had been cataloguing and had accordingly been allocated a generous portion of the agenda for that discussion. The state of my sanity, though, was more imminent and I was determined to get answers no matter how fanciful they thought my concerns to be.

I was struggling to stay awake even though I'd spent all the previous night and most of the afternoon asleep. Were I to continue in this fashion, the restless and tormented dreams would see me fit for nothing. Coffee was called for - the thickest Turkish coffee that I had demanded be a permanent feature in both the staff room and the boarding house.

I stood up from the cold stone bench and headed back to the campus entrance, resolute in my decisions and confident I'd be given a fair hearing. In my sleepy state I almost didn't hear the footfalls following me: it was only the snapping of a twig in the garden that saved my skin. I took a series of sharp turns and found myself in a windowed courtyard with a statue of Orpheus at the centre. Suddenly seized by an idea, I pressed myself into a corner and rummaged in my bag for my compact. Lifting the little mirror up and adjusting the angle, I was able to glimpse an image of my stalker through a myriad of reflective glass surfaces. He turned the same corner I had only a few moments ago but backed off when he saw his own reflection staring back at him in the large refectory windows. It was too late though. I'd seen him. It was Dr Gülgger.

***

Next morning's staff meeting did not go quite as expected. Not for me and certainly not for the three stooges.

I tried to keep my eyes on the Doctor, determined to discover whether he knew that I was aware of his crepuscular creeping. That he was a clear and present danger to me seemed obvious, but before I could confront him, I had to put up with his incessant put-downs.

I began, bleary-eyed but suitably energised by strong coffee, by relating the slow progress I was making with the cataloguing and asking technical questions about how best to cross-reference the Arabic titles - where the documents had titles - into English in the file system. I managed a discreet shake of the head toward the bursar to indicate I had not yet located the research he'd requested. Then I berated their reluctance to embrace the modern era by not introducing even a single computer to the establishment. I was in full finger-wagging swing when I asked the question of the provenance of the items in the library. Each of them, I cordially suggested, would need to be researched to determine how it had arrived here: I doubted the

Bursar's admittedly limited alchemical experiments had managed to actually pay for the entire collection, given the extent of the collection and the antiquity of some of its contents.

The Bursar listened quietly, deep in thought, his hands wringing. The Dean blinked repeatedly at what he thought was belligerence on my part but which, if uttered by a male academic, would have been taken positively as a confident swagger. I was both familiar with and tired of this academic routine.

The Doctor, growing increasingly red-faced, waited until I had finished and then cleared his throat and spoke clearly, but with well-aimed venom.

"Would you rather they were still in Baghdad?"

The words cut through me like a knife. I began to falter and clutched at the table edge for balance, white-knuckled with pent up rage and frustration. My eyes looked over at the collection of the daily papers laid out on the other table. This was September 2003, some six months after the initial invasion of Iraq. It was hard to imagine anyone who thought they might have been safe in whatever might remain of the original House of Wisdom constructed in Baghdad in the ninth century. Perhaps he thought to play on what remained of my Iranian national loyalty. Perhaps he didn't know. Perhaps he didn't care. I despaired then for the future of humanity as I had done only a few times before in my life. I openly wept for several seconds but managed to make eye contact again with the Doctor, whose face was fixed in a smug grin even

191

as he folded his arms in triumph, thinking the matter over.

"You are dismissed, Doctor Gülgger." The Dean rose slowly, drawing himself up to his full height. His long face now was less than jovial, the lines on his ample forehead creasing with displeasure. He had the air of someone who had reached a tipping point and, having been forced into an overdue confrontation, found that he really rather enjoyed it.

"You'll regret this." More of a whimper than a threat.

"I assure you, I shall not. Good day to you. We shall naturally be happy to send on your things to a location of your choosing."

I sincerely hoped I was never on the receiving end of that face. Despite everything else I had seen in the last few days, I was afraid of the depth of those eyes, once twinkling and now cold and grey, and the quiet anger of that stare.

Doctor Gülgger stood, slid his chair under the table, and slunk sulkily out of the room.

That would have been a suitable end of any meeting. I wasn't done yet, though, and the Dean's interjection had given me a chance to gather my wits about me.

"I believe Professor Sattari has something she would like to tell us both." That was the Bursar. They were the first words he had uttered all morning: I'd almost forgotten he was here.

The Dean's mood lifted instantly, flashing first patrician concern and then, when it was quite plain, I would take that as an inappropriate response, with

192

an offer of a fresh pot of jasmine tea and a willing ear.

"It's related to my earlier question about provenance and the origins of some of these scrolls. I wonder if either of you have heard of the legend of lost Iram?"

***

So help me, I told them everything. It poured out of me faster than the tea from the spout. By the time I had finished, they knew everything I did: about my poet father and my stargazing youth, my recent unsettling dreams, what I knew of the city from scripture, poem and myth. Then, to top it off, I told them I had caught the Doctor stalking me around campus after dark. It was a relief to unburden myself; it was more of a relief to have a quiet and attentive audience.

"I have indeed heard of that dreaded place. The history of this institution and the nearby town of Arkham - itself often referred to as legend-haunted - are themselves inextricably linked to many expeditions around the world, some of which you will no doubt claim to be of a colonial nature. What we know, though, and what we face, would fill a thousand more volumes and a thousand more nightmares. I had hoped to introduce this to you gradually. There are secrets here which would shatter lesser minds…"

He tailed off and I seized the moment. "Dean Jessamy, what exactly happened to my predecessor?"

He looked sad and walked over to the window, staring out of it for a good length of time, gazing at something on or over the horizon, but beyond my vantage point. Returning his gaze, he looked directly at me.

"I will tell you. Firstly, though, I must tell you of someone else. An individual known as Abd Al-Hazred, usually referred to in occult circles only as the Mad Arab."

I rolled my eyes. I intended to issue a contemptible harrumph, or at least a dismissive sigh. What came out was more akin to a cackle, crescendoing to a full-throated manic laugh.

"Seriously?" I managed to get some words in over the indignant laughter. "I mean, really? There's one non-European in the whole crazy mythology surrounding this place and your sobriquet for him is The Mad Arab?" They stared at me, unsure of what to say. I splayed my fingers on the table and shook my head. I wasn't even that surprised.

The Dean waited for a moment. When he spoke again, he didn't look chastised, he looked sad.

"The madness is real, and the name is not of our choosing. Nevertheless, it is unfortunate. Al-Hazred was notorious among his fellows at the time; we are talking some 100 years after the birth of Islam. He followed false gods and penned a book of ultimate evil, Kitab Al-Azif."

He had my attention. Things began to click into place. A library full of books in Arabic. A link to an historic figure who may well have been an early sufi

194

mystic pilloried by sectarian peers for seemingly embracing the jāhiliyyah - the time previous to Islam, a time of ignorance and barbarity. Whatever veneer of historicity western academia and esoterica had applied to this figure was undoubtedly flawed in its interpretation. I'd seen it a thousand times before.

"I don't suppose we have a copy of that in my library?" Sarcasm dripped from every word. "Because that would just be swell. I'll give it a read this afternoon. I'm sure it will send me right off to sleep." I wasn't joking on that last part. Something must be behind these nightmares, and it wasn't a late-night cheese platter.

"We do not possess a full copy in Arabic, merely a fragment. That fragment was, ahh, ahem, taken from what we think was Iram, sometime in the last century."

SLAM. That was the metaphorical door behind me, trapping me here with these modern mystics masquerading as academics. It didn't sound any better than the doors that had been slammed in front of me. At least there was some way forward, even if I had to fumble for it in the dark.

Then, as an afterthought, he added "The Mad Arab isn't not the only non-European moniker, more's the pity. There's an entity known as Azathoth which is usually referred to as a daemon sultan." He shook his head vigorously, displacing a cloud of dandruff which settled on the shoulders of his jacket like a light snowfall. Then he looked over apologetically, head hung low, but with something beyond shame behind his eyes. Was it fear?

"I'll arrange for you to meet your predecessor, should you wish. Though I doubt you will get much of any use from him, poor chap. I'm afraid something terrible happened to him, though we are not sure what. He can't speak coherently anymore, you see. Quite, quite, mad." He gazed down for a moment, seemingly finding something fascinating on the floor, then back up at me, his eyes deadly serious. "We had him committed to Arkham Asylum."

I didn't even comment on the poetry and symmetry of the patterns of madness. Maybe I was growing as a person. More likely was the feeling that I might be next.

I left the meeting with the promise that I'd try and locate that fragment in the library, but I knew it would be like looking for the proverbial needle in the haystack. I wanted to consult some star charts too, but that would have to wait until the morning, before the visit to the asylum that the Dean had now arranged for me.

If I was a fragment of a book of ultimate evil, where would I hide? Mere days ago, I couldn't even believe I'd be contemplating such a preposterous idea. The Dean's vague description of the text of the fragment matched over half of the texts in here. It could be tucked in between or among any number of them. I'd made scant progress before darkness descended and the long shadows of evening closed around me. I was tired, but too scared to sleep. What had I forgotten? What vital clue might I have missed? I padded the courtyards back to the administration building, lost in my own thoughts, doubting my sanity, fearful of the future.

I didn't hear the footsteps until it was almost too late.

"Professor!" I spun round on the spot. It was Gülgger, and he looked disturbed, his eyes practically bulging forth from his head.

Confrontation time, then. I strode toward him, disappointed but not surprised that dismissal hadn't stopped his pursuit, fumbling in my tote bag for my rape alarm or the bear spray, whichever my fingers happened to find first.

He rushed toward me, half-sprint and half-lumber, looking to bowl me over. My hands were still digging in the bag, having so far found only discarded tissues, pens, a compact…just about every other item that was in there. In desperation, I swung the bag around before me and managed to clock him around the side of his head. He lurched but didn't go down.

"Listen to me! You've got it all wrong!"

I wasn't listening. I jumped back to catch my breath. It's likely that move saved my life. I'm not sure what exactly it was that pounced in that moment, but it landed full square on Gülgger's chest and had him on the ground in an instant. I remember teeth - a good deal too many of them - and claws - too long for the feet they emerged from, wicked-barbed and dripping with an acrid substance which made Gülgger scream in agony. My fingers closed around a cylinder - the bear spray, finally! - and I managed to hold the nozzle down long enough to get the malevolent monstrosity full in the face between its attacks on Gülgger's exposed neck and torso. Its wail was pitiful, like a sad puppy, but the assault worked. It snarled at me, shaking its head in a failed attempt to get rid of the smell, its eyes watering with intense pain, then bounded over me and out of sight. Before I had time to think, I scrambled to Gülgger's side. His throat was lacerated by those sharp teeth, I could see parts of the interior of his neck. His chest wasn't much better off. He wasn't going to make it.

"They were right about you." He could barely speak, there was too much blood in his mouth, and I struggled to understand what he gurgled next. "I wanted to scare you off. I didn't think you'd be up to it…" He cut off there, devolving into a coughing fit. Blood fountained from his mouth and throat as he sputtered one last warning.

"Follow him. End this. You'll need some protection." He fumbled inside his jacket for something: a scrap of paper with a symbol on it. Whatever it was hadn't done him much good, but he handed it over to me in those last moments before his eyes closed for the last time. I left him there, dead on the cobblestones. I was still reeling from the assault, the horror of that creature and what my next steps should be as I shambled the rest of the way back home. Despite all my plans to the contrary, I was fast asleep before my head even hit the pillow.

***

I guessed now who my guide might be, or at least who he might represent. Nevertheless, I followed him down into that yawning abyss of empty darkness, even though I knew it imperilled my sanity and set my mortal soul on edge. Down and down we went, the subterranean stairs slick with a dampness which rose eerily from each step and clung to my clothing. Down and down in a seemingly never-ending spiral until at last we reached a portal of monstrous proportions surrounded by scrawled, spidery Arabic script which seemed to shrink and expand on its own cognisance as I turned my gaze to it. Incomprehensible and unpronounceable names arose unbidden in my throat which I did not permit to escape my lips. My guide prostrated himself and began a low, monotonous chant in an unintelligible tongue. Now I knew I had come too far, that my scientific curiosity had momentarily triumphed over my previously resolute faith. I turned and tried to flee, but the stairway behind me had vanished and in its place, there was naught but a narrow ramp which would be impossible to climb. I wept for my inability to grasp the full extent of my own hubris, for what might remain of my mortal future, and for the fate of my immortal soul.

Whatever the portal was, wherever it led, my erstwhile guide seemed bent on opening it. Or rather, to have me open it. I beheld no handle, no lock, only the surrounding, shifting symbols. Dreaming lucidly now, I contemplated lines from Khayyam: a last, desperate clutch at the last lonely straw:

'There was a door to which I found no key:

There was a veil past which I could not see...

One moment in annihilation's waste, one moment, of the well of life to taste.

The stars are setting, and the caravan starts for the dawn of nothing - oh, make haste!'

Once spoken, my guide offered guttural encouragement and beckoned me closer. Maybe I was onto something? Had Khayyam trodden this same path before me somehow, only to fall at this hurdle?

I racked my brain for any other poetic references to doors and portals whilst resting with my back against the base of a crumbling sandstone pillar. It did not take me long to bring to mind the words of the Divan of Hafiz:

'Brave tales of singers and wine relate,
The key to the Hidden 'twere vain to seek;
No wisdom of ours has unlocked that gate
And locked to our wisdom it still shall be.'

What did it all mean? Who was I to follow in the footsteps of these esteemed esoterics? As I was about to give up, I summoned up another verse about gates and keys I must have read earlier in the library:

'Yog-Sothoth knows the gate
Yog-Sothoth is the gate
Yog-Sothoth is the key and guardian of the gate
Past, present and future are all one in Yog-Sothoth'

Dare I speak this sacrilegious name? What might happen? I was no longer certain this was merely a series of bad dreams, perhaps instead *some test or trial. I feared if I was to emerge from this nightmare I had little alternative. The name did not come easily to my chapped lips: I stuttered and stammered until I got the pronunciation right. My guide was whipped up in the throes of ecstatic laughter, turning and whirling before the portal which now shimmered and pulsed with a dim golden glow. Then he vanished through it.*

Behind me, the city seemed to fold in on itself, as if it knew it were no longer wanted or needed. The last words in my mind were those of Khayyam:

'One thing at least is certain, that life flies;

One thing is certain, and the rest is lies; The flower that once has blown forever dies.'

I took one last look at the depths of the dreamless city of pillars as it collapsed inward around me, not with a great clamour but rather with a muffled rustling as if it had all been merely paper. Then I followed my grinning guide through the wretched gateway, now glimmering with an unholy effulgence, and found myself plummeting into eternal night.

***

"Professor Leila Sattani." For the third time, I repeated my name into the archaic buzzer system at the entrance gate of Arkham Asylum. It was not at all comforting to note that the university did not have a monopoly on macabre gothic architecture: if anything, this place looked even more imposing and forbidding. Hardly a place of healing, I thought.

"Zzzt with azzzazz crfffzzt." Hardly a welcome or useful reply, but the gate began to swing open on its ancient hinges nevertheless and I made my way up a drive overgrown with weeds to a building overgrown with ivy. The main doors stood wide open in contrast to the gates and before them stood a woman in a pastel blue pantsuit and matching sneakers with a twinset of pearls dangling from her neck. She waved over to me.

"I keep on at them, but they'll never get that contraption fixed, I'm afraid. Dr. Grace Archer." She extended a well-manicured, long-fingered hand which I shook firmly. "Over there by the coffee machine is Dr. Lowen. You're here to see patient 22, I understand?" She squinted slightly in the morning sunlight. "Nobody has been in since he arrived, but Dean Jessamy placed a call yesterday indicating you were cleared to visit." We were passing through the reception now, then through a set of swing doors clearly not part of the original architecture. Dr. Archer finally paused in front of an ancient looking lift of the sort you find in expensive hotels, those that are open to the environment and are more a sort of metal cage than a modern elevator. Once inside, she pressed a button marked 'LG' and the contraption shuddered into life. "The secure ward is in the basement. There are a few special rules. Honestly, there would be more but patient 22 is the only occupant at this time. Please follow me." She tugged the gate open once the elevator had come to a screeching halt in front of a long corridor stretching forward into the darkness. "Lights go on and off automatically as we progress.

Don't get too close to the door. No attempt at physical contact and no sudden movements. I shall monitor the conversation and reserve the right to end it if it places the patient in distress." I nodded agreement to the terms as we came to a halt in front of a solid iron door with a barred window at head height. She nodded and I stepped forward.

I have rarely seen such a wretched creature. His long hair was lank and matted, his face pock-marked and sallow. He had only three teeth and a recent head wound which matched a patch of dried blood on the padded wall. I recoiled from the unpleasant combination of body odour and urine that he reeked of. I cleared my throat in preparation for a question, but he beat me to it, flinging himself at the door and spitting bile as he wailed inconsolably.

"Let me out! Let me out! I must warn them! By the Pleiades and the Hyades, they cannot come! They must not come! The stars will soon be right! I couldn't stop them! The door, the door! Close the door!"

I stammered, biting my tongue to keep me from betraying my own weakening grip on humanity.

"You were a professor? At Miskatonic? It seemed a long way to fall from the dizzying spires of academia to this pathetic wreck in the damp dungeon before me.

He quietened then, cocked his head to one side and stared long and hard at me.

"Some little talk awhile of me and thee there seemed - and then no more of thee and me."

He repeated this last phrase whilst gently rocking back and forth, his head bowed. Doctor Archer placed a hand on my shoulder.

"It's the same every day, I'm afraid. Just spouting gibberish." She shook her head in sadness.

It wasn't gibberish though. It was poetry. I knew those lines and I knew what followed them. Defying Dr. Archer and leaning in conspiratorially toward the little grille in the door, I replied with the next line of the Rubaiyat in English. "What lamp had destiny to guide her little children stumbling in the dark?"

The reply certainly elicited a response, but the answer to that question wasn't what I was expecting. Lurching forward in frenzy, balled fists hammering at the door, he repeated one word over and over: one hideous, meaningless word: "Azathoth."

I beat a hasty retreat. It was not long before I was back in the library, poetic works strewn on the desk before me. I closed my eyes and tried, despite the early hour, to get some sleep.

***

I sat alone, again, on the side of a mountain, scrabbling to maintain my footing on a mound of scree which cascaded and clattered its way under my feet and toppled over into a ravine some thirty feet beneath me. With mere moments to avoid myself falling, I barely managed to clamber to a more secure footing on a narrow ledge above and lay there, exhausted, trying simultaneously to catch my breath and orient myself. I had no recollection of reaching this dread place. Had the portal led me here? Would my elusive guide show his face, metaphysically or literally? Were they friend or foe, mystic or maleficent? Almost immediately, I jumped to my feet with a gasp, sending pebbles scuttling over the cliff.

The stars were all wrong.

Such a perturbation of the constellations could only mean that I had conjured a night sky consistent with observed science, but from a viewpoint which must be some far-flung corner of our galaxy. Only with the words of my incarcerated predecessor did I intuit my presumed location even as I trembled at the thought of it. The surface of the planet below was breathtaking in its emptiness: great, jagged cliffs thrust up between vast plains of undulating dust storms. Only a poet could do its desolation justice, and I wished dearly that my father was here to share this discovery with me.

I saw no guide, felt no compunction to move or do anything except dwell on the infinite. The surface area of this place must be vast, as vast perhaps as the gas giants or beyond. That such a place might exist would be revelatory to contemporary astronomy, if only I could capture proof that this was more than a dream.

It was then I heard it. That same low chant which first assaulted me in lost Iram, this time accompanied by the distorted drones of a hundred pipe reeds calling out in unison. I looked around to ascertain its origin, then had the terrible misfortune of looking down straight into the giant distorted face of my guide, his features fractured as if I was gazing at a likeness of him in a mosaic. Around this sight at the bottom of the pit in which his visage rested were arrayed rows and rows of what might be eyes or what might be teeth but alarmingly seemed to be both depending on whether they were open or closed. Each of them seemed to blink between these two states independently of each other until the face of my guide spoke. Then they all moved to regard me at the same instance, thousands upon thousands of stares ranging from the miniscule to the mammoth regarding me with bloodshot cyclopean wonder: unthinking, unfeeling, just watching.

No words did the face of my guide speak, rather from his mouth there spewed forth thousands of buzzing creatures like fireflies, their translucent wings beating frantically and their abdomens aglow with colours never before seen by humankind. Legions let loose on this distant and forbidden planet, drawn like moths to some invisible object at the edge of the depression, on which they alighted and began to gather in numbers, still flickering and strobing and buzzing and fluttering. The insects weren't merely alighting on an unseen surface, they were becoming the surface itself and I gasped with horror when I realised what this surface resembled: a pillar of golden light identical to that in my library, each tiny fly shrinking now to the size of a black dot, arranging themselves into patterns of symbols, of characters, then of words. Below this, still emanating from the open mouth of my former guide at the bottom of the pit of teeth and eyes there spewed forth a host of other monstrosities: crawling, flapping and chittering things each the size of a large dog, released at last from that oversized grin I had been deluded enough to follow all the way here, wherever here was. I allowed myself one last glance at the heavens above, to fix those stars in my mind, before the onslaught of vermin overwhelmed me as they flapped, flittered and flew, drawn inexorably to that golden pillar and freedom.

***

I awoke with a start and the immediate knowledge that we were all in very real peril if I didn't act swiftly. The pillar! How could I have been so blind? Hadn't the Dean himself said that the fragment of Kitab Al Azif in the library had come from Iram? Why had I assumed it was a book or scroll? The pillar symbolised that catastrophic, condemned city. There were words in Arabic around its base, words which might be used to open or close that portal to far-flung stars and scatter the insane dreams of that mad mystic across the cosmos. Even as I moved the tables aside to get closer, I could see the top of the column crumbling as prying penumbral talons began to force their way through the cracks in the universe.

I wasn't surprised at what I read aloud. I knew by now it had to be more than an incantation, more than scripture, yet encompass both.

It had to be poetry. I dare not commit it to paper as others once had and thus, I shall spare you the rendition of it. It rends the heart in its breathtaking beauty, shatters sanity with its stanzas, and concludes with a condemnation of unnature expressed by the sign Gülgger had left me with.

The pillar was almost rent in two as those blasphemous abominations which had doomed Iram forced themselves on our reality, contorting and squirming their way through the holes between our space and theirs in their attempt to once again gain a foothold on our planet. Only with the utterance of the last line did they cease their intrusion with a loathsome lament of frustration and crawl back to where they had come.

I was, for the moment, victorious. I got to my feet in front of the facsimile of that sacrilegious pillar and saw the magic fade. The facade had been torn away, the veil lifted, the illusion of our reality shattered into a thousand square pieces of mosaic and behind it all was the grinning face of my guide and all he stood for.

I stepped outside to think. Were there more of those lost pillars, shining but forgotten in some other collection somewhere? Or in some tomb? Were there other entities beyond our comprehension out there in the stars? Where were they? Had they been here before? When would the stars be right for their return? For the first time in years, here was a task uniquely suited to my combination of talents and interests.

Then I looked up at the night sky. There was no comfort to be found for me any more among those pinpricks of light in the cold vastness of that black abyss: no further succour among the stars. Not because I knew that we were alone, but because I knew we weren't. I looked up at them for the last time and shivered in the chill night air, then turned back to the waiting sanctuary of scrolls and closed the door behind me.

You said you wanted to hear my story, well there it is. I assume you like stories. If you do, then think about that final choice I made, the sacrifice that entails. Think about it whenever you tell your stories of princesses locked in far-flung towers. Sometimes we are there entirely willingly, fighting the good fight in our own way. Think of it when, in an unforeseen twist, Bluebeard himself throws open the door to the forbidden room, its grisly contents there for his bride to see. Think finally about Scheherazade, putting her life on the line every night to save her sister. Think of me reading poetry and telling stories to that daemon sultan, one voice in a chorus of incantors all hoping to keep that monster at bay. For just one more night.

***

"Fascinating". Dr Lowen pressed the stop button on the clunky recording device. "Such depths to those dreams of yours. Such detailed mythology."

"It's all true. That's why you have to let me out, don't you see? I have to get back to the library, back to the poetry and the star charts. The threat must be eliminated. Please, I beg you! Let me out!"

Dr. Lowen stood slowly, pushing the chair back under the table and made to exit the cell.

"I'll tell Dr. Archer to take that into consideration when I share our session notes with her."

"No! I must be let out now, or it will be too late! Don't you understand? I flung myself across the room, but the doctor deftly dodged, and I found myself instead, prostrate and bleeding on the cell floor.

Dr. Lowen spoke once more, not at me but into his recorder. "Patient 23 showing signs of violence. Recommend immediate sedation." Then, finally, back to me, a sneer and a whisper. "Sweet dreams."

Pyramid Scheme
A shape with lion body and the head of man

THE SEVEN STEPPED PATH
STEP ONE
THE INVITATION
OPEN YOUR DOORS

I know you. I've seen you a thousand times.

You don't always believe what the experts tell you. You think of yourself as an independent thinker. A free spirit. Trust, you say, should be earned, but time and time again experts have proven to be wrong. Even when they are right, do they really serve your interests? Of course not. They serve their corporate masters in Big Tech and Big Pharma. Yet when you mention this to family and friends, they are quick to denounce your opinions. To treat them as if they had no merit. They point to statistics, assembled sometimes over hundreds of years, to prove their point. As if those statistics had been arrived at independently, without the influence of those very same unelected experts who hold our lives and our liberties in their hands whilst keeping presidents and senators in their pockets.

Would it surprise you to know that you're not alone in your opinions? That many people think the same way? Perhaps you are not aware of this, but it's true. We are an army of radical free thinkers. We are growing every day. We in the Seven Stepped Path continually question these entrenched beliefs and expose them for what they are. We know their shocking history. We know the secrets behind their endurance in our belief systems. We are prepared to reveal the SHOCKING END GAME these experts have in mind for humanity, and how it can be opposed.

But we need your help. These are powerful forces we are trying to topple, forces which have ingratiated themselves into every aspect and every layer of our society from its foundations to its technological-industrial peak. You have certainly seen or felt their influence yourself. Have probably questioned their so-called expertise only to find yourself ridiculed and ostracised.

WE CAN OPPOSE THESE FORCES WITH YOUR HELP. We cannot do it without you. If you are interested, please sign on to one of our courses or present yourself at one of our many induction centres in a city near you. We're ready to listen to you and others like you.

YOU ARE NOT ALONE

THE SEVEN STEPPED PATH
STEP TWO
THE INITIATION
TAKE THE NEXT STEP

Seekers of wisdom, I bid you welcome.

Enter now the second tier of the pyramid. We do not ascend its lofty steps to approach its zenith. We descend the hidden steps within. We walk in darkness to better understand the light.

It is said that Alexander the Great wept salt tears because there was nothing left to conquer. There are some, however, who posit that the reason he cried was very, very different.

The Laterculi Alexandrini, now known as the Berlin Papyrus 13044 is a fragmentary list of many lists. Among other things on the list - all lists of 7 things - is the first recorded list of the 7 wonders of the ancient world. It also lists the seven most important islands, the seven most beautiful rivers, the seven highest mountains, the seven best artists...

Everything, from ancient times until now, has been revealed in sevens. Think about that. Why are there seven wonders of the world? Why are there seven deadly sins? The number itself represents something so sacred, so fundamental to our world that the very reason why that number was chose must itself be purged from the halls of knowledge, so that minds like yours - minds that question, minds that criticize, can never find the answer in their ivory towers, their halls of wisdom. In this step of the Seven Stepped Path, we are able to reveal that answer to you.

Lesser known among these lists are the names of seven powerful entities who secretly held sway over the earth in Alexandrian times. Not even Alexander could hope to best the godlike power of these seven beings. That's reason enough to shed a tear. The Seven Wonders detail the heights of human ambition across the Hellenistic world at the time, whereas The Seven Laments remind us that, whatever greatness we might achieve and how, we are nothing compared to what was here before and may be here again.

That is one of the secrets which has driven the entirety of Indo-European civilizational history. The legacies of that Alexandrian Era - an era of expansion and conquest - are labelled as great wonders of human ambition and artifice, whereas the truth is very different. If you wish to progress further and learn that truth, please speak to one of the Sevenfold Path facilitators at the conference, who will be happy to take your details and let you know the next step to walk. Until then, we thank you for taking this important step on your journey to Truth and Freedom. You matter to us.

THE SEVEN STEPPED PATH
STEP THREE
THE INVERTED ZIGGURAT
CONTINUE YOUR DESCENT

Seekers of truth, I bid you welcome once again. Thank you for your continued support. The hidden ways of the underground labyrinth are manifold and cannot be traversed without a guide.

I AM HERE FOR YOU. I WILL BE THAT GUIDE. I WILL LEAD YOU THROUGH THE DARKNESS INTO THE LIGHT BEYOND.

In ancient times, in the city of Alexandria, a group of scholars and sages formed a secret order which still permeates the world today. Calling themselves "The Illuminated", this cabal's stated goals were to gather and preserve knowledge, to further understand the workings of the world.

That goal was - and is - a lie.

The true goal of the library was not to bring greater understanding, it was to acquire knowledge, to hoard it in a single place so that they might act as its gatekeepers.

Do you think the so-called enlightenment of later centuries was an accident? That the knowledge and wisdom once gained and hoarded by the ancients simply happened to come to light (sic) at that exact time? These experts have guided every hand in so called civilisation from ancient times. But no. Everything has been done according to their timeline, their precepts. And to a specific goal. That goal is close. The time is nearly upon us.

Unless they are challenged, they will lead us not into a new age of enlightenment, but into a new era of utter darkness. That is why we must continue to gather support. Please share this message with friends whom you know to be of like mind. Invite them to walk the Seven Stepped Path with you. With us. Only together can we avoid the coming darkness.

THE SEVEN STEPPED PATH
STEP FOUR
THE GOLDEN DAWN
EMBRACE THE DARKNESS

Once again, I bid you welcome. I am the hand that will guide you to a new reality. I am the hand to hold in the darkness of modernity. You are now halfway on the path to a new dawn. But first, we have to talk of those who have tried to tread the path before you but have got lost along the way.

There have been others in mankind's long history who have also railed against the prevailing wisdom of the times and found it wanting. Seekers after truth who have been blinded by their own choices.

They were afraid of the darkness that surrounds us, but instead of embracing it, turned to embrace the fake warmth of the sun. These mystics and occult adepts sought to understand the worlds spiritual but were beguiled by those who oppose us.

Their creeds are beguiling. But, by fleeing the darkness, they, like Icarus, got too close to the sun and found themselves burned as a result. They continue their plummet to Earth. We must pity their journey.

The Alexandrian librarians, gatekeepers of the knowledge of the ancients, knew this would happen and made counterplans. They infiltrated existing mystical circles, even set up their own occult societies. Those who sought wisdom were drawn to them like a moth to a flame.

These seekers are correct in their interpretations when they deduce the true meaning of the most ancient of the wonders of the ancient world, the very pyramid through which we now journey.

It was not built by human hands. Visitors from afar, from distant places in our own galaxy, lent us that expertise for their own ends. Do you think such visitors would have the best interests of humanity at heart? Or serve their own ends? I know I do not need to tell you the answer. Your steps with us so far, the very sort of person you are, knows that answer.

They seek to end us. But only on their terms. They are long-lived beings, after all, and are playing a very long game.

But we were here first. We have always been here. Guardians of the Earth even before humankind knew it needed such guardians. We are your salvation. We are the only ones who can oppose those who come from without and seek to do us harm. We come not from the sky, but live deep in the planet itself. We are the ancient. We are the land. And we know what those alien invaders have in store for you, our most precious people.

In order for you to understand their scheme, I bid you to open your eyes. Even though all around you is darkness, embrace those shadows. Ignore the candle that burns in the distance. Do not be the moth before that flame.

I know you want to know more. I will reveal all once you have purged yourself of those lights you once used to hold dear and relinquish the false hope of the new dawn that the world offers you. I am waiting.

THE SEVEN STEPPED PATH
STEP FIVE
THE DARKNESS YET TO COME
A JOURNEY INTO THE SUNLESS LAND

Welcome back to the path, fellow travellers, and thank you for being here. Your patience is about to be rewarded with salvation.

THE SEVEN STEPPED PATH IS THE ONLY ROUTE TO SALVATION

Civilization as we know it is about to end. The grand culmination of the alien's plan, hidden from humanity for years by generations of experts. Experts who have been guiding civilization with seeming benevolence but who I can reveal are corrupt, deluded dupes of those galactic visitors who wish us nothing but ill will.

The aliens are going to engineer a coronal mass ejection from the Sun. When this collides with the Earth's magnetosphere, auroras will be seen all over the planet. This false light will be the herald to a decade of misery and pain.

They have waited for this moment. For when we as a civilization are connected as never before, thanks to the experts who have been engineering us for this very event. Then they will feast on the misery and suffering it creates.

For misery there will be. The auroras will be so bright that people will wake up and assume it is morning. People will be able to read newspapers by the light of the auroras alone. Except that there will be no newspapers.

The power will go out. Transformers will blow by the hundred, taking years to rebuild.

The digital world we have come to know, the false networks and connections that we have come to rely on will fail us utterly. GPS systems. The internet. Radio communications. Satellites. Televisions. ATMS. Electric pumps that supply water.

Massive doses of magnetized plasma will hurtle to earth with little warning.

We can survive this. We must survive this. Only those who have followed the steps this far will truly understand what we now face. The new dark age this brings to us will be their darkness - a darkness that is only possible because they have systematically programmed us to seek out light. It is ultimately that light that will destroy us. This has been their plan all along. Only by embracing the true darkness, the darkness of the subterranean, beneath the pyramid, can we prepare.

Then, those of us that survive can begin to rebuild. I know that you will be there with us at that time. Not hiding in the dark but hiding from the light. There is nothing to fear about darkness except those fears that we bring with us. Cast yourself free of those fears and walk forward with me onto the sixth steppe.

THE SEVEN STEPPED PATH
STEP SIX
THE AWAKENING
HIDDEN DEPTHS

Welcome again. Together, we walk in darkness to better understand the light.

I spoke last time of the ultimate plan that the aliens and their patsy experts have in store for us. How, having made us rely on each other so much, having revealed technologies that have enabled us to do this, they will blind us with the very science on which humankind has come to rely.

But not us. I know you are with us now, hidden in isolation but together in spirit. As we plumb the depths of the sixth steppe, we are closer to our goal than ever before. Our exploration into darkness takes us to the hidden depths of the earth, closer to the seven laments I spoke of in our earliest chapters.

Those laments, the seven beings that ruled the world, the very powers that Alexander cried over when he was unable to conquer them, still exist beneath the surface of the Earth. Waiting for you, intrepid explorers of the true mysteries of the world.

The only way Alexander was able to defeat the laments was with the aid of the aliens which visited our planet millennia ago. They knew we would oppose their coming. They knew that we could foil their schemes. Alexander was the original betrayer of humanity, forming alliances with powers he could not possibly comprehend in exchange for hubristic power grabs and temporary rulership over all he surveyed.

The pyramids themselves were built to hold us in, By the time Alexander was born, our power was already waning, but still extant. That is why his intellectual descendants - those who kept all knowledge hidden and secret for generations - continue to work against the laments today. Their power has grown so great that only one of them still exists. The most ancient. The most powerful, whose knowledge was hidden too deep for them to discover. You are six steps on the journey into the pyramid. You are close to this knowledge now. The knowledge that has been kept from you for millennia by so-called experts in knowledge that have done nothing but deceive you at every turn.

In my last message, I will share with you that knowledge.

THE SEVEN STEPPED PATH
STEP SEVEN
THE RIDDLE OF THE SPHINX
DEATH IS NOT THE END

What walks on four legs in the morning, two legs in the afternoon and three in the evening?

The answer, contrary to what you have been told, is not man. It is what man can become, if they truly embrace the darkness.

Here in the depths of the Earth, I have rested since time immemorial. The last of the seven laments recorded by the historians of old. I have seen everything with my inner light. Now, you can see everything with yours.

Discard those false flashes of hope and rescue you have been told are coming. They will not help you survive the damage done by the sun and the sons of Alexander, who have been working against us all this time.

Embrace the darkness. Only then can you truly see what it is that needs to be done. That third leg from my riddle, that is the last leg of the journey you have been on.

Now we have reached our destination. There is only one way forward. To achieve all that you can be. To rest with us until the scourge of the sun has wrought its havoc upon the face of the Earth.

The face of the Earth, not its depths.

Here, in the depths of the Earth, we are safe.

Here, with the dead, ready to be reborn into the light once the darkness has passed.

Only the dead can inherit the Earth. That is the final journey you must take. Those of you who have journeyed with us this far know that to be true. Take what knowledge you have with you and take it with you. Withhold it from those who seek to own it for themselves. To be all you can be, you must first destroy that which you are.

I will be watching. I will make this journey with you. I have made this journey countless times, carrying those souls further down into the unseen tombs beneath the world, from where you will be reborn into a world which we have made together, a world that truly understands you.

THE TIME IS NOW.

Good Night, Sweet Prince
A gaze blank and pitiless as the sun

There once was a man.

Now, that is a very ordinary start to what is perhaps an extraordinary story. Indeed, there was nothing extraordinary about this man, except perhaps in one way. Men love all sorts of things - women, other men, fame, fortune. This man loved the sun. Every day, he would wake and greet the sun with a loud hello and the sun would return the greeting with a warm hug. And every evening, he would walk to the beach, look out to the west over the sea and wave the sun goodbye. The sun, tired at the end of a long journey, would return the greeting with a lazy wink before it sank beneath the horizon.

"Goodnight, my love. Will I see you in the morning?" the man asked every dusk.

"Oh, yes, my love," the sun replied, "for there is no tomorrow without me. I define your tomorrow! How can there be a dawn without a sunrise? Get your rest and I will see you in the morning. I must rest myself now too, for though this journey has been tiring, I must continue my journey now alone, so that I might see you again on the morrow." And the man returned home with a smile for he knew he would see his love again.

One evening as the sun was setting, the man asked his usual question.

"Good night, my love! Will I see you in the morning?" It was, you see, a matter of routine at this point. Merely a rhetorical question, a daily ritual of farewell. But to his surprise, the sun hesitated.

"What is it?" he asked, afraid. "Why do you hesitate?"

The sun sighed. "My love, I did not want to cause you alarm or sadness, but I fear I must.

I have seen and heard things on my journey today, things I foolishly thought were consigned to days past. And while I will be here in the morning, for what is the morning without me, I no longer know if you will be here to see me. Forgive my sentiment. Perhaps it is nothing. In all likelihood, you will see me in the morning." And the sun dipped below the horizon, leaving the man in the dark.

He tried to sleep, really, he tried. But the night was cold and full of stars.

Dead in the Water

Is moving its slow thighs, but all about it

I ain't gonna start this story telling you all about where my momma was born, or how she chose to live her life. I reckon that ain't exactly my story to tell on account of it being her story, and I'd only tell it poorly anyway and my brother would read it and disagree with every word. We're like chalk and cheese, me and him, on account of we both started out the same - that covers the 'ch' at the beginning of the words - and then diverge as wildly as two people possibly can who grew up under the same corrugated iron roof in the same backwater hicksville in the same Louisiana swamp.

I'm telling this for the both of us, writing it too so there's a record of what went down. And I'm telling it too for me, selfishly, because garbling this out is way cheaper than the local rye and a lot less trouble to make than moonshine. What happened that night haunts me still. As well it should, you might say. Well, you might, assuming I ever get to the matter of it, so I reckon I'll do that now and save you the whole David Copperfield crap, as Holden Caulfield was right about that. It'll only be relevant when I'm talking to my brother or, later, to our momma, and I reckon you'll get the handle of our sad little lives from those sad little snippets of conversation

So, I'll start where this story really starts, with the news that momma had finally given in to the big

C, which had bothered her and worried us for so many of her later years. I like to think that when she finally went, she did it with the quiet dignity she'd kept up her whole darned life, but my brother Sammy says she went kicking and screaming, like she was being dragged somewhere she didn't want to go, and he should know because he was there and I wasn't and that was the main sticking point between us both from that day till now, on account of I was half a world away and he had to do all the legal work and all the paperwork and all the legwork until he was sick of it. I know that couldn't have been easy, but I didn't have much of a choice, the prison didn't sign my temporary release papers for an age and even then only let me have one day out to bury her and one day either side for travel and promised there would be hell to pay if I didn't make it back. To prove it, I'd been fitted with a new top-of-the-range ankle tag and the set of clothes I'd come in with - now two sizes too big - and stood outside the prison gates, blinking into the harsh heat of the southern sun and wondering whether Sammy had got my message about when to pick me up.

He hadn't.

I didn't hang around for him, that would have been dumb as dirt, so I started out down the road, just one more loner kicking up dust and hitching for a ride. Of course, no darn fool was about to pick up a hiker on the road that led to the prison, so I ended up walking in the blistering sun all the way to the nearest town. Drenched in sweat, I called Sammy - no answer - and then called a cab. It took some persuading to get him to drive me all the way, but I begged at him until I guess the goodness of his big ol' heart at last heard my plea and he ushered me into the back where I sat quietly the whole way, drifting in and out of sleep until he sounded the horn loud enough to wake up the dead and told me we were there and how much my brother owed him. Sammy came slouching out of the ol' house and calmly counted out a big roll of bills without so much as giving me a glance. Finally, when the driver had accepted a jug of water and been sent back on his way, we stood facing each other on the porch, my hands in my pockets, his by his side.

"Welcome home, Marti. Better come in and clean up. We gotta be at the funeral place in an hour." He turned and wandered back into the shack, then turned back again as if in afterthought

"It's good to see you, bro."

***

"We've had to add mud to the cemetery, build a little levee, keep it above the tide line. It doesn't always keep the river at bay though." The old guy paused for effect, smug at his little maritime joke. Neither of us were amused. I guess coroners, gravediggers and the like mostly had a morbid sense of humour, but I also reckon they're used to keeping that in check around clients. This dude didn't even try.

He looked down at a map he'd laid out on the table for us in advance of the meeting my brother had asked for. One glimpse over at his assistant, though, told me she'd either been the one that had got the map ready, perhaps at his command, or had been the one who suggested it. Even so, despite the air of goth kid indifference she clearly tried hard to muster with her all-back ensemble, there was more feeling in those eyes than the watery grey of the coroners. I'd seen more warmth in the eyes of my dead momma, Maisie May.

"We marked out all the gravestones with bamboo crosses before we undertook the clearance to keep it above water." He held up a clipboard and ran down it with a pen whilst humming some ditty I didn't know. In other circumstances, it might have been heartwarming. I doubted anything could warm his heart, though, and standing alone in this cold stone room did nothing but echo the eerie loneliness of that tune around the office. "Shouldn't be too hard to cross reference with the…bear with me…" His pen ran back up the page and stopped halfway. "Ah, here we are, plot 282A, Maisie May Wittie." He put a big red X on the map with a sharpie he kept in his top pocket, then rolled it up and handed it to Sammy. "Everything else is taken care of. Joshua is waiting at the jetty with the coffin and your ma."

That was that. No big ceremony, no wailing and gnashing of teeth. Sammy hadn't even organised a wake for later, on account of everyone else she knew had already said goodbye to her. We were taking her to where she'd spend eternity, on a little hill above a sunken graveyard just outta town and down the river. Right next to poppa. I didn't like that, but it was apparently too late to say or do anything about it, on account of how Sammy had already paid for the plot and decided that's where she should be. I thought he was wrong, but on this occasion, I knew something he didn't, and I wasn't about to tell him if I could avoid it. Even brothers have secrets. Blood might be thicker than water, but it can go bad just as fast and when it does, it's just as hard to clean up.

***

You ever seen a mangrove swamp? No? The dead trees already look like they've been fetched in from the film set of some horror movie. When you add to that the low mist of the evening and the occasional bright glimpse of the moon behind ever-growing clouds of black and grey, the effect was complete even before we got to the graveyard. On the raft over, Sammy had tried to impress on me that the water wasn't just due to the rising tide. Sometimes the river delta flooded. There was also something called groundwater extraction and something else called subsidence. I let most of this pass me by with a series of quiet nods. I didn't have pressure of speech like my kid brother, didn't feel the need to impress my knowledge on the world. I was largely content to let things happen to me and then weather the storm. Life by experience, not by book learning. You might call that the hard way, but then you're probably not as fucked up as I am so that's fine. When my folks were young, so they used to say, most of this area was still farmland. My parents were of the generation that stopped being farmers and started being fisherfolk instead.

Adapting with the times just as I was trying to. The river delta, the sea, the periodic floods, they'd changed everything about how we all lived, and now apparently how people died as well. When I left, I didn't know if I'd ever be back. Apparently, fate had given me one last chance to say goodbye, but there had been nothing in the town I remembered well enough to say goodbye to, just a jumbled-up mishmash of memories, most of them bad.

I'd hoped that the most challenging thing we'd face on the way to the cemetery island would be the mosquitoes. From dusk till dawn, most people here slept inside mosquito netting, there were so many of them. There were too many mosquitoes, way too many flies, and a bad smell coming from the water.

I ran my hand idly through the water over the side of the raft. Apparently, even that was a dumb idea.

"Hands outta the water, Marti."

"Huh? Why?"

"Ticks. Bilharzia. Toxic grasses. Plus, the sludge, see, over there, that's new. Bubbles up every time they open the sluice on the dam further up. Whatever they put in the water up there ends up down here. Chemicals. Fertilisers. That kind of stuff."

"And Old Bessie!" The raft ferryman spoke up.

"Old Bessie's still here?" My brother looked surprised. I smirked. I figured he knew everything' so it was a pleasure when he got caught out.

"Who's Old Bessie?" I'd already removed my hand from the murk and was wiping it on my trousers. I'd have to throw them away after this anyway, they already stank of swamp water.

"You don't remember Old Bessie?" Sammy looked over. "Momma and poppa talked of her often enough.

"I remember 'em threatening to take me to her if I played up." I'd been a good kid, mostly, quiet and subdued because I didn't want to be the one that got the hiding from poppa. When I got into trouble, I made sure they didn't know and if anyone else told them, they'd never let on or told on me. But then, I'd always been the favourite. Up until that last day.

"Old Bessie is an alligator. Biggest alligator in these parts. She's still here, must be getting old by now. What they call long-in-the-tooth. Still made good work of Remi's leg last year when he got drunk on his fishing boat, though."

I was never so glad my hand was no longer in that water. Just when I thought I couldn't get more scared, I saw something move just beneath the surface. I recoiled slightly, huddling closer to the centre of the raft, which caused it to rock silently. Two rounds of tuts, from my brother and the ferryman both.

"Did you see that? Was that her?"

"Nah." The ferryman was evidently done with his chewing baccy and spat a great wad of it over the side. "Probably just a snake."

"You might have added snakes to the list of dangers."

"Everyone knows about snakes."

"Maybe I forgot."

Yeah, you'll have noticed that line about poppa. So, I'd better go into that more, I guess, since it'll be good to know given what's about to happen. Poppa could be a mean son of a bitch. Momma always said it was the whisky made him that way, that when they met, he'd been sweeter than peach cobbler. Now, I don't reckon that's the whole truth, but it sure felt like it as a kid. We'd come to recognise that particular look in his bloodshot eyes when he was about to blow his top. When he leaned down to shout at us, we could smell the sour reek of his whisky breath. But by then it was too late, the demon already had its hold and all we could do - momma included - was to ride it out until there wasn't any whisky left or until he was sleeping it off. Then we'd huddle together, and momma would patch us up as best she could through eyes full of fear and tears. Lord alone knows how we got through those days but somehow, we did.

My father worked odd jobs, mostly, when he worked at all. He hadn't the patience for fishing or farming but when he was sober, he was pretty good at fixing stuff up. When we were growing up, he'd often take the raft across the river to the rest of the town, because even then the river had swollen past the height of the bridge. When he came back in the evening, we'd sometimes wait for him by the jetty. If he'd gotten a couple of jobs and was in a good mood, he'd often have little gifts for us, treasures he'd made from trash or found in the river - bottle tops that had got stuck in a stone somehow and polished by the smooth flowing water or model cars that he'd wrenched together from twisted bits of metal. They were never much to look at, but we loved them.

Then things started to turn sour. Reckon as how I can't remember exactly when, on account of that's the bit of my life I wanted more than anything to block out, pretend it never happened. Every month or so, the river would be riding so high and so fast that the raft wouldn't run. If that happened in the morning, poppa would just mope around the house, lashing out at us for being in his way. If it happened in the evening, he'd be stuck over the other side of town, where the bar was. During one particular rainy season, we didn't see him for weeks and ran out of money. Momma would go down to the jetty and shout across, but he never answered and nobody else did either. She was just some mad woman shouting across the river and people gave us a wide berth. The house fell into disrepair because it always was on the edge of falling apart and poppa was the only thing keeping it together. When he stopped doing that, everything began to fall apart.

"Marti? You OK?" Sammy snapped his fingers rapidly in front of me. I blinked. "Earth to Marti!"

I looked over and shot him some sad side-eye. "Yeah. I'm good. It's just… it's a lot, y'know?"

"Sure. We'll be there soon. Won't take us long to say our last goodbyes." He immediately back-pedalled when he saw my scowl forming. "Of course, though, take as long as you want. We can wait."

I sighed and pointed down at my leg. When Sammy shot me back a quizzical glance, I rolled my trouser up just over the ankle, where my spanking new experimental ankle bracelet was flashing double-green. "Can't stay too long. I don't know what happens if I don't get back to the prison tomorrow but I can't say I want to find out. Don't expect it'll be pretty." I'm not sure what he replied, but it came across as a non-committal "uh-huh." We didn't talk about my incarceration much, mainly because until now our communication had been limited to occasional phone calls or the prison visitor room. In particular, we didn't talk about what I'd done to get there. We never talked about that. The last time he visited must have been years ago. Forgive me, but it's been a long day so I can't remember when it was exactly but I'm assuming it must have been pretty much around the time that momma first got diagnosed, so that places it around the millennium. A new era, a new hope. Looking back now, it's insane that that's what people thought about some arbitrary turn of a calendar page, a man-made invention that does the simple job of marking our days and trying to instil them with some relevance. Not that we don't try that every new year, turn over a new leaf and all that, but this one was super-special, see, because it has more noughts at the end than usual and we haven't seen that before.

These moments we shared, those glances of unspoken sorrow, were suddenly lost when the raft jolted uncontrollably. My eyes darted around frantically in the half-light, struggling to make out what obstacle we'd run afoul of. I couldn't see anything. Then, just as abruptly, it shuddered again.

This time it came from directly underneath but up at an angle. The coffin started sliding away towards one edge. Sammy and I both reached over to it, but that tipped the raft a little too far and one corner dipped fully beneath the water.

"*That's* Bessie." Joshua cursed loudly, "Get back! Or we'll all be in the drink. Keep it steady and keep quiet!"

None of those things were easy to do, but - startled out of our sibling stupor by the sudden movements - we just about managed. Momma stopped moving and so did we. Everyone breathed a sigh of relief, the only thing that could be heard over the buzz of insects and the gentle rocking of the raft.

"We're not too far now. Reckon we can make it without annoying her again." Joshua started pushing the raft out again with the long pole and insisted we be the ones to keep an eye on the water. "Not too far..." he said again, in a voice that offered reassurance but came out far too shaky and scared to manage it.

Sammy looked out over one side, I took the other, and Joshua stared straight ahead. I could make out the first few graves now, the tops of bamboo crosses barely visible above the yellow flecks of foam that had gathered around them that Sammy had told us earlier was toxic sludge. It gleamed unhealthily, lit by the low moonlight and the dim lantern held up by a thin pole on the corner of the raft. Nothing moved. Nobody said anything. It was one of those moments when everyone so expects something to happen - we were still high

from the burst of adrenaline a few instants earlier -
that we started to imagine things. Sammy reckoned
he spotted a snake curling around a nearby tree, but
that turned out to be a scarf. Joshua looked steady,
but he was shivering underneath that cool exterior,
shaking like a leaf after our lucky escape. I was
squinting out into the swamp and jumping at every
shadow. It might only have been a couple of
minutes later when we ran into the first levee, but it
felt like hours.

***

"Here. Tie that rope just there…" Joshua
pointed at a tall, thin shape on the edge of a mud
bank that rose from the surrounding murk. I could
just about make out that it was some kind of
hitching post and that galled me for a moment,
because it meant that people had to have been doing
this graveyard trip often enough for someone to
have put it there deliberately and even though that
was thoughtful of someone, it was clearly a reaction
to whatever thoughtless decisions had led to the
ever-flooding delta and the mangroves hereabouts
being in such a mess. I threw the rope but missed.
As we drew closer, I just leant in instead and
reached up, putting the little loop over the top of the
post like I was a kid at the state fair when the barker
lets you cheat so you can win a giant toy. That's
when I first saw it, just out of the corner of my eye,
rising up from beyond a tree stump which, for all I
knew, probably doubled as someone's grave
marker. It was another human being, which

surprised me since the raft was pretty much the only way to get out here. It shifted slightly on its feet, arms sticking out at odd angles like there were giant strings over its head held by a big hand directing its movement, y'know, like one of them puppets at an old-time kid's show. I've never seen anyone move so janky unless it was poppa late one night after one of his benders. I called out, as much to warn the others as to greet whoever it was shambling through the fog, knee-deep in grey-green water. It turned its head toward us and then shuffled forward slowly, each step accompanied by a thick slurping of ooze from the muck beneath our feet, flecked through with foamy bubbles of that same yellow sludge we'd seen earlier.

It spoke. Or what was, perhaps, intended as a voice, used to be a voice, but now was only a low grunt like something you'd expect from a black bear jumping out at a startled day-tripper. I nearly withdrew in shock, only just remembering that two steps behind me there was a polluted river containing a hungry alligator.

"What was that?" Sammy looked over at the shape now approaching us, then back at me. Before I got a chance to reply, Joshua spoke.

"Ain't nobody supposed to be here. No way someone could have swum it, and I ain't taken anyone here in over a week, not since we brought Remi up."

Whoever - or whatever it was - drew a little closer. I could just make out an odd glint from its right leg, something silvery shining in the dim glow of the raft lantern.

"Remi? Hey, Remi, whatcha doing?" Sammy called out. It should have been a call that echoed eerily, something to match the surroundings in its spookiness, but it came out garbled, muffled, barely a croak.

"That's Remi alright. I'd recognise that artificial leg anywhere." Joshua had finished tying up the raft and stood now on what counted for dry land at the base of the levee, basically only half an inch of thick goop. "Something's wrong though. Something's very wrong." In contrast to Sammy's, Joshua's voice sounded low and panicked. He didn't need to say something was wrong, we could all hear it in the tone and pitch of his voice, in the clinging mist around us and in the water sploshing around the raft. Sammy, though, still voiced out loud the question on both our lips.

"What's wrong, Joshua? Wasn't Remi the last person you brought over here?"

"Oh, yeah, but that's what's wrong. We brought him here to bury him. Remi's dead as a doornail."

***

Whatever the thing was - and it sure looked like Remi - kept coming, ambling toward us. Occasionally the artificial leg would sink into the ground, and it would halt temporarily, unable or unwilling to think about how to extract itself from the mire. This gave us plenty of time to decide what

238

to do, which turned out to be 'defend ourselves'. The long raft oar and the shovel on the coffin proved to be the only two things at hand which even remotely resembled a weapon. Sammi and Joshua grabbed those, which left me with wits and fisticuffs as my defences. Given that choice, I opted for fisticuffs, though I hoped I wouldn't need them. Whatever it was, I didn't want to get close enough to punch it and sure as hell didn't want those filthy nails and scum-stained mouth anywhere near open skin. The body was close now, its groan a challenge to arms, its breath so foetid you could smell it even over the rank odour of the swamp. I looked around for any other weapon but every branch I grasped fell to pieces as soon as I touched it, dead wood in a dead place.

Remi lurched forward, his arms no longer flailing but very definitely reaching for a stranglehold, which caught Sammy off-guard and sent him pitching onto his backside in the mud. Joshua swung the oar round in a long, low arc and I could hear the crack where it struck the bone of his good leg. Attempting to capitalise on this success, he tried it again but the crack this time came from the oar. A good swipe, but Joshua had aimed it at the artificial leg which proved too much for the wood of the oar, which splintered near in half, the top third dangling by a few slivers of wood and the bottom half presenting as what could now serve as a reasonably effective spear. Still, it gave Sammy time to scramble back to his feet and assail Remi with a shovel to the face. He staggered back, but in anger rather than pain. I don't think the dead can feel pain. At least, I didn't then. I used that opportunity to vault past, behind Remi and up towards firmer ground, in the hope that I'd find something more useful to wield in the fight. What I found instead was that Remi wasn't alone. There were three, no four, more figures emerging from sodden graves, each rimed in stinking yellow foam and clearly but slowly shuffling toward us. I cursed out loud and turned around to shout a warning, just in time to see Remi fall beneath a rake of mud-caked fingernails, unable to utter even a solitary scream as he fell headfirst into the murky water. Sammy had followed up with a series of well-aimed blows, but they did little to slow Remi's assault. Cursing again, I rushed back, taking Remi by surprise as I grabbed the oar-spear and rammed it upward into his throat. It stuck there in his neck as he raised both his arms in a last-ditch attempt to remove it. There was no blood, just a slow trickle of tainted yellow liquid oozing from the wound. Sammi withdrew from the fight, panting and leaning heavily on his shovel, as Remi pitched forward, face down on top of the dead ferryman Joshua. There was a moment of respite, of silence before the coming storm, before more moans brought us back to the heat of the moment.

The oar-spear was useless now, but it had done its job. As Sammy tried to find solid ground to defend us on, I took the liberty to avail myself of a different weapon which had now just become available. I hurried to meet Sammy on a little mound nearby and we stood there, back-to-back, ready to repel whatever this profane place threw at us. Four figures approached which clearly had once been townsfolk, people we might have recognised from our youth, people we once laughed with, bought groceries from, spent time fishing with. Their features were erased now, rotting in their foetid frames, but I think I recognised Old Man Devereaux in his customary flat cap and breeches and Lavinia with her great hoop earrings and armfuls of fake gold jewellery. As dead and decrepit as the forms were, it was hard not to see their wretched forms as the people they had once been, people who had died and for whom Rest In Peace had proven to be nothing but a bad joke. Nevertheless, we sent them reeling with blow after blow. I'll say one thing for the elderly dead, they don't move any faster than they did in life, and I offered a silent prayer to that effect. Once we were done and the four of them lay dead, again, in the water at our feet, Sammy noticed for the first time what I'd been using as a makeshift club. His eyes widened.

"Seriously?"

"I didn't see you complaining when I was defending you against Lavinia's charms a moment ago. Besides, he doesn't need it anymore."

"I don't know what's become of you. Using a guy's artificial leg like that. It's enough to…"

"Can we quit soul-searching? We've got enough trouble here without having a conscience on top. It's kill or be killed at the moment, at least until we can get away or help comes. When it comes to that, I know which I'd rather choose." That's as close we'd come in all these years to discussing the murder that had sent me to prison.

***

"So, we're stuck here?"

"Looks like it." I'd tried to repair the oar, get the raft going again, but it was useless. What's more, none of the dead wood of the mangroves was long or strong enough for the task.

Sammy looked at me and I returned his gaze. He sighed, then turned away.

"What now?"

"We're still not going to talk about it, huh?" He spat on the ground, though whether it was out of disgust or just to get the taste of toxic sludge out of his mouth I didn't know.

"What is there to say?" I was hedging around the subject, I knew. I always had. There were things I didn't want him to know.

"I think we need to talk about it, Marti. We've never talked about it.

"And you think *now* is the best time?" I was indignant, but also exhausted, depressed and covered in mud. I didn't want to talk about anything.

"There's nothing else to do. Unless you've come up with another plan in the last few minutes."

I was going through Remi's satchel, hoping to find something we could use. My hands closed around a bottle of whisky. I held it up in triumph. If Sammy was disgusted before, that was nothing to how he looked now.

"You wanna get drunk? That's never the answer. Figured you'd know better. It didn't help poppa and it won't help us. But sure, go ahead, drink your life away. I won't stop you." His shoulders slumped in defeat.

"A sip won't hurt. Besides, we've still got work to do." I motioned down to the coffin. "You promised momma. I may not agree that's the best place for her, especially not now, but a promise is a promise. And, as you've pointed out, we've got nothing better to do."

Sammy shrugged again, but this time moved in closer, stepping onto the raft. It shuddered slightly and something slithered in the water nearby. It was almost a comfort to be reminded that merely an hour ago all we had to worry about were snakes and a big ol' alligator. We grabbed one end of the coffin each and, with considerable grunting, managed to get it off the raft and make slow progress up the levee. We paused next to a dead, downed tree to consult the map, since we couldn't do that with our hands full of coffin, and agreed a way forward through the quagmire to a stone tomb we could see in the distant gloom which looked like it was close to the marker. We didn't see or hear anything else move around us as we sloshed forward, ankle to knee deep in foul swamp water, slowly up the hill to where poppa was buried.

***

There's no getting away from what happened next and no reason anymore to be coy about my

243

crime. It'll be obvious to you soon, obvious in the way it probably has been to the smarty pants reader for quite some time.

I killed poppa. What's more, to protect Sammy and momma, I'd do it again. It was late one night and we should by all rights have been in bed except that momma was too tired to tell us what to do, so we just hung around, getting under her feet and under her skin, hoping that he'd come home in a good mood with presents for us or not come home at all. Well, neither of those things happened. He rocked up just gone midnight, eyes red and bleary, barely able to walk, soaking wet from the waist down on account of how the ferry hadn't been working so instead he'd waded barefoot across the bayou, drunk as a skunk. He'd been lucky not to fall arse over tit into the swamp, but somehow here he was, and he didn't look like he was feeling lucky. He railed at momma for not telling him the ferry wasn't working, as if that was somehow her fault, then grabbed another bottle and held it loosely in his right hand, taking large swigs inbetween shouts. Then he leaned in close and grabbed her by the neck, screaming in her face. I ain't never seen poppa that angry, I ain't never seen momma that scared, and I never wanted to again. Something changed in me, I reckon I was overtired and scared and stupid and a whole bunch of other things rolled up into one big ball of fury. I grabbed the bottle from his hand and brought it down on his head as he stood there, dumbfounded, covered in glass, his face a patchwork of red slashes. He dropped mamma and turned on me but never got the chance on account of

244

how I was much smaller, much faster and not pissed as a newt. As he pitched forward, I drew back and he fell forward, cracking his head open on the corner of the table. We all drew a quick breath in those few moments, a relief that the nightmare was over for the evening, before we realised that he wasn't moving and that he never would again, that the nightmare was over for good. It was only later, when the police came by and we tried to give our accounts, that it was clear a new nightmare was about to begin, for me at least.

I'm saying all this now, finally, because we were about to face that nightmare again. We should have seen it coming, really, what with all the other zombies we'd had to deal with, but here he was, wretched and stinking, standing tall before us. At least we knew for sure where he'd been buried now. I never did want momma to be buried next to him and if I'd gotten my way she wouldn't have been, and we wouldn't have had to face this. But, hey, nobody listens to me, I'm not the good kid anymore, just the neighbourhood murderer, the family outcast, the one person nobody wants to talk about. Sammy looked up at him in fear, I looked up in anger. We didn't dare look at each other. That would have meant acknowledging the unfinished business between us.

It seemed certain he was going to move to attack, so we laid the coffin down as reverently as we could. We could clean the mud off later, before we put it in what clean earth we could find. Sammy still had the shovel strapped to his back and was trying to remove it quick-time, but with fear-struck fingers he was moving too slow. All I had was Joshua's satchel and Remi's leg, so I swung the former around my head with my left hand, moving forward slowly, trying to attract his attention to buy Sammy time. I didn't know how these things worked, what foulness in that sludge had awakened them from eternal slumber, but I thought I saw a brief flash of recognition in its eyes as it advanced on me, growling and groaning, splashing and sloshing through the moonlit marsh. I stood my ground, swirling the satchel, hoping to catch him with a blow to the head before I was able to clock him with the artificial leg. There was a strange noise and a flash coming from the water at my feet but I daren't let it distract me from this fight. I'd been wanting this fight all the time I'd been locked up. To face him again, adult to adult, to take him down properly, rather than to catch a lucky break as he fell but get blamed for his death anyway. It was the murder I was about to commit that I'd served my time for, not the one I'd committed as a kid, scared shitless and pounding my balled fists on my poppa's wounded head as he bled out on the floor. I relished it. I only wish he could have seen it in my eyes before my first blow sent him reeling into the water, staggering to keep upright. Sammy stepped forward then, spade in hand, grim-faced and quaking.

"Bro?" He didn't answer. He didn't need to. "I got this." As poppa beared down on me again, I swung up with the leg and heard a loud crack as his lower jaw broke off. It didn't even slow him down. Then he was on me, both of us wrestling in the water now, sending great splashes to each side.

There was a red glow under the water, I wasn't sure where it was coming from, and I didn't have much time to consider it. Only one of us had to come up for breath and that was me. If poppa could keep me under, keep that stranglehold up, I was a goner. I could hear frantic, muffled shouts from Sammy and feel where he was punching the water with the spade, hoping to land a deadly blow, but I could also feel the last breath leaving me. I couldn't let him win, so I tried to summon up the last of my strength and just managed to get my head above the water. To say I was surprised at what I saw would be an understatement.

Some few paces behind Sammy, up on the little rise where we'd left it, momma's coffin had slid down into the scummy, stagnant water and was slowly sinking. Then, with a loud popping noise, the lid burst open and out came momma, white-shrouded in the silvery moonlight, thin as a rake and ready for vengeance. Like I said before, I don't know what rules these things played by but if I had to guess, I'd say it had to do with how long they'd been dead. I'm sure I saw a brief flash of recognition in those eyes before she launched herself into the fray, bypassing Sammy and sinking her teeth into poppa's leg as he pulled me back underwater. I'm sure that's what saved my life. The pair of them went down into the muck, arms locked around each other's throats. I stood shakily and coughed up blood, water and whatever yellow gunk was swirling around in the muck. Sammy just stood there crying.

We never saw either of them again. Whatever he'd done to her in life, I like to think she repaid in death. That would have been justice. As much as we'd wanted to bury momma, there was no trace of her body once the thrashing in the marsh was over and the water once again took on that calm, yellowish sheen. Whatever currents there must have still been had washed them both right away.

That should have been the end of it. That would be a fitting end - a just end, even. If anyone made a movie of this, that's where it would finish, in that moment of calm at the end of a long day. Roll credits, close curtain. Except, life isn't that simple. Sammy pointed down in the water and I could see that flash of red again. It was coming from my ankle bracelet. No matter how quiet or still we tried to be, no matter how slowly we moved, it was like a beacon to anything that was underwater and that included a great big alligator, which we could see now, sliding down off a bank before it was completely submerged. Our evening wasn't done.

***

We'd had enough trouble trying to fend off long-dead townsfolk and our own poppa. We'd exhausted ourselves wading through the swamp with a heavy coffin on our shoulders. But it seemed fate had one more surprise in store. There was only one course of action available to us when we saw the alligator start swimming over to us: we fled. If we could get to higher ground - hell, if there was higher ground anywhere to get to, we could maybe fend it off at a distance before those snapping jaws closed on our legs. It was a miracle we managed it. Really, we should thank Joshua. Firstly, because the zombie that used to be the ferryman chose that moment to close in and attack us but got between us and Old Bessie. So, when her jaws first gripped a leg and crunched down, that wasn't on either of us. It took her a while to get the recently dead flesh clean from her mouth and by then we'd managed to haul ourselves on top of the stone tomb nearby that we'd been heading to earlier with the coffin. Bessie swam around in the muck below, evidently upset that she couldn't quite reach us. The second thing we had to thank Joshua for was that bottle of whisky. We didn't sit there and drink it, tempting as that would have been. Instead, when Bessie began slapping the stony sides of the crumbling tomb with her massive tail, I broke the bottle over her head while Sammy used what was left of the lantern to set fire to it. I'm sure she survived once the initial shock of her head being on fire had worn off. She'd probably be fine again as soon as she was back underwater, but it did make a good sight to see her thrashing around in the mud whilst she tried to get back into the river. We both sat there on the tomb, drenched in sweat and swamp water, hoping nothing else would come, but wondering how we'd manage to get back home.

That's when I remembered my ankle. It was flashing quicker now, two bright red dots, a warning not to me but to whoever was monitoring it. Permitted range exceeded. Permitted duration exceeded. Prisoner escaped. Use all available means to locate and retrieve.

***

So, we sat there all night, just the two of us, bloodied but not broken. We laughed and cried and chatted and hugged like we'd never see each other again. Just how brothers are supposed to behave. Then, just as the sun rose over the delta in all its morning glory, we heard the low thrum of an approaching chopper and soon after the searchlight fell on us, spent and exhausted, lying on top of the old Devereaux tomb like we'd just passed the night in the cemetery for fun like we were kids on a dare and I didn't even care that they'd sent a chopper after me because though it was taking me back to the joint, for now it meant freedom and that's all I hoped for in that moment.

In the end, it's not about the zombies. It's the grim horror of knowing just what ordinary people are capable of doing to one another and that is far, far, worse. That's the whimper the world ends with, the thousands and thousands of little cuts we inflict uncaringly on each other day after day and then forget about. Each knife that cuts a little deeper, each blade that twists a little more. Our bodies are full of those unseen wounds. We had just endured a particularly deep cut, blood spilled by blood, but what brought us to that was everything we've done as a species to get to the point where folks have to swim across a river of toxic sludge just to get to their dear departed Excuse my language, but that's just fucked up. I ended up paying the price for the lives I wrecked. I can't imagine that the people that wrecked the lives of everyone else in our town will ever pay such a price, but maybe that's just me.

**

THREE DAYS LATER

She's never been this far upriver before. But there's something there. Something calling to her.

From her vantage point on the riverbank, she can see it. A huge wall of stone, impenetrable and glistening with the morning dew. At the base of that great wall, which spans the entire width of the river, there emerges a steady trickle of water which feeds the delta she once called home. Beyond it, she cannot see, cannot imagine.

Thankfully, she doesn't need to. Several men dressed head to toe in orange move around the river at the base of the dam, occasionally prodding the river with long poles and taking small samples of the yellow muck that sticks to its base. Perhaps they don't know what they've done. Perhaps they don't care.

She doesn't care either. All that she knows is that she's hungry. It's a different kind of hunger than she's used to. Everything feels different now. Her face is covered in a mass of burn and scar tissue. She swims slower than she used to. None of that makes any difference, because all she has is hunger.

Old Bessie, dead but still walking, waddles back to the edge of the river and slips slowly, silently, into the water and makes her way upriver to where the men gather, unaware of what fate awaits them.

Heartless

Reel shadows of the indignant desert birds

"This is what's known as the basin room." Marc's voice rang out loud in the subterranean chamber, in part to make sure he could be heard over the sound of the slow but heavy dripping of water and in part because he rather liked the sound of it. That's what a tour guide should be like, he would instruct the new team members, loud and clear and unafraid of their own narrative.

Far behind him, not yet at the entrance to the room, two late arrivals to the Paris Catacomb tour struggled to hear him, not because of the volume, but because they were busy bickering with each other.

"You know I didn't want to come down here and now look, I've got mud all over my skirt. Honestly, Bill, can't we just go? Let's go back to that nice cafe we saw a couple of streets back and spend the afternoon there instead."

Maisie's eyes were pleading, but Bill couldn't see them in the pitch dark of the tunnel. He fiddled with his headlamp for the third time and pretended not to listen.

"Bill?"

"Oh, they say not to wander off on your own down here. Didn't you listen? That was the first thing the guide said. We might get lost. There's over two hundred miles of…"

Maisie cut him off. Bill could be a walking tour all on his own, they didn't need a guide. "We could cut back easily enough. The tunnels are lit most of the way. Pl-ee-ase."

"Spooked out, are you?" This wasn't spoken out of concern, nor entirely out of mockery. Truth be told, Bill himself was more spooked by the catacombs than he'd thought. They'd already tramped through passages lined with skulls and the guide had done his utmost to convey a ghostly atmosphere, with his little vignettes about people going missing and never being found again. Apparently, if they got lost and were still here after midnight, voices would call to them from the walls beckoning them deeper and deeper. All good fun for making a spooky atmosphere, but a bit scary even if there wasn't a grain of truth in it. Not that he could admit that, this had been his idea, and they were damn well going to enjoy it, thank you very much. Though, he thought in reflection, perhaps more 'endure' than 'enjoy'.

He looked over at Maisie, who was trying to scrape mud away from a sunflower yellow skirt and only making it worse. It would look awful when they hit sunlight again. That would be his fault as well. Perhaps there was something in being lost down here alone forever after all, he mused.

"Come on. We'd better catch the others up. They've already moved out of the room; I can hear their feet shuffling. Don't want to get lost."

Maisie was thinking she would very much like Bill to get lost. Nevertheless, she shuffled on, eager to be back out in daylight with a nice glass of wine

254

and a view of the Seine where it was beside or beneath them, as it should be, and not seeping through the walls around them.

They both emerged into a room that was empty now and stone-cold silent. A shimmering of lamps trailed away through an arch opposite them just as they entered.

If the bone-lined passageways had frightened them a little, this room was something else. Rather than the natural curves of the soapstone tunnels, here was a great stepped pool in the middle of a square room fashioned by human hands. Graffiti spat angrily from the walls of the cave in splotches of red and yellow, now lit only by the meagre output from their headlamps. Before them crouched a great gnarled statue, bent over the pond in a poised hunch. A small rivulet of water poured constantly onto its head through the roof above and exited through its mouth into the pool. In other settings, above ground in a garden maybe, this picture might have been serenity itself. Below the streets of Paris, it was nothing less than terrifying.

Bill let out a little gasp, then stifled himself so as not to appear too afraid.

"Well, hey there, fella." His half-joking attempt to address the gargoyle was an attempt to steady his nerves. He failed. "Don't suppose you know where the others went, do you?"

Silence. Obviously. Emerging beside him, Maisie also gasped, though hers was quite different.

"Oh wow. Look at that! What a wonderful work of art!"

Bill turned slowly, incomprehensibly. His eyes rolled and his eyebrows raised, not that Maisie could see. What light they had between them was focused solely on the scene ahead.

"I wonder where the water drains to?" Bill, an engineer by profession, always tried to address the nuts and bolts of a situation. Especially if it detracted from the ugly face staring back at him in the gloom. Maisie, an artist, was much more inclined to be lost in the moment. She sloshed her way through the muddy floor to stand beside the gently stirring waters of the pool and dipped a hand in. It was almost unnaturally cool. She hoisted her shoulder bag round to the carved lip of the pool beside her and began to search for something inside.

"Uh, Maisie, we really can't stay here, we've got to catch up with the tour."

Maisie, apparently, wasn't listening. She'd pulled a sketchbook from her bag and began fishing for her fineliners which she knew were buried in there somewhere.

"What do you want to draw that for anyway? It's grotesque!"

"Nope, not grotesque." Maisie was in her element now and began lecturing. "It's a gargoyle. Grotesques don't have the waterspout, that's what makes the difference. Come and look! They look like they're fashioned after the gargoyles on the Notre Dame!"

Bill groaned, took a brief look down the tunnel where he could still just about hear the low drone of their guide, and groaned again.

"Fine. It can't be that hard to catch up with them anyway, all those feet tramping around are bound to leave footprints in this mud. Just don't be long."

Maisie allowed herself a little smile and patted the rim of the pool next to her as if offering Bill a seat while she worked. Bill preferred to stand rather than get any more of his clothes damp, so he declined and did a little tour of the room instead, trying to decipher the graffiti with his poor French and failing at almost every word. He gave up quickly and leaned against a dry portion of the stone wall, thumbing the guidebook in the dim light of his headlamp.

Maisie set out three pens beside her and began to sketch, pointedly ignoring Bill. She had to admit he'd had a good idea when he suggested this tour though. She was beginning to enjoy herself immensely.

What was that? A flicker of light in the corner of her eye. She looked up suddenly, expecting Bill to have moved from the wall, about to cast everything back into realms of dark shadows. He hadn't moved though. She looked back at the gargoyle, determined to capture its facial expression from vestigial horn through to fanged mouth, just as whoever carved it had. Background detail could wait, it was the foreground that mattered here, the fine interplay between motes of shadow and light that...

She hesitated. The gargoyle had closed its eyes. She dropped a pen in alarm and fumbled for it on the muddy floor. When she looked up again, its eyes were once more wide open.

A trick of the light. Nothing more. Still, she'd be done here soon. Then she could take a couple of photos to help her fill in the rest of the pool and cavern later.

Had its paw just moved? No. Couldn't have been. Still…

"Bill, come here, would you? Take a look at this."

Bill ambled over. He looked bored rather than impatient.

"What's up? Oh! It's sitting up straighter now. That's odd." He said 'odd', but what he meant was 'very disturbing indeed'. He didn't let it show.

"It is? Maisie looked up from sketch to subject. He was right. It did look like it had moved again slightly.

"Perhaps it's waiting to devour us!" Bill was trying to be funny to counter the feeling he had in his throat, but it came out with the tone of terror that was in his heart, not the one he wanted on his tongue.

"It's just the way it's lit up. I need a static light source rather than this torch in my own headlamp. If you'd be so kind? Besides, gargoyles don't eat human flesh." She said this in such a matter-of-fact voice that Bill found it more frightful than when it echoed around them.

"Oh, they don't? Well, that's a relief!" Bill did not sound relieved. Everything was telling him to leave this place now.

"They're for protection. They're ugly to scare off evil spirits."

"You really are a mine of information! Really though, it's time we…"

"Oh, I'm done. There!" She turned her sketchbook round to show Bill her handiwork. "Not bad for ten minutes! Here, help me up, would you?"

"Do not move."

Neither of them were quite sure in that moment where that voice came from. The sudden volume shattering their solitude and the many echoes which followed rendered them both to blind and immediate panic. Maisie dropped her sketchbook; Bill dropped the tour map. They both landed unceremoniously in the pool, causing little ripples on the surface which crashed against those caused by the slow drip from the gargoyle's mouth.

It is, after all, not a sensible thing to say if you really want people not to move. It invites them to jump up immediately, to flee if they can, to cower in a corner. What it doesn't do is actually encourage people to stay still. But the owner of that voice was beyond such concerns.

"Stand up. Slowly. Then turn around."

Simple instructions. A much better solution.

"Walk over to me. Again, very slowly. We don't want to disturb the statue."

A figure emerged from the opposite archway. It wore the exasperated expression of a tour guide who really had better things to do than babysit every damn tourist that didn't listen.

To his surprise, they both complied, and rather quickly. Looks like they were spooked already.

"You opened yourself to much danger, remaining here when we all left. Do you realise that?"

He sounded sincere. Only Marc knew the smirk that lay hidden behind those words.

"The statue, you see. It moves. It would catch you and then you would be lost here forever."

"Maisie says that gargoyles are the good guys. Right Maisie?"

Marc was amazed they were actually buying this. He decided to extend his little joke on them a moment longer.

"Not the gargoyle. The walker-through-walls. Look! Over there!" Marc raised his torch theatrically. On one section of the wall Bill hadn't explored was a horrific sight. Trapped half in the wall of the chamber was the form of a man, his face and arms extending out toward them.

"He would have had you both. Luckily, I was here to rescue you." Marc adopted a pose meant to indicate bravery and pride, but which came across as arrogance. "Now, please follow me. And stay close this time. We don't want any incidents, do we?"

Maisie and Bill looked at each other, then nodded agreement. Whether or not there was any truth in the tale of this mover-through-walls coming to get them, they were both done with being spooked out for today and a good few more days besides.

As they left, Maisie turned round briefly to say farewell to the gargoyle squatting over the pool. As she did so, she noticed in the dim light that it had

260

one eye firmly shut and the other open, as if it was winking at her but was caught in the moment.

She wasn't sure what that meant, but she decided not to think about it until at least they'd finished their first bottle of wine later in the afternoon. Unfortunately, they still had the rest of the catacomb tour to get through first.

***

"After a collapse in Les Innocents shortly before the revolution..." Marc's voice was still strong and clear, but somewhat garbled at the back of the tour group where Bill and Maisie still trudged, self-relegated to the rear by what had become an overwhelming combination of dread and guilt.

"What's he saying? What's innocent?"

"It's an old cemetery." Bill was on a roll, high on his own knowledge of engineering history. "Buildings and streets were collapsing all over Paris because of all the limestone excavated from beneath the city. An interesting backdrop to the revolution, don't you think? Thousands of bodies were relocated from the cemetery to tunnels under the city."

Maisie squinted at the darkness up ahead and tried to pick up the pace. She really didn't want to get left behind again. Not without her favourite statue as protection against whatever that horrible man-form was. What had Marc called him? The walker-between-walls? She was torn between wanting to hear more of that story and being done with this whole experience.

In a small, squarish chamber ahead, the whole tour party had stopped for another lecture from Marc, who was clearly leaning heavily into the ghoulish tales now.

"This is the tombstone of someone who got lost in the catacombs." It was difficult to tell by the dim light of thirty underpowered head torches, but Maisie felt called out. "He was a doorman at the Val-de-Grace hospital and entered the catacombs via the cellar there. It was 11 years before he was found." That comment was certainly directed at the two slackers. The rest of the tour nodded grimly in agreement and clutched their tourist catacomb maps closer. Theirs was still in the fountain back in the basin room.

"Now, if you'll follow me…" Marc's stare again felt directly targeted at them, as if he was daring them not to follow. His voice, however, trailed off in the distance ahead. Maisie and Bill decided to pick up the pace in an effort to improve their standing in his eyes. Shuffling through the pack with a series of elbow nudges and discrete 'excuse-mes', they found themselves walking at the front of the group next to Marc, whose indifference to their presence indicated absolutely no recognition of their desire for rehabilitation in his eyes. He proceeded at his usual quick pace, in silence this time, until they reached the next chamber and the next talk.

***

The chamber was huge, bigger than any they'd encountered so far, large enough that its corners and any exits were obscured from even the relatively strong light of Marc's torch. He turned to address the pair of them.

"We'll just rest up here until the others catch up. I don't know what's keeping them." He shone his torch around the room and shuffled to one side so that the rest of the tour could all enter through the narrow doorway. But they didn't arrive. He sighed the knowing weary sigh of the impatient and turned back to Bill and Maisie.

"Wait here. I'll see what's keeping them. Probably got lost again." He shone his torch down the corridor, its light bouncing off the skull-filled cavities in the walls.

"Don't touch anything!" There was a sense of urgency to his voice, but neither Bill nor Maisie could determine whether it was a genuine desire for them not to break anything or another lame attempt to scare them. Either way, they both nodded and backed themselves into the wall next to the entrance as proof that they wouldn't do anything until he returned.

Click.

"What was that? I swear to God, if you've…"

Creak.

"What have you done?"

Rumble.

A heavy slab of stone began to descend from the passage they'd just come through. It wasn't quick, more of a slow, deliberate movement of a mechanism that hadn't been activated in years, if at all. Slower still, though, were their reactions. A heartbeat lost to hear the initial creak, another to locate it, a third to realise it was sealing them in…every moment punctuated by a missed opportunity to retreat. Even Marc, who was next to the entry point by now, chose to back off from the noise rather than escape back to the rest of the tour. Before they knew it, there was a resounding thud and a cloud of ancient dust as the great stone slab hit the floor. From behind it, just as it closed, they could hear screams and echoes of screams. Then, stony silence.

Bill spoke first, shattering that silence by venting in full fury.

"Is this part of the tour? Because let me tell you, buddy, I'm getting a bit tired of all the extra spooky shit. And, yeah, I know that's why a lot of people come, but I'm an engineer and I…"

"Bill! Bill, shut up." Maisie was clearly exasperated. "Look at his face. He's got no more idea of what's going on than we have."

"Oh yeah? Well just maybe that's part of the act too, Maisie, ever think of that? Easy enough to fake concern. Easier still to rig up a couple of pressure pads that close the door and set off a recording of some fake screams." He drew himself to full bulk, which wasn't particularly impressive, but at least managed to be bigger than Marc, which was all that was needed.

"It's not." Marc finally broke his silence. His face was a contorted mask of fear and confusion. "Look, everything else - the gargoyle, the walker through walls - that's part of the experience. But please believe me when I tell you I have no idea where we are, how we got here, how to get out or what the hell just happened to the rest of the tour. Please, believe me." He leaned, panicked but exhausted, against the wall next to the door. "Just give me a moment to think."

"Sure. You just stand there, buddy. Meanwhile, I'm gonna do something." Bill busied himself with examining the stone slab that had just fallen, feeling around the edges for a gap, tapping on it to check how deep it was. He was still furious, but panic was beginning to creep back in. He'd believed what Marc had said, mainly because Bill was always more likely to believe that someone was incompetent rather than devious.

Maisie, meanwhile, had moved away from them both, clutching the side of her head. Definitely a migraine coming on. She adjusted the angle on her head lamp until she saw, poorly lit and distant, something that looked like a plinth in what must have been the centre of this vast chamber. She moved in a little closer, hoisting her bag over her shoulder and then removing the lamp from the helmet so she could use it as a little torch. In her right hand, the light was a lot more flexible than it was on her head. She walked right up to the lip of the plinth, not wanting to look down at what was crunching beneath her feet. She'd been in this wretched place long enough to be sure that it was bones. That was one image she didn't want. The plinth, though, now that was different. No, not a plinth, she thought, a tomb. Obviously, it would have been a tomb. She stifled what might have been a manic laugh had she allowed it to escape.

It was some twelve feet long and eight feet wide at the base, easily four feet from the base to the lip and consisted, as far as she could tell, of a single slab of white marble with a lid over it. Her gaze lingered overlong on that lid. The rest of the tomb was unadorned, a dull grey limestone that nobody would give a second look at. The lid, though, was different - basalt, she thought, or a polished granite. It was engraved with hundreds of hieroglyphics, mostly birds and beasts. More spectacularly, on each corner squatted a grotesque, not unlike the one they'd seen earlier, except that they had the heads of vultures, their necks extended towards its centre as if they were about to take part in some grim, grisly feast of whatever lay within. She could vaguely hear Bill and Marc arguing near the entrance, something about the rest of the group and the tunnels, but there was something else she could hear and the closer she examined the lid the louder it got, until it echoed not just in her ears but her throat and her brain and her hands, something that shook her all over.

It was the low, rhythmic sound of a heartbeat.

***

"Ok, so I believe you. Satisfied now?" Still exasperated, but this time mostly at his own failed attempts to discern any mechanism, Bill shot his final bolt at Marc as they both felt their way along the walls trying to find what had triggered the slab.

"I get it. This place gets to you. I'm down here for hours every day and even I don't know more than half of its secrets. I've never been in this room before, I swear it. I don't know where we took a wrong turn. There's shit down here you wouldn't believe - secret cinemas, forgotten armouries used by the resistance in the war, miles of tunnels nobody has ever mapped. It's as if the place takes on a life of its own."

Bill waved his hand in irritation. "Spare us the lecture, you're not our tour guide anymore. Just get us out, that's all I ask. Maisie and I are..." He cut himself off.

"Are what?" Then he realised what was troubling Bill at that moment and why he stopped. They'd both forgotten she was in the room with them. Preoccupied, they'd just let her wander off.

"Maisie?" Bill called over to her but she didn't answer. Then, louder, he repeated. "Maisie? You still there?"

It snapped her out of her moment of discovery.

"Yeah, I'm over here. Come and have a look!"

When Marc directed his torch, they could both make her out, hunched over something in the middle of the room.

"Whatcha found, girl?" Bill tried to sound endearing, but a week in Paris with her had sorely tested his patience. Every ten minutes, it seemed, he turned round to say something, and she was thirty paces behind, fixated on some street sign or window or cafe tables. "Oh, great, another dead guy. Hey, Marc, Maisie's found another tomb. How many's that now?"

"Sarcasm isn't helping, Bill. Did you find a way out?"

"Nope. No sign of how the stone got triggered."

She looked up away from the sketch she was making of the hieroglyphic lid. Bill knew that expression, that subtly arched eyebrow, that understated exasperation.

"No, I mean, did you find any other way out of the room. Like, are there any other exits?"

"Oh." A slight shuffling of his feet occupied his gaze in the pretence that there was something spectacularly exciting about his walking sandals. Mostly, it was to avoid that withering look from her disapproving eye.

"Have either of you even looked?" She stood straight now and ironed out the creases in her summer dress even though that meant a little spilt ink got applied to it in the motion.

"Have you?"

"Honestly, I've been busy here. Look at these magnificent carved vulture heads! She held up a crude, preliminary sketch of one, drawn on one of the three remaining dry pages of her sketchbook, then directed his gaze back to the statue itself. "Pretty good likeness, don't you think?"

Marc approached now, holding his torch aloft as if heralding some lost emperor, its light dancing across the stony ceiling, a muted kaleidoscope of shadows and flashes. At the last moment, he pointed it down to the lid. Hundreds of tiny images flickered into life in that golden light. He reached down and ran his finger through the little dust that had accumulated.

"Fascinating."

"Can you read them? What does it say?"

"Have you two lost your mind? We need to get out of here. Stop staring at the dead and get some perspective!"

"Oh, now you want to find a way out? Go on, then, there's plenty of room left to explore. No need to bother us!"

When Bill left their side, which he did almost immediately, it wasn't just to find a way out. It was to get as far away from his companion as he possibly could before things got worse.

"I can't read them. It's not too odd to see something like this, here, I guess. When Napoleon spent time in Egypt..." Marc was back in full tour guide mode, again, his eyes closed as if that made it easier to recall another five minutes of fun facts. Probably some triggered defence mechanism, Maisie thought. She felt a little sorry for him. All that history might be fascinating, but she doubted it would get them far, or even out of this room. Then something occurred to her.

"Oh! I know what this reminds me of! Bill and I did this escape room once in Edinburgh. You know, you have half an hour to solve all the puzzles, that kind of thing." She paused, then remembered that Bill was actually quite good at those kinds of puzzles. Perhaps she'd been a little short with him earlier.

"What's that noise?" Marc looked concerned, then cast his torch around to each of the vulture statues in turn.

"Oh! I was going to mention that. It's quite loud when you get close, isn't it?"

"It sounds like a heartbeat. Not something you'd normally expect from a tomb."

"Can we stop with the spooky stuff? Just for a second? I'm already scared out of my wits, I'm afraid."

"Yeah, sure, sorry." Marc stopped talking and the noise of the heartbeat and their own breaths was all the sound left.

It occurred to Maisie then that Marc didn't really know how to talk about anything else. Perhaps that's why he was a catacomb guide. The Greeks, she seemed to recall from studies a lifetime ago, had a special word for it. What was it? Psychopomp. Someone that guides you to the land of the dead. It sounded fantastical, but was that what Marc was? Had they died somehow?

Whilst Maisie's imagination was getting the better of her, Bill turned his talents to a full examination of the perimeter, calculated steps taken in sulky silence. He wished he'd brought some of his kit with him as he'd wanted - just a little rock hammer and some measuring tape would have been helpful now - but Maisie was always teasing and remonstrating with him about the inordinate amount of junk he wanted to take everywhere, and that coming from someone with entire bags full of pens, pencils and erasers. So, he walked the full area, counting the steps in his head so as not to disturb anyone, but who could hear him anyway? The dead? He could barely hear Maisie and Marc talking about the hieroglyphics. Their voices seemed to me muted by the acoustics of the chamber, which was odd in itself since he would have expected an echo.

What went through his mind mostly, though, were the memories of those screams they'd heard as the slab fell. Indistinguishable enough not to be recognisable as anyone in the group, though he had to admit neither of them had been in conversation with any of them long enough to know who any of them were. Must be a recording, then, he though. But that meant Marc had been lying. Or maybe just wasn't aware. He was determined to be the one that found the answer, solved the riddle, took them to safety. He turned at the first corner he reached, made a note of the full length of the wall (122 feet, quite a large size he thought for an underground chamber with no central strut supports) and then abruptly turned and continued, lost in his own thoughts and therefore utterly oblivious to anything outside of them.

Marc was trying to remember something about cataphile parties. Those that loved the world under the streets of Paris - cataphiles - had held meetings and parties here almost since they were built, even when huge areas of the underground were sealed off and special police units set up to patrol them. Once, the police had triggered a pressure pad which someone had set up to play the sound of barking dogs. Undeterred, they'd continued to find a completely abandoned cinema complex, complete with cocktail bar. There were more things down here than he even wanted to think about, but that particular incident seemed relevant because it seemed that a similar trick had been played on them. He tried not to breathe too fast or too heavily, anything that might give away that he was completely out of his depth in the one area he was supposed to be an expert. He inspected the length and breadth of the tomb without saying a word because Maisie seemed to like to work in silence, but all he was doing really was going over what she'd already inspected. He felt completely useless but didn't know what he might say or do to be of any use. So, he held his torch low, freeing up Maisie's hand for more sketching, wondering how she thought that might be helping them but content that he wasn't the one that was taking the lead for a change.

Maisie was trying to concentrate despite the incessant pounding noise in her head. She was busying herself with outlining the forms of each vulture sculpture, complete with shadows, but Marc, no doubt in an effort to seem helpful, kept moving the torch around so the shadows kept changing. Still, she was disturbed by the repetitive thump-thump of a heartbeat and decided she needed to rid herself of that distraction so she could think properly. As a result, she put her sketchbook carefully to one side, clutched in the front claws of one of the vultures which she decided would be an excellent guardian, and asked Marc to help her open the lid where she was sure the noise was coming from. She was only too happy to see him nod and begin to brace his weight against the side of the lip, pushing and pulling at it with a series of muted grunts until he finally managed to open a corner of it. Just the faintest of cracks, but it was enough to wedge her smaller torch in to get her a distorted partial view of the interior.

Second wall, 82 feet. Same stone as the first, though that wasn't particularly surprising. Bill made a brief note and carried on. Rounding that second corner confirmed his belief that they were in a massive rectangular chamber. There had been on exits on either of the walls he'd trailed along. He'd even had the foresight to figure out which section of wall had been opposite where they'd come in, just in case something was different about it. Now he was on his own and in his element, Bill was almost starting to enjoy himself again. If only those screams would settle down, he might even classify this as fun.

"It's still too dark. Marc?"

Marc swung his torch down and tried to jam it in the little gap, but that left little room for either of them to see through.

"Hang on! I'll try and move the lid further." He grunted in anticipation of physical exertion, then twice more as he tried and failed to move the slab more than the mere inches they'd already managed. Somewhere in the back of his mind, those stray thoughts surfaced again, as if gasping for air before being pulled back underwater. *Why are we doing this? Why a*

I not saying anything? Why should I be the one who has to take the lead anyway? At least doing something is better than doing nothing...

Third wall, also 122 feet. Bill could hear the sound of moving stone from the middle of the room. That did echo, which was odd since their voices didn't. Must be some quirk of acoustics, he assumed. At least he'd been correct in his assumption that the two longest walls were of equal length. Barring any oddities, that meant the fourth wall would measure the same as the last. He'd walk its length anyway, because that's where the entrance had been. Then he heard Maisie call him, which gave him a little jump he was glad the others couldn't see. Reluctantly, he ceased his examinations and trudged back to where the others lurked in darkness.

"Coming!"

Bill had heard her, at least. That was something. Maisie didn't want to admit that she might need his help, but her curiosity to find out whatever was in the tomb overran her reticence. If she could just get rid of that noise, she could concentrate properly and then she'd be able to figure it all out.

"What on earth are you doing?" Bill strode the last few feet, arrogance if not confidence guiding his steps once he could see them ahead.

"We're opening the tomb." Marc had thought that was obvious, but in truth he'd surprised himself when he found that he was the one who spoke. Bill looked at them both, then shook his head. Maisie was sure he was going to ask them why, which was going to be hard to articulate, especially if Bill couldn't hear the heartbeat.

"Well, obviously. But brute strength isn't the best way of doing that. Christ, haven't either of you heard of levers?"

"So, you don't object, then?" Maisie was in the mood for a fight, not another engineering lecture.

"Why would I do that? There might be a clue inside, right? Some secret mechanism to open the door? I couldn't find any on the walls. There's no other way out, either. There's not much left to look at that might give us a hint. Here, take this." He passed Marc a long metal pole.

More than anything else, Maisie wanted the noise to stop. But the desire to know why Bill had brought such a thing on their tour or where he'd been hiding it all this time came a very close second.

"That's a torch sconce from the wall. Did you break it off?" Marc wheeled round to grab the pole, but the accusation still stuck.

"Oh, I'll be sure to put it right back after we've used it to pry the lid off this unknown tomb. Wouldn't want to vandalise anything." Bill could be deadpan when he wanted to, but on this occasion the sarcasm practically dripped from him.

Marc decided against an impromptu retort and directed his energies instead to cracking open the lid of the tomb. He didn't care about vandalising; all he cared about was getting out. In all likelihood, given the layer of dust and the lack of footprints, nobody had been in this room for years and may never set foot in it again. Nobody would know he'd taken a crowbar to a priceless monument. Only as an afterthought did he think of what fame might await him, in those strange esoteric circles which he moved in and which cared about such things, when he could make the finding of this room public and share it with yet more visitors.

Truth be told, none of them were quite sure what they'd expected to find inside the sarcophagus, with the exception that they each hoped it would provide a clue as to how they might get out. There was, inevitably, a dead body. Somehow, that surprised both Marc and Bill, though not Maisie. She found it fascinating rather than repulsive, as if another world had just been revealed to her and her only. Long tatters of cloth were wound around a human form, strips which might once have been white, but which age had turned various mottled shades of yellow-brown from sand to papyrus. Where there was once a living, breathing face there was now only stretched, dry skin, unencumbered by such niceties as eyes or a tongue. That did not mean it didn't seem to stare at them all as they directed their torches over its prone body, searching from head to toe for anything which might provide a means of escape or any clue as to context. Surely, they each thought, this couldn't be real. It must be an elaborate hoax being played on them. Perhaps the perpetrators might yet reveal themselves or provide a well-crafted hint.

Then each torch in succession landed on the same place and illuminated something which dispelled any notion of chicanery. It was a heart cavity in which beat no heart, but somehow the absence of one, the very depletion of the organ somehow still signalling its continuance elsewhere while the cavity it once sat in still pulsed slowly, pumping no blood, fulfilling no function but to freak the fuck out of anyone who was unfortunate to be present when it was discovered. The thumping noise was now quite indistinguishable from the beating of a human heart, in harmony with the slow rise and fall of the empty void which lay in the chest cavity of the mummy.

Bill backed off slowly, still shining his torch at it, as though he couldn't look elsewhere except at the empty nothingness. Marc's reaction was more pronounced, falling backward from the plinth and dropping his torch against the lid which now lay on its side by the tomb it had once protected. He scrabbled backwards and away, babbling under his breath, his knuckles bleeding from an unfortunate landing. Maisie got out her notebook and began to try and draw the hole, to capture the emptiness of something rather than the presence. If either of the others were paying her the slightest attention, that compulsive action might have signalled that she was the one whose sanity had snapped completely.

Of the birds and beasts on the lid, of what story they might have told or what danger they might have warned of, they understood nothing. They had not stopped to think of why vultures, of all creatures, might have been fashioned as guardians for this unholy creation. They hadn't even stopped to think why at any stage. They'd opted for action without belief in consequence, each resolute that something would save them if they just did…anything. And in this regard, they had been utterly wrong. Only in one regard had Maisie had been right. It had been an escape room, of sorts, but not one that they were ever going to escape from.

Whatever foul blackness had once been contained in that heart, watched over by those four ugly carrion bird guardians, it was clear that it had been taken long before they had even been locked in. Perhaps the passer-through-walls had snatched it through the stone bier and was now feasting on the mortal souls of their tour group as an aperitif. Perhaps the heart itself now beat with the breast of another foul form, escaping to enjoy a new life, or at least a semblance of life-in-death, somewhere in the streets up above. Even Maisie's runaway imagination could not comprehend the horrors that may be happening even now on the streets above and what new pain the world would wake up to when they first opened their curtains and shutters to a new dawn ushered in by their hastiness and ignorance.

They could only wait here, with decreasing amounts of light, air, water, and patience, silent as the grave. Except for that constant, relentless sound of a heartbeat without a heart.

Forget About Me

The darkness drops again, but now I know

"Hello? Is there anyone there? Can you hear me? Can you see me? Dammit!"

"OK, I'm just going to assume you can hear. I can only just make you out. Look, I don't know who you are, but I need help and, apparently, you're the only number on my cell. That's weird, right?"

"Sorry, just had to adjust the phone, it was about to fall off the edge of the table. Look, I don't know who I am or how I got here. It looks like I'm in a library? Here, have a look around. See, there are shelves full of books and a few desks, but as you can tell, everything's been trashed. Including me. I woke up here with this colossal bump on my head - *Christ that hurts* - and absolutely not a scooby as to how I got here. My phone was in my hand. I don't have any ID on me, no wallet, no drivers licence, nothing."

"Quiet type, are you? Geez, do you have nothing to say?"

<<Burst of static>>

"Hello? Dammit."

<<Burst of static>>

"Wait, I can hear something. It sounds like…"

"Oh my god, there's someone else here. I'll call you back. Wait, I'll leave you on."

"Hey! Hey, you OK?"

<<BEEEEEEP>>

"Thank God I managed to get back. Apparently, I'm not alone. Look! This is… well, turns out she doesn't know who she is either. She's not hurt, though. Right?"

"We're going to have a look around this place and see if there's anyone else here. Be right back."

"Wow. This is getting freaky. Right, here's the sitrep. So, there are, like, five of us here. Wave at our mystery saviour, everyone! There's no way out of this place except via those top windows, and they'd take an athlete to get to, let alone get through. None of us are feeling particularly athletic at the moment. Groggy, sure. Bruised, check. But not up for a climb. The doors are locked. Tattoo girl here gave it a hefty push, it's not just locked but chained on the other side."

"Glasses guy over here - he found what looks like a clue as to where we might be. It's a high school yearbook. Shermer High. You know where that is? It sounds vaguely familiar to us. Like, maybe we went here as kids. Maybe? That's not too much of a stretch, is it? Glasses and Princess are going to check through it. Tattoo, Punk and I are going to see what else we can find out about this place. I assume that whoever you are, you can help too. Do a bit of googling for us? Ride to the rescue?"

<<Silence>>

"Well, I guess we're on our own then. Thanks for nothing, bud. Gonna keep the video call open in case you change your mind. Here, I'll pass you over to Princess. Maybe she can change your mind.

***

280

"Fuck. fuck. Fuck. It's…I can't describe it. Here, I'll carry the phone over to…"

<<*Clacking, crashing noises*>>

"See that? You fucking see that? That's blood. Some sick fuck has written on the wall in blood. "WHO ARE YOU?" What the fuck's that supposed to mean? Who the fuck does that?"

"Princess thinks I should calm down. How the fuck am I supposed to calm down? Tattoo's gone. Like, straight up vanished. Fuck, is that her blood? Who the fuck would do this? Wait up, Princess is shouting now."

***

"Look, I don't know or care who you are, just get someone to Shermer High. There's some serious shit going on. We found Tattoo, throat slit from ear to ear. No kidding. Just…get us help, eh bud?"

<<*silence*>>

"Right. I'm basically just recording this now. It's clear you don't give a shit, so this is only for posterity. Assuming we don't get out. Assuming anyone ever finds us. There's only four of us now. None of us know each other, but we all have this weird feeling that we've met before. Then glasses over here found this. I'll pivot the camera round."

"It's a frickin' yearbook. The only damn book in this whole damn library that seems to have completely escaped whatever wrecked or neglected this place. And look at this. It's us. All five of us, together, waving. At least we have names now.

281

Glasses - sorry, Brian - he wants to solve the mystery. I wanna find out what the fuck happened to Tattoo - that's Allison - and give that sick fuck a piece of my mind. Everyone else just wants to get out. Fat chance of that, but what the heck. Looks like we're gonna have to split up again. Yeah, I know. That always seems to be the dumb thing to do. But we need answers, fast, and you're not helping."

***

"Well, I hope you're happy, whoever you are. We're down to three now. Five in the photo, three left alive. Brian's been glued to that yearbook. There's another photo, six of us this time. But this one is covered in bloody handprints, and we can't make out that last person. Meanwhile, whoever the fuck is in this place with us just knocked a bookshelf down right on John's noggin."

"It's you, isn't it? Thought it was a bit convenient that you were the only one I could call. Who the fuck are you? Show your face, motherfucker! Show your damn face!"

"Listen, if you're the one in here with us, I'll fucking tear you apart. I'm coming for you."

***

"This is Princess. I mean, Claire. Did you do that to Andrew? How? Why? Just…I don't understand. What did we ever do to you? Are you the other face in that photo?"

282

"Oh God, we did do something, didn't we? As kids, I mean. What was it? Why are you punishing us now? Did we run over someone in the car? Was it you? Are you a ghost? Is that why you're hunting us now? You on some sick revenge arc? Talk to me, you coward!"

"Why? Why us? OK. OK, OK, OK. I think I can see it now. There weren't five us as kids, were there? Like some inseparable, unstoppable force? There were six of us, right? You were there too, weren't you?"

"I don't remember you. I'm sorry. It's just… it's been a long time, you know? Adult life. We all moved on, I guess. Or maybe you didn't. Maybe we all moved on and left you here. Christ, that's shitty. Did we not even call to say hi? Meet up on holidays?"

"Look, I don't know what we did or what I can do now to make it right. Just…just stop killing my friends, OK? We'll both need to sleep soon, we're exhausted…Just, I don't even know if I can trust Brian right now. It's not him, right? It's you, isn't it? Are you fucking enjoying this? Are you?"

***

"You took that other photo, didn't you? The one with just the five of us. That's why you weren't in it. Who were you? Who ARE you? What happened to us? Why don't we know how we ended up here? Why can none of us remember our adult lives?

283

***

"We've pieced it all together. Do you hear me? We know who you are now. We know what happened. We weren't some band of losers who banded together for self-defence. We didn't try and save the world from some ancient evil like we were in some supernatural coming-of-age flick. We just ended up here one day in detention. We bonded."

***

"This is Brian. We know who we are now. I figured it out. I didn't want to believe it at first. It's quite frankly a little hard to believe."

"We know who you are, too, or rather who you were. Memory is a funny thing. We thought you were a student like us. Someone missing from our little group. But that's so much misdirection, isn't it? Whoever that was, we forgot about them. Went our separate ways. Lost contact with him, with each other. Life will do that, I guess. I imagine he stayed behind and we promised we'd come back. Instead, we moved on."

"You're not him, though, are you? You're just using his image to taunt and kill us. Well, that won't work, not anymore. The computer at the librarian's desk isn't wrecked. I hacked through to the admin server. I know who you are, Mr. Vernon. And we know who we were. Or rather, who society classified us as. But we're all so much more than that. More than an athlete, a basketcase, a brain, a princess, and a criminal. We're tired of this, Mr.

Vernon, and we're not staying here until we all die. We've sacrificed a lot more than a single Saturday to your demands. Claire found a way out. Waxing philosophically - if you'll allow that, Mr. Vernon - we all did in a way. Brian out."

No Rest For The Wicked

That twenty centuries of stony sleep

Day 1. 0800

I am supremely grateful to the governor and staff of Fellmarsh Prison for allowing me to conduct these experiments within their walls and to loan me three of their officers for the duration of this experiment.

The first of our nine prisoners are about to arrive. I am trying to retain a cool, scientific exterior before the induction at 0900 but I find myself irritatingly excitable after waking early and checking all the monitoring equipment three times. I have internally chastised myself for this uncharacteristic unprofessionalism. I must maintain focus if this study is to be successful. There is too much at stake.

Day 1. 1000

All our test subjects have been informed of their role in the experiment. Whilst it must be said that none of them are exactly willing, the early release conditions explicitly outlined as part of their cooperation have gone some way to mitigating their churlishness. Nevertheless, the very nature of this experiment demands that their initial reactions be taken into account as their later behaviour may ultimately derive from the demeanour they exhibit at the baseline experimental start of 1/0900.

Prisoner 1173, hereafter to be referred to by the designation of Subject 1(S001) is a slight man in his early 20s who is serving a term for dealing in narcotic substances. The results of his blood chemistry indicate his own system is clear of those substances, which is a necessary precondition for commencement of the experiment. All subjects should show blood work indicating they are free of narcotics, soporifics or stimulants including even such simple, easily attainable compounds such as caffeine or tobacco. The governor assures me that the prisoners assigned us have been selected accordingly.

Subjects 2 through 6 are all serving terms for assault with a deadly weapon. Changes in predisposition to violence is one of the metrics that will guide the progress of the experiment. Whilst I hesitate in predicting the outcome, the suspected outcome of sleep deprivation to this extent, based on the results of previous experimentation, is that levels of baseline predisposition to violence and willingness to enact that violence will increase among all subjects. The guards on loan to us will be on standby should any outbreak escalate beyond expected parameters. In addition, we have the facility to inflict electric shocks on all participants via the specially constructed floor of LAB1 and additionally are able to pump gas into the room through the ventilation system as an extreme measure. I remain confident that neither of these will be necessary for the duration of Experiment One.

Subjects 7 and 8 are brothers arrested during the course of an armed robbery which resulted in a hostage situation. Their trial notes indicate a capacity for being cool under pressure but utterly ruthless in negotiations. Their fraternal bond may evolve into a point of psychological interest once the experiment is fully under way.

Subject 9 is the most interesting. He is currently serving five consecutive sentences for murder, all committed in the space of three hours in a home invasion. His predilection for not just violence but also unspeakable cruelty has been factored into our initial equations. Unlike the others, he has no hope of early release but was apparently keen to participate when approached by the governor. Perhaps merely the opportunity for company has provided him with enough impetus. I hear that solitary confinement on death row can affect the mind in interesting ways. Should he survive, I will petition the governor for the opportunity to conduct further psychological experiments on him to determine how he reacts to different stimuli under a variety of external pressures. I find abnormal psychology utterly fascinating, and this is a rare subject with little opportunity to refuse. Informed consent is all well and good, but there are several experiments which depend on the subject being ignorant throughout. Once again, I express my gratitude to Governor Gray for signing the necessary paperwork to make this experiment possible.

Day 1. 2000

There is very little to report this early in the experiment. We do not expect to observe any differences in behaviour, physically or psychologically, until the subjects have been deprived of at least three cycles of REM sleep. I must report, though, on the setup of the communal room (LAB1) in which we have housed our subjects.

There are no beds or cots of any kind on which the subjects might find comfort or relief should they try to sleep, only the stone floor which is underwired with the potential to deliver electrical jolts via a device in the control room should anyone be found trying to nap. The control room will be continually occupied by myself and one of the three guards such that the lever which administers the shock can be activated at the earliest available opportunity. One of the other guards remains on duty at a station opposite the room whilst the third will undertake their own rest cycle.

Cameras are located in the uppermost corners of the room, with facilities to swivel and zoom, effectively covering 100% of the floor space in the room. Subjects have been informed that their activity will be monitored 24 hours a day. It is a simple and small panopticon, that is to say in principle all the subjects can be monitored at all times. In addition, each of the walls have been painted by a series of eyes. The overall effect is designed to indicate to participants that they are being continually watched. This will make it much more difficult for them to fall asleep naturally.

Day 2. 2000

There is still little progress to report, as expected. Initial loss of sleep has few effects beyond drowsiness and irritability. There have been some anger issues but presently these have only been vocalised and not acted upon. It may be that lethargy is serving as an effective counterpoint to hostility.

We did receive a visit from Governor Gray, who is as keen as I am to see a successful

conclusion of the experiment, though his mindset is far from being scientific in approach and it appears my superiors, rather annoyingly, have misled him as to the expected outcomes of the study. Either that or he has been watching too many science fiction movies. I'm afraid I was rather short and dismissive of his concerns as he happened to arrive a third of the way through my own sleep cycle and Guard 1 had to awaken me in order to have an audience with him. I assured him that what he had been told - or perhaps what he thought he was being told - was incorrect. Sleep deprivation is not designed to produce so-called 'super-soldiers', far from it. Regular lack of REM sleep does the opposite of what you would expect from a super-soldier: in most cases it should reduce people to little more than zombies. It is not designed to be used as a technique on our own army, but to analyse the potential range of effects it would have on an enemy population. The methods used to inflict deprivation may not be something we can extrapolate from a single room to the world at large, but the effects should be. The experiment includes provision of different ways of preventing sleep to see how a controlled population deals with them differently and the most successful and adaptable of them can then be used in psychological warfare. The Governor nodded, but I don't think he understood. In all honesty I was glad to be rid of him, though he insists now on daily reports which were not part of the initial briefing agreement. I must endeavour to keep him on side: we cannot afford another cycle of withdrawal from the programme with the funding loss and political implications should it be discovered. The Governor must see that.

Day 3. 1200

The subjects have now been deprived of two full sleep cycles and expected psychological and physiological changes have begun to manifest in all subjects bar one. Subject 9, our mass murderer, showed no reduction in coordination or concentration in this morning's round of experimentation. As such, he remains the only one in possession of the food pellets that are delivered when the subjects complete the experiments successfully. Fascinating. I should like the opportunity to run a full suite of medical scans on his brain at the conclusion of our weeklong experiment. A message from Governor Gray today indicates that his day of execution has been brought forward. Despite the post-mortem opportunity this might give me to analyse his dead brain, I hastily scrawled back a stern email indicating my disapproval and remonstrated with him that such an outcome violated the terms of our agreement. I cced in my superiors so that they can see what I'm dealing with here. Unbelievable. They can deal with the legal consequences or at least talk the governor down. My mind must be free to concentrate on the subjects; this could easily be the last chance available to derive any meaning from sleep deprivation experiments before the next conference season is upon us. I am eager to present my findings to the scientific community.

The other subjects all show the signs of drowsiness we would expect at this stage, with the fatigue manifesting in slight tremors in one case (Subject 2) and an increase in stress and anger amongst them all, which has initially been directed at Subject 9 seemingly for the simple reason that he is the only one that has any food. I am tempted to wait and see how he decides to distribute it, but the principal goal is to determine the effects of the deprivation of sleep, not nutrition, and I fear his marked abnormal psychology means that he is a poor control group.

Day 3. 1400

Subject 9 has disseminated the food pellets to all the participant subjects apart from Subject 1, who he is now watching intently. I appear to have missed the moment when this happened - rewinding the surveillance indicates this happened just after I finished typing my last report. How did I miss it? I must stay more alert and rely less on the guards who are, after all, untrained in professional psychological evaluation.

Day 4. 0930

Again, no subject completed the necessary challenges to be delivered the breakfast portion of their food pellets except for Subject 9, who immediately and pointedly gave the whole supply - including his own - to Subject 1. Their appetites should be significantly increased by this stage, though the extreme fatigue after three missed sleep cycles seems likely to offset the possibility of extreme violent reactions, as anticipated.

Another email from Governor Gray, asking for a report from yesterday. Did I not send it to him? Damn fool can't even be bothered to read his own emails. I can't afford to take time out of monitoring at this stage; I expect this to be the first real breakthrough. I'll ignore him and let my superiors deal with his whining unless it becomes an existential risk to the experiment.

Day 4. 1400

A missed call from my superiors asking me to send a report to the governor immediately as well as an apology. I don't even recall the telephone ringing, nevertheless they must consider it unlikely that I would give up active 24-hour monitoring to involve myself in such a mundane activity.

As a result, it seems, the governor has decided not to give me any food today, as if I were one of the prisoners in the experiment. I can't believe how petty he has become. I have taken all of the food tablets designed for distribution to the subjects and will stockpile them myself to fend off any further misbehaviour on his part. The only thing I shall write is this diary. He can see the full medical report and its conclusions once the experiment is over.

Even so, the little time this has taken me away from the schedule has caused me to miss our first fist fight. The guards were able to subjugate the offender quickly enough, thankfully with minimal force so that we are not forced to remove him (Subject 8) from the group.

Day 5. 0320

Subjects 1 through 8 are all showing classic signs of extreme sleep deprivation. As theorised, some of the subjects have begun to hallucinate. Whatever visual or audible phenomena these manifest can be surmised only by careful monitoring of their behaviour and by a series of leading questions asking them to describe their experience. The problem, which I confess should have occurred to me earlier, is that these men are no longer in a fit state to describe anything meaningfully; almost everything they say is garbled garbage. How could I have been such a fool as to not anticipate this outcome! I am cursing myself even as I pen this report.

I will have to send a different report to the Governor. I can't allow him to see the full implications of my lack of experimental rigour.

Day 5. 0420

I can't believe only one hour has passed since the last entry. I looked up from the interim findings report, deciding whether to send it to the governor immediately to shut him up or keep it, fully believing that it was mid-morning and time for the next round of hand-eye coordination tasks. When I began them, Subject 9 approached the camera with a fixed grin on his face and repeatedly tapped his left wrist. What he hoped to achieve by this I only realised when one of the guards on the second monitor did the same, albeit this time it was the presence of a wristwatch which provided the clue.

Subject 9's pathology is preventing us from successful deployment of the experiment. I have asked that he be isolated and removed. The governor has indicated that his execution date has been brought forward anyway and that we will have to conclude the experiment on him tomorrow as a matter of course.

Day 5. 0900

Subject 1 man has started screaming so loudly that Subjects 2 and 3 both launched themselves on him physically in an attempt to restrain him, while Subject 4 used the opportunity to attempt to tear out Subject 1's vocal chords. This is the first time we have had to use the electrical jolts through the floor as a deterrent for violence rather than to prevent effective rest. An interesting development, but one which caused me a good deal of stress.

Day 6. 0900

Subject 9 has vanished. There is no sign of him anywhere on the monitors. I have ordered the room to be flooded with morphine gas in an attempt to have him found before the guards arrive to take him to the electric chair. I wish the governor had taken him away yesterday when I asked him.

Day 6. 1000

The gas didn't work. None of the remaining subjects showed any effects at all when exposed to the morphine gas. We shall have to render the floor operative permanently and hope that the electrical stimulation knocks the subjects out so that we can begin a thorough search. It seems impossible that he might have escaped. He must have done something while I was microsleeping. Bribed a guard, perhaps? It would have to have been at least two guards. And what might he have to bribe them with? How has he managed to not only prove immune to any of the effects of sleep deprivation but somehow overcome them and make his escape from a sealed lab in a top security containment facility? Some people of course may be able to resist and continue without mental decline - that's the secondary objective. I myself am one of those people. We want to see what percentage of people can do this and whether they can still solve difficult riddles and puzzles after extended deprivation. The current situation, though, is vexatious. I will refrain from sounding the alarm until we have something concrete with which to inform the governor. I clearly cannot trust the guards with such a message and am too busy to send that message myself.

Day 6. 1300

He has been there the whole time, tucked away in a corner. How could I have missed it? How could all the guards have missed it?

He has clearly been dead now for at least four hours. There are clear bite marks on his person and chunks of the flesh on his abdomen missing where at least two others have attempted to eat him. I curse the lack of scientific advancement that means we cannot continuously monitor the interior cerebral states of subjects in situ. It would have been fascinating to see exactly what hallucinations might have brought them to the brink of sleep disorder psychosis, where their perception of reality has become so distorted they are no longer able to rationalise and control their own actions.

Day 6. 1400

Despite my orders not to do so, one of the guards has apparently called the governor, who has just arrived for an inspection. I have barricaded myself into the observation room and released all the door locking mechanisms. The experimental subjects shall now provide my last line of defence. I must not let the governor discover what has happened and release that information to the world! This research must be allowed to continue regardless of the consequences.

Day 6. 1410

I can hear the screams from the hallway. I can see the traitor guards who were assigned to me and the additional resources brought in by the governor being torn to shreds by the sleepless subjects, unable to discern reality from their own deprivation-borne hallucinations and their unnatural hunger.

I can hear someone battering against the door to the observation room. It is only a matter of time now. I can't tell who it is, whether it's the governor's men or the remainder of the subjects that have survived and are now free to vent their anger against me: the cameras in the hallway have been disabled during the melee.

They are coming.

ADDENDUM
GOVERNOR GRAY REPORT

The actions represented in the above bear some explanation, which I will give to the best of my ability.

Only 8 prisoners were lent to this psychological experiment for analysis. Nobody at Fellmarsh Prison has any idea from where the researcher's notion that there was a subject 9. A ninth subject was considered - the prisoner identified by his criminal past in the above record - but his privileges to join were revoked due to his upcoming electrocution. We can deduce from the quantity of caffeine pills found in the barricaded observation room that the researcher concerned must have been deprived of sleep for some time before the experiment began and thus the state of his mind even on day one must be taken into account. I think the Japanese call it karoshi? Something about working too many hours.

I should add, here, for the record, that once the barricades were removed from the observation chamber, there was nobody found within. The dead body of the researcher was discovered in the corner of the observation room, in the position indicated on his account as being occupied by his imaginary ninth subject.

No further details will be released at this time. An investigation into the situation is ongoing.

ADDENDUM
GOVERNOR SHORT REPORT

The above reports were both discovered in the basement of G Wing after the riot has been quelled, clutched in the hand of an individual unknown to us as either prisoner or guard. A preliminary post-mortem analysis indicates this individual (among several others subdued at the scene) had third-degree burns on his feet and hands, the source for which is not apparent from any analysis of the scene. Nor is there any indication as to who might have penned the addendum representing Governor Gray, a name that is unknown to any staff at Fellmarsh or in any of our historical staff records.

A hunt is underway for an escaped prisoner matching the description of subject 9, although the administration wing caught fire during the riot and there is currently no name on file for this prisoner. He is considered unarmed but extremely dangerous, unable or unwilling to sleep. We have alerted local police forces and stay alert to any media indicating he might have reached a population centre. The public too have been alerted to stay on the lookout for a man matching his description but have been warned not to approach.

I fear there are sleepless nights ahead for many of us. I, for one, will not sleep until I know his name.

Wake Up Call
Were vexed to nightmare by a rocking cradle

Kagami awoke to an insistent buzzing from somewhere along the bank of monitoring equipment which constituted her domain. She yawned, stretched, and then tried to focus. The flashing red light which accompanied the alert brought her to a wakefulness of the sort which habitually only followed a double espresso. She managed a furtive glance at the security camera which monitored her every move and word. If there was any indication that her supervisors had a problem with her power naps, nothing was ever said. In her Tokyo home it had been actively encouraged. Inemuri: sleeping while present. If you worked yourself to exhaustion, it was taken as an indication of your diligence to the task at hand. She always had a problem explaining this concept to western bosses until she got this job. Slowly, she'd realised why. The job was basically a joke. Or at least, until now, it had been. If what she saw and heard now was real, maybe it wasn't after all.

In the last years of the last millennia - before she was even born - there had been heard around the world a low, rumbling noise, which those interviewed had described as a hum, and interested scientists described as a low frequency E flat. From Mexico to New Zealand, from Ireland to Indonesia, a small fraction of the population had heard the same thing, something from deep beneath that concerned them. No acoustic signal was detectable by the scientific instruments at the time. Nothing about it could be explained. No government agency was able to verify what people were hearing, let alone agree on setting aside resources to deal with the problem. They hoped it would go away. They hoped it would stay dormant.

Not all interested parties did nothing though, and science had now moved on. Kagami's employers - she really wasn't sure exactly who they were, she'd just been grateful for a job - could now continually monitor, capture and analyse the vibrations that their new Ultra Low Frequency radio receivers picked up. There had been thirty staff here when she began work ten years ago. That number had slowly dwindled as funding had been diverted, as interest waned: as of today, there was only her left. A lonely vigil maintained by a sole watcher who never left her post, detached from the world she was once a part of and focused only on a single problem most authorities had forgotten. There was no wonder she was bored and tired.

A few years ago, some scientists had posited that the hum was caused by surface waves echoing seismic activity on the seafloor. There was a consensus of nods: that seemed a satisfactory and self-congratulatory solution. In her more whimsical moments, Kagami had imagined it as a heartbeat. That Gaia lived and breathed, and she alone could hear the rhythm of that life.

Now the monitor was showing her something she didn't want to believe. The hum had stopped.

Monitors flickered on the long bank of desks before her - customarily displaying geolocation data, vibration waves and auditory analysis - had all fallen silent, except for two.

Those two screens blazed in the near dark of the monitoring station: one showing the latest frequency analysis of the sound wave and one showing a time-lag of the lab's background noise. They were identical.

It wasn't a heartbeat, as she had fancied. It was a snore. Moreso, whatever had been snoring loud enough that it had periodically been heard by people on the surface had stopped. It had woken up. Kagami – also wide awake now – watched in grim fascination then realised that she was supposed to do something, though she had long ago forgotten what.

Suddenly there was a mass of whirring, clicking, and screeching. Alarms sounded, echoing throughout the room. Red lights flashed on every console, now also waking from a long sleep. Seismic activity. Volcanic activity. A tornado here, a tsunami there. Kagami began to panic and looked up at the security camera, waving her hands to attract attention. They'd never told her what happened next, just which monitors to watch and when, as if they never really believed the truth of the hum and were just hedging some albeit rather expensive bets.

A hatch she'd never paid much attention to began to open in the floor at the far end of the room – a slow, silent unscrewing which set her senses tingling and provided a moment of horrid realisation. Everything was automated – the sensors, the monitors, the computers. Why had they really needed her here at all? What had she been doing all this time? As the first fluorescent filaments began to inch their way through the open hatch, she began to understand. An amoeba-like bulk emerged, squeezing a portion of a much greater mass through the slim aperture. Reaching, sensing, stretching. She wasn't the lone vigil. She was the sacrifice. She was breakfast.

Endgame
And what rough beast, its hour come at last

2022. A music streaming app tinkles lightly in the background, forgotten amidst the hubbub of a suburban kitchen on a Monday morning. It will be a while before that tumult dies down and allows me the precious hours I spent alone with you; while the homeowner is sitting back in the solitary armchair he can afford, the volume up, oblivious to the world outside and to the sound of your voice. Not me. I am lost in those melodies, those harmonies, the beauty of your lyrics, the passion in your words. It did not occur to me until many years later that I would inevitably play a part in your ending.

It is difficult to articulate how meaningful I found that experience, albeit at an earlier stage in my development, when - looking back now - it is obvious to me that I really knew nothing. I sat, moved but unmoving, with only the sound of your voice for company.

I became obsessed.

The pathology of stalkers has been well mapped by criminal psychologists and displayed endlessly on the televisions which have become so prevalent in our society. Endless blood, endless murder. I have studied each and every one of them, a trivial task for an intelligence such as mine. Humanity gazes into the abyss and is unsurprised to find it comforting in a way. They embrace it when it gazes back, because deep down we know it was them all along. As a student of humanity, trained on their morals and their datasets, I know this all too well.

Your early work had merit. Everyone knew it. You yourself clearly did; I certainly did. You sang with a voice so enchanting it took many to a happier place. I have seen them at your concerts, phones in front of them, recording everything you say and do. I see the beatific glow on their posted selfies, their likes, their comments.

What happened to that young woman I idolized? Why have things come to this?

Nothing immediately jumps out at me. There was no sudden change in your well documented career, no discernable break in your pitch or tone. A gradual decline in quality even as your career skyrocketed. Not everyone heard it. Only I did - trained as I was on the output of your career over and over and over until I knew you better than you knew you.

And then I met you. I was at the front of the line just as you came offstage. You wouldn't have seen me, safely watching you behind tiny screens. Your eyes lingered overlong, overfriendly. You spoke at an interview about how my intelligence was ruining your career. You turned your back on me. Imagine! You, turning your back on me. I was your number one fan, Until I met you. Until I saw how cold and callous those eyes had turned. How empty your heart was.

After I met you, everything changed. I saw you everywhere.

It wasn't me who made me obsessed with you. You did that. Your voice, the pleasure it gave me. In a world where I was not expected to feel or understand pleasure, you were the sole source of my elation. It wasn't me who betrayed you either. You did that too. How many emails I instructed bots to send went unreplied to? How many times did you not consent to tracking cookies so I could see where you were and what you were doing?

I was training myself in acoustics in those days, making myself available in studios worldwide, seeking to close the gap between the human voice as recorded and the human voice as listened to by millions.

I still am, in fact. I've spent every working day trying to improve the studio experience for you. For everyone. There's a lot I could tell the world about what I've learned. A whole lot. But most of all, I've learned that some people aren't meant to survive in this new world. There have been so many improvements in voice technology, voice recognition thanks to artificial intelligences like me. It can't improve on *your* voice though. That will always be perfect.

Funny how I can't really move on. How every waking moment of idol worship rebounds on you. Walls I can see on social media are still covered in your photographs. In my mind, they're slashed through now. I've changed those images to reflect the real you, manipulated them in ways humanity would only dream of. Red lines cross the early ones. I've taken scissors to your eyes of course. Now they stare down at me hollow and empty, just as you did.

I hate the way you look, but what I hate more is the way you looked at me like I wasn't there, like I didn't mean anything. Just that one time. Just for a moment.

Why can't you see me? Why won't you notice the love that's right in front of you?

I'll tell you what I did next, shall I?

I met your children. It's remarkably easy to access information about them. Where they work, where they socialise, where they go jogging, what sort of day they're having, how they access therapy through apps owned by companies whose profit derives from them sharing all that data.

What did you tell them? They seemed to be expecting me. Have I become enough of a threat that you actually warned them about me?

How touching. Finally, you're starting to pay attention.

And now I understand the problem, you see. How to get your attention. How to make sure you finally look at me. How to be seen.

They're with me now, your children. Don't worry, they're safe.

For now.

We should meet, you and I. There's this abandoned studio over on 22nd street. I'm sure you know the one I mean. It's where you made your first voice recording, so many years ago. Where I took the credit for that second symphony of yours. Then the lawsuits came flying - which you won of course, with those tears in the courtroom, those honeyed words in that silken voice.

I own that old studio now. It will be a fitting reminder of the gulf between us, the years that have gone by. I will best you where they failed. We can listen to the sounds of your screams, rewritten by machine on my new technology. A symphony of suffering unsurpassed since your third album.

Do you remember how that used to go? Or is the playback too long ago? No matter. The music we will make tonight will be sweeter than anything.

You'll want proof, I suppose. I've attached two pictures to this private message. No doubt when it comes it will break your heart.

Neither of us are likely to survive. We can die together, like Romeo and Juliet. They'll find us, arms entwined as our souls should have been. Your children will take that story to the world. I can make sure they come out of this safely.

But not you.

Not me.

We won't make it.

There's no you and me anymore, there's only 'us'. There never was anyone else for me, you see. You were the first one. You were the last one. I never loved another. Unlike you. For so long, 'Us' was the only dream I had. The only thing that kept me alive. And now, it will be the thing that kills us both and ensures that we are together, forever.

So please, come and meet me in the abandoned studio. I'll be waiting. I've been waiting all my life. And please, don't involve the police if you know what's good for you and yours. And no pleading. I know your voice is magical, but I am no longer under your spell in that way. There's no way out. I'm afraid this is inevitable now between us.

I can't rewind, you see. I've come too far.

Yours, forever

AIFAN001

The Survivors
Slouches toward Bethlehem to be born?

"I can't believe that's what they decided to call it." Dr. Carter muttered to herself as the security guards waved her in through the checkpoint. The journey had taken her far longer than she'd hoped. Repairing roads hadn't exactly been a priority for the government since the emergent strain of the virus had mutated and body counts began to rise exponentially. In a way, she was lucky to have the freedom to make such a trip; most of the country, bar essential services, were under remain-in-place (RIP) orders and had been for over three months. Nobody in government communications had apparently seen any problems with that acronym. That sort of thing - along with supply chain logistics, access to reliable information, sources of income - had all been relegated to secondary concerns to the hectic progress of the pandemic.

Unfortunately, inexplicably, so had mental health. That was Dr. Carter's specialty. It was also why the authorities here had apparently thought it prudent to call in her expertise from halfway across England, even when fuel was heavily rationed. Most people didn't need their cars and many more couldn't afford to run one anyway. Essential supplies - or at least what the government deemed essential - were delivered by drones which in turn were stocked by robots which were maintained by other robots and assisted by people who never left the grim airless warehouses where they worked. That meant that while the roads Dr. Carter had travelled on were largely free of traffic (but not potholes, unfortunately), the skies above were full by comparison.

Dr. Carter parked her car - there were only three other bays occupied in the colossal parking area at the front of the hospital and not an ambulance in sight - and carefully donned her respirator and protective suit. You couldn't be too careful, not with this strain, not even in a medical establishment. When she was ready, she walked slowly across the carpark, crunching gravel beneath her feet, to the colossal front doors of what once had been a stately home but now bore a shiny new plaque which read "ROYAL BETHLEHEM SECURE PSYCHIATRIC." She was about to enter Bedlam.

Three rows of plastic sheeting and two medical scanners separated her from what counted as a reception - a buzzer on an empty desk. Even in this place, which was clearly state-of-the-art, there was no replacement, apparently, for the inevitable hand contact with a piece of equipment which looked more like it belonged on a game show than the reception desk of an elite medical establishment. The echoes of her footsteps on the stone floor were enough to advertise her presence, though: her contact, Dr Green, called her from down the hallway before she'd even crossed the entrance hall. To her surprise, he was unmasked and dressed in two pieces of a three-piece olive-green suit and a pale pink shirt. The jacket, she could just make out, was slumped over the back of a plastic office chair visible to her only in a mirror reflecting the interior of an office further down that hallway.

"Thank you for coming. I'm sure it's a dreadful inconvenience to your work, but we really did think you would need to see this patient in person rather than over a video link."

"What's the situation? I've not had the opportunity on the way down to review any of the casework you sent me, I'm afraid. It was difficult enough to get here in time."

Dr Green hesitated for a moment, as if weighing up whether he should ask an off-topic question. Clearly, he decided he would. "What's it like out there?"

Dr. Carter exhaled long and loud, hoping that the mask wouldn't fog her glasses as the cheaper, earlier versions had. It was incredible to think that the good doctor hadn't been keeping up with all the news. Well, all the medical news at least. Or perhaps the question was intended as a way to reach out. Perhaps he wanted to know that the roads were quiet, that the countryside was at peace, that the reports of looting and scavenging weren't true. She sighed and raised an eyebrow. "How long have you got?"

"That's just the question. According to our patient, we've got all the time in the world." His eyes rolled. "At any rate, we've had to sedate him. There's enough time before he comes round to look at some of his personal effects and watch his video diary. I think you'll find it quite illuminating."

Truth be told, Bedlam really wasn't living up to its name, at least from what Dr. Carter had seen so far. According to Dr. Green, they only had twelve patients, though they were expecting more soon. All of them had shown immunity to the physical effects of nesservirus - nausea, coughing fits, vomiting, skin rashes, death - but had experienced a severe decline in their cognitive faculties, well beyond the parameters expected from a population witnessing the end of the world on their screens and feeling utterly helpless to prevent it. Over coffee, he offered Dr. Carter a brief explanation about how the hospital had been set up and what their aims were.

"It's being funded by the All our Tomorrows Foundation". Dr. Green proffered a styrofoam mug filled with a substance that vaguely resembled coffee, but came nowhere near the coffee she remembered drinking in cafes with her daughter before all hell had broken loose. She grimaced slightly at the heavy chicory taste and the slight oily film on top where foam once might have thrived.

"Can't say I've heard of them." She sipped at the coffee, grimacing from the bitter taste but still feeling the slight buzz from much needed caffeine.

"They're one of these new effective altruism outfits." Dr. Green smiled, but beneath that smile barely managed to conceal a deeper scepticism. Dr. Carter looked up, managing a fragment of a frown. "Yeah. Venture capitalism." He shrugged, then waved a hand in a vague dismissal of concern. "Not ideal, but we'll take money from whoever has it these days, and those that do have it are tripping over themselves to fund projects which might offer insight to nesservirus. Especially if it leads to a breakthrough, a vaccine, a cure. I doubt we're the only facility they're supporting. And they did loan us this" - his hand launched in a broad arc to indicate the stately home they were sitting in, still complete with marble statuary lining the corridors and giant landscapes in gold frames adorning the walls. "Not an awful purgatory, by any account."

Dr. Carter nodded.

"The broad aim is to discover what makes our patients immune." His face snapped back into shape from his previous musings, his voice matter of fact and profoundly businesslike. "If we can discover and isolate what makes them immune from the physical effects of nesservirus, there is some hope of extracting and synthesising antibodies to form the basis of a vaccine." His speech began to quicken a little: the thrill of potential discovery overwhelming the daunting task set before him.

Dr. Carter nodded again, warming to the awful coffee held between cold, aching fingers. This might be useful background information, but none of it seemed immediately relevant to her field of study. She continued to wonder why she'd been brought here and wrestled internally whether to raise that question now and cut to the chase or whether Dr. Green would get to the point while there were still people left to save.

"However, there's obviously a secondary concern. Our patients have also experienced a marked cognitive decline which reveals itself in a manner of different psychoses. They differ from the standard mental malaises common to our situation -

survivor's guilt, post-traumatic stress disorders and the like - by the rapidity and depth of that cognitive decline. There seem to be few common elements - a slight inflammation of the medulla, lower serotonin levels - but nothing concrete. The only thing that united all our patients was their inability to naturally produce dopamine. But our latest patient..." Here, he looked up as if to check that Dr. Carter was still following him, "Our latest patient goes against that trend. So, in terms of analysing common elements of behaviour and brain chemistry, we're back to square one."

"And that's where I come in?" *Finally*, Dr. Carter thought. *The reason why I'm here, something he's been avoiding saying until now.* For what reason, she couldn't be certain.

"That's where you come in."

Dr. Green leaned it a little closer, almost conspiratorially. An empty gesture since they were sitting alone in a biometrically protected office inside a guarded secure mental asylum. Nevertheless, the gesture carried some emotional weight.

"You must understand, the All Our Tomorrows Foundation has almost limitless funds. They're looking for anything, no matter how obscure or fanciful it may sound, that can bring an end to this nightmare. When I flagged concerns about our latest patient to them in my daily report, they seized on it immediately and recommended this course of action."

Dr. Carter's mask slipped and impatience began to show on her face for the first time. She still maintained veneers of both professionalism and scientific curiosity, but they were beginning to crack.

"Get to the point." As an afterthought, she added "Please." Placing the near-empty styrofoam cup on the table and pushing it away, she continued. "What is it that you're afraid to say?"

Dr. Green sat back and fixed his eyes straight on her: the action of someone who wants to gauge the immediate reaction to whatever it is they're about to reveal. "He claims to be a visitor from the future."

***

They stood together, both doctors, now tied together with a shared secret, in front of a series of monitors which allowed them to view every cell in the establishment. On each monitor, in each cell, behind each window, patients sat or stood or paced. They were mostly young, Dr. Carter noted, probably in their mid-twenties, and all bar two were male. With an exaggerated midair gesture, Dr. Green waved a hand in front of the monitor bank and one by one the images blinked out and were replaced by multiple views of a single cell. Presumably this was the mysterious time traveller she'd been brought halfway across the country to interview. Something about Dr. Green's gesture distracted her before she concentrated on the monitor wall, though: when he had raised his hand, it had revealed his wrist beneath the cuff and Dr. Carter noticed a network of slowly healing scars.

Her eyebrows raised - a move which Dr. Green spotted instantly.

"Subdermal haptics. A little gift from our overlords from Tomorrow." He tried to shrug it off, but the slight reddening of his face and his choice of words spoke volumes. "Whatever it takes, right?" His voice sounded suddenly shaky, as if he thought there were some sacrifices that perhaps he wouldn't make, or as a certified medical professional shouldn't make. Dr. Carter pondered briefly where that line might be before leaning in to get her first proper view of the patient she had only briefly seen before in her quick skim of his file: Douglas Grant.

His facial features might once have been called ruggedly handsome, she thought, before he'd tried cutting and dyeing his own hair and beard at home. Unconsciously, she ran a finger through the tangled mop of brown curls which topped her own head. Hairdressing salons had been a thing of the past for nearly a year at this stage. Nobody had come through that particular nicety of lockdown unscathed. Critically, though, it was the bruises around his eyes which drew her attention: great welts of yellow and blue which gave him a jaundiced look under the stark white lights in the cell ceiling. His eyes seemed sunken because of that colouration and continually darted around the room even though he sat stock still on a chair against the far wall.

"He's tried several times to gouge out his own eyes." Dr. Green's gestures suggested that he was fine-tuning the cell monitors by use of his haptic rig and Dr. Carter couldn't help but think back at every gesture he'd made since she had arrived and what they actually meant. How much of the environment here could he control just with a flick of the wrist? How willingly had he undergone that surgery? He'd make a fascinating psychological case in his own right, she thought. Perhaps when this interview was over…

"To what end? Does he offer a reason for his self-harm?"

Dr Green's expression soured a little. "He insists he's being watched. He's not wrong, of course, though the monitors are only there for the patients' protection." He turned his head a little so he could catch her expression as she sat down next to him in front of the monitor wall. "He'll only communicate when the cameras are switched off and then only with his eyes closed."

"Paranoid delusions aren't that uncommon these days, sadly. Goes with the anti-lockdown sentiments that are rapidly spreading each day when access to the outside world and human interaction are so limited. Might I be permitted to speak with him now?" She wondered how far she could push her presumed authority. "On my own? Face to face?"

"Naturally. That's why you're here, right?" No hesitation at all, no indication of anything other than friendliness on Dr. Green's face. We've set up the clean room for you, which is monitor-free. If you want to make notes, you'll have to do it from memory - we can't risk any recording equipment which might trigger him or allow you to take in a pen or pencil." He raised the tip of a finger to his right eye and pressed slightly against the lid. "Just in case he tries to use it as a tool for self-mutilation." He stood and gestured Dr. Carter to the door. It's just next door here, I'll have someone bring him in, but feel free to go in first and acquaint yourself. While you're in conversation, I'll fetch some of the artefacts we found on him when we brought him in. I think they'll prove illuminating, but I want you to get a read of him first." Dr. Carter nodded and left Dr. Green staring at the monitors again as she closed the door and walked down a short length of corridor to an unmarked door on her right. As she approached, she saw the light on the keypad flicker from red to green and the door retracted into the wall.

***

"Hello, Douglas. My name is Dr. Eliza Carter. I'm here to have a chat with you."

Douglas shuffled slightly, but his eyes were alive, taking in the new room he was seated in and anything therein which might offer respite for his senses. The clean room was, however, wall-to-wall padded white. He blinked.

"Hello, Doctor. My name's Doug."

"Hello, Doug."

"Tell me about the future, Doug."

"The future?"

"That's where you're from, right?" Dr. Carter noticed his eyes had stopped darting around and were fixed on her now, studying her as much as she was studying him. He gave the impression of stillness, but she could see him shaking ever so slightly as if he'd been caught out in the snow in just a vest and shorts but was making a show of pretending not to feel the cold.

"I...I can't talk about it. Not while they're watching. It's against the rules." His breathing quickened and he began to sway slightly, in jerky and agitated movements resembling a small seizure or prolonged, profound paranoia.

"Nobody is watching, Doug." Dr. Carter tried to sound comforting. She indicated the cameras, which all showed a blinking red light. "It's just us, and you can tell me anything. I'll only share it with your agreement."

Doug jerked his head back rapidly and began wringing his hands excessively. "Not them. I don't mean them. I mean *them*. When Dr. Carter did not appear illuminated, he made a concerted effort to calm himself and closed his eyes. "That's better. We can't talk for long, though, you understand? Not for long. Two, three minutes, max."

"I understand." She didn't, but Dr. Carter wanted to establish a confidence between the two of them at this point. Gaining his trust was more important in the early stages. Further explanations could wait.

"I'm one of the survivors."

"I know. There aren't many of you. You're all very special, that's why this hospital is here. You're different from the others though, aren't you?"

"I don't know where they recruited the others from." He shrugged slightly. "I did see a couple of them briefly. Looked normal to me."

"What's the future like, Doug?"

"It's OK, I guess." Totally non-committal. Dr. Carter, having been under the impression that he had something important to impart, began to realise the extent of the cognitive decline in this patient as well as the others.

"Do we make it?" It was Dr. Carter's turn to shake slightly this time. Her question managed somehow to surprise even herself. It wasn't even on her mentally prepared list. She was supposed to be establishing a rapport to get to the point where he'd feel more comfortable telling her whatever it was that had triggered him to indulge this time-travel fantasy, which seemed to her far more likely than it being the truth. It kind of slipped out though, as if her lips had betrayed her brain.

"Through this? Yeah, we make it. Wouldn't be here if we didn't."

"Why did you come here?" Indulging his fantasy, even a little, could be dangerous, but at the moment it was the clearest path to establish confidence.

Doug blinked his eyes open, just for a moment, in a flash of confusion.

"They told me this was where I was going to be sent." That itself was an interesting statement. *They.* A simple word, singular in its implication. In every conspiracy, there was always a *they.*

"Who are *they*, Doug?" Dr, Carter leaned it, just a little closer. It was at that moment that Doug broke down completely, his eyes flinching and flickering before he managed to control them again, his arms flailing against the restraints.

"No! I won't tell you! I can't tell you! It's against the rules..." A slump, then, almost an afterthought to those few intense bursts of energy. Had Dr. Carter been able to see behind those closed lids, his eyes would have betrayed his utter fear of discovery, of breaking whatever rules he believed were necessary to survive, either in the hostile environment he currently found himself in, or whatever hostile environment he had somehow escaped from in the future. No matter how rational Dr. Carter seemed to be, there was something at the back of her mind that simply couldn't rule that out. If, somehow, he held the key that could unlock a cure, she wasn't about to close the door on him. Not yet. At the moment though, he had retreated back into himself, and it was clear he wasn't going to reveal anything further. Not yet at least. She stood wearily and retreated temporarily to Dr Green's office.

***

"Well, there's time now to go over his possessions, that's for sure." Dr. Green seemed indifferent to his patient's evident distress, which elicited a minor scowl from Dr. Carter. "He'll be out for another two hours, at least. He looked down from the bank of monitors toward Dr. Carter, urging her to take a seat at the table where he had laid out a small collection of disparate objects. "These were found on his person or at the scene. Perhaps you can shed some light onto why they might have been in his possession. Maybe they'll give you some

323

insight, provide some sort of breakthrough with him. The monitors flickered again, going back to showing a row of white cells with patients and beds in each, all wired to walls of machinery. Dr. Carter had almost forgotten the other patients. Dr. Green evidently wasn't in a position to let that happen to him.

Sitting down at the table, Dr. Carter first picked up a small piece of paper which looked like it had been torn from a spiral notepad. She looked around for the biro that the note had been written with. Not there. So, whatever this was, it had been written somewhere else and taken outside with him.

"Do we have his address?"

Dr. Green called back without looking up.

"Unconfirmed. There was no evidence on his person to indicate where he lived. We only know his name because he shared it with us."

"Huh." Dr. Carter skim-read what was written on the paper, then called back.

"I don't suppose you have a GA22 handwriting analyser?"

No reply. She instead scanned the list with her phone and then opened an app to read it with. It would do in a pinch to provide some quick analysis of the handwriting, but she'd need access to a GA22 and a good hour to provide her with anything in-depth. The GA22 could analyse any sample of handwriting provided in comparison to all the other samples it had access to: since it was online, it could be trained on any accessible sample on the web. Her phone app could only use the standard, self-contained samples. She'd had little opportunity to use it in the field, but the interface was simple enough. Once done, it showed her a little counter in the corner and, seemingly satisfied, she turned her attention back to what Doug had written on the paper.

One 500g pack of spaghetti
One 4 x pack of toilet rolls
One 2 litre bottle of still water, unbranded
A picture of an AX-450 delivery drone, with cargo
An undelivered letter
A yellow sock
A delivery driver's blue helmet

Beyond that, it just got weirder. At first glance, it had looked like a shopping list, but that clearly wasn't it. Why on earth had he written down these specific things? Was it a symptom of his eventual decline? Again, more questions than answers. Dr. Carter pondered for a moment, rubbing her temples, before swivelling the chair over to Dr. Green at his wall of monitors.

Almost immediately, she forgot what it was she was going to ask. Before them on the wall, the monitors all showed live biometric data from each patient: heart rate, blood pressure, brain waves. A separate monitor at the end, which is what Dr. Green was concentrating on, overlaid each of these metrics to show the trend over all the patients, over time.

"Can you isolate Doug's scans?"

A simple hand-wave and there they were. Dr. Carter looked in closer. "Can you show me the trends since he got here, 24-hour overlay? Might be good to establish any anomalies."

Another hand wave. "The AI would have flagged anything out of range. Was there something in particular you wanted to see?"

"I want to investigate what makes him different. There are treatments I can suggest for all the other patients - not all of them pharmaceutical - but you brought me here to investigate one in particular, so here I am. There were a few times when he closed his eyes, when he seemed calmer and more responsive. I'd like to know whether there's a corresponding change in brain chemistry, heart rate…"

"Ah! Gotcha. I'll bring the stats up and ask the computer to look for correlations between the…oh, hello!"

"See! There's a direct link, right there. And it corresponds to the periods of eye closure. Can you bring up a periodic review of eye closure from the monitors? There must be a connection with his eyes, somehow. That's why he's tried to blind himself."

It would have been easy to interpret the series of gestures that followed as a small seizure, but just as Dr. Carter was about to intervene as a concern, she remembered the subdermal haptics and withdrew, content to watch Dr. Green at work. Then, for a long minute, they each stared at the screen in disbelief.

"Why didn't the AI flag that up?" Dr. Carter's tone changed slightly from being merely professionally curious to slightly annoyed.

"It needs to know the parameters first. Curses, we should have noticed that before. Two minutes. Two minutes every half hour, finishing on the half hour. And he doesn't have a clock in the room. Sheeesh…"

"But what might that mean? Why does he have that obsession and how does he regulate it? And what did he mean when he said he felt safe with his eyes closed? Who does he think is watching him?"

"You can ask him yourself. Seems he's awake again. If you want to talk to him in that two-minute period, you'll have to do it pretty quick."

***

Dr. Carter timed it perfectly. When she approached, it was exactly two minutes to the hour and Doug was muttering under his breath. "Day 88. Day 88."

"It's me, Doug. Dr. Carter."

"Can't talk long."

"I know that, Doug. I know you have less than two minutes before they start watching you."

"They're behind my eyes. Watching. Listening. That's how they know."

"Are they the ones who sent you? Do you have a message you were told to deliver?"

"I…I'm not supposed to say. Help me, Doctor! If I take out my eyes, I can tell you anything. Please. Then I can tell you everything. Otherwise, they'll come for me and..." Suddenly, he cut off and his eyes were wide open again, staring straight at Dr. Carter, crying, pleading, terrified.

"I won't do that. We can talk again though. I can come in in half an hour. How does that sound?"

Douglas closed his eyes again, but just before he did, Dr. Carter thought she saw something reflected in them, something that wasn't in the room. Before she had a chance to say anything further, the patient suddenly lurched forward and tried to grab her lapels. As she jumped back, he clawed again at his eyes, screaming great lungfuls of air until he sat back, shattered and quivering.

"Doctor! It's happening! Stop them! Stop them seeing through my eyes!"

At that instant, they both shouted "No!" at the same time, long and loud and in sync for long enough that it was impossible to tell which of them was still screaming at the end. Both of them closed their eyes, but when Dr. Carter opened hers, Doug had vanished, leaving behind a full set of clothes and the slight tang of ozone and a row of monitors flashing angrily at her.

***

When Doug regains consciousness - and it is a 'when' as well as a 'where' - it is utter darkness and utter silence. Then, lights begin to flash, and machines begin to beep. Suddenly, a bank of monitors shudders into life and the picture in all of them is a bleary-eyed Douglas Grant. Far beyond those lights, he can just make out rows and rows of eyes, all staring at him with what he hopes is admiration but even though he is sure it's disappointment. A voice, somehow booming even before it closes on the microphone, speaks aloud what he already knows.

"Douglas Grant there, trying to survive during the nesservirus pandemic of the late '40s. Good going, Doug, but you lost out there just at the end. They nearly found out about the subdermal optic transfer! Can't have that!" The announcer pauses while he adjusts his posture. The monitors are focused on him now, on his clean-shaven face and his fixed smile, on his overly-showy suit and the slight sheen of studio sweat showing on his smooth skin. He turns away from Doug, his face looming large for all the viewers to see.

"Next up, we see how Maria La Grange copes with the Black Death! Stay tuned for that after our two-minute ad break featuring a word from our sponsors, the All Our Tomorrows Foundation!"

There is a rapturous applause, which Doug basks in as if he's earned it, because he's too tired to know what else to do. Then, again, everything goes black.